BYSTANDER

MIKE STEEVES

BY STAN DER

BOOK*HUG PRESS

TORONTO 2022

FIRST EDITION
© 2022 by Mike Steeves

Library and Archives Canada Cataloguing in Publication

Title: Bystander / Mike Steeves.
Names: Steeves, Mike, 1978– author.
Identifiers: Canadiana (print) 2021037246x | Canadiana (ebook) 20210372478
  ISBN 9781771667104 (softcover)
  ISBN 9781771667111 (EPUB)
  ISBN 9781771667128 (PDF)
Classification: LCC PS8637.T4314 B97 2022 | DDC C813/.6—dc23

The production of this book was made possible through the generous assistance of the Canada Council for the Arts and the Ontario Arts Council. Book*hug Press also acknowledges the support of the Government of Canada through the Canada Book Fund and the Government of Ontario through the Ontario Book Publishing Tax Credit and the Ontario Book Fund.

Book*hug Press acknowledges that the land on which we operate is the traditional territory of many nations, including the Mississaugas of the Credit, the Anishnabeg, the Chippewa, the Haudenosaunee, and the Wendat peoples. We recognize the enduring presence of many diverse First Nations, Inuit, and Métis peoples and are grateful for the opportunity to meet, work, and learn on this territory.

For Nikki

'Everyone readily assumes that he himself couldn't do anything evil, because after all he's a good person!'
—Robert Musil

'The honourable life is like timing. One might not have a talent for it.'
—Karen Solie

PART ONE

I used to think that if I ever had to face a moral crisis or was confronted by a matter of life or death—the sort of grand ethical dilemma you might read about or see on TV—not only would I know what the right thing to do was, but I would actually do the right thing. I dreamed up melodramatic scenarios where I said all the right words and had all the right opinions. Whenever I heard about a disgraced public figure, I told myself that given the same wealth, power, and fame, I would've handled a similar crisis with grace and dignity. Whenever I watched a war movie, I identified with the hero who somehow managed to preserve their common decency throughout the most degrading circumstances the civilized mind has come up with yet, and not with the sad, desperate, and craven characters who served as scapegoats, the ones who invariably wound up doing something depraved and horrific. I watched the heroes sacrifice their lives for the lives of others and I told myself that's what I would do. That's who I would be.

I wasn't naïve. I knew that if I were ever to experience what it is like to be a celebrity or politician who has been publicly shamed and humiliated, or if I had to live through something on the same scale as World War II and the Holocaust, it was highly unlikely I would do anything heroic, or that I would conduct myself in the dignified and graceful fashion, which has been so rarely on display throughout history that it exists more as a myth or a fantasy than a feature of humanity. Still, I was convinced that at the end of the day, when push came to shove, in the final analysis, when all the chips were in, I was at heart, at base, at my core, a fundamentally decent person, even if the real reason I lived a morally blameless life was simply because I hadn't been given the opportunity to do any real, lasting harm. I saw myself as the sort of person who would pull over at the scene of an accident and offer to help, even though I never had. I fantasized about volunteering at a homeless shelter, and while I never acted on these good intentions, I told myself it was only a matter of time. 'I'm too busy,' I would say. 'You have to look after yourself before you can look after other people.' Without ever having done anything that could be described as courageous or heroic, I somehow convinced myself that given the right circumstances, the appropriate context, I would live up to the ideals that still persist in our culture, even though they have been shown to have played a large role in many of history's bloodiest wars and atrocities, and I was convinced that in any moral crisis, or life-or-death situation, I would never behave in a cowardly and morally bankrupt way, like the characters in movies and on TV shows who stand by and watch, or run away, or stay silent and do nothing while the hero is sentenced to death, or has their home taken from them, or their children are abducted.

But now I know that if I am ever faced with a test of my courage, or character, or moral instincts, that I will probably fail the test in the same thoroughly predictable ways as everyone before me has failed.

Last year, after spending nine months on a work assignment in a foreign city, I was called back to the home office. My job involved a lot of travel. My company sent me all over the world, and I became accustomed to the perks of living in a foreign city on an expense account. Because I was willing to go anywhere at a moment's notice and for long stretches of time, I was able to distinguish myself in what might've been an otherwise unremarkable career, and I was rewarded with colonial-level luxury whenever I was on assignment. Travelling for work was a way for me to get ahead without having to do much else aside from travelling. Despite the ubiquity of international business and the frantic way people are ceaselessly shuttling back and forth across the globe, my clients were always grateful when I travelled to meet with them, even though all I did was buy a ticket and sit on a plane for a few hours. My friends and family were impressed too, imagining that all the meetings they had to do for their work, the excruciating small talk, and the mindless drudgery, would somehow be redeemed if they took place in a foreign city. 'You're doing great work over there,' Roger, my boss, said to me after one of my first foreign assignments, when I was really only doing a passable job at best, and, as he knew, the work I was doing wasn't anything special, and certainly not challenging. An open secret of my profession is that even though we all make a show of the crazy hours we keep, and the nonstop pace we maintain through a workday that starts with a client breakfast and ends with client cocktails, the truth is that the work itself, of which it must be said we do very little, could hardly be described as difficult or challenging, and even though popular culture appears to be having a moment with my profession, and professional life in general, it's not an exaggeration to say that I'm little more than a well-paid cog in a very luxurious machine. The reason I was sent all over the world at a moment's notice and set up for months in the most exciting and glamorous cities had nothing to do with my talent, or skill, or competency with certain systems and programs, or my fluency in abstruse professional jargon, or even my facility with interpersonal affairs. The truth is that I had the right look, so they gave me a job.

But after a few years of this global business lifestyle, I started to get tired. When you're starting out in my profession, you have to be willing to do the road work. Some even seek it out. For a while it can be fun to indulge in the executive-class lifestyle, but eventually you can't hack it anymore. You settle down, and fade into the good life. 'I don't understand how you do it,' Roger said to me after one of my extended foreign assignments. 'I used love it,' he said, 'but I wouldn't be able to do it now.' Roger saw his career in terms of progress, or stages, and his time at the company as a set of distinct historical periods. But there was never anything going on in my life that gave it a similar shape. I was unmarried, single, no kids, and I knew that if I stayed in one place for too long there was a risk that people might notice how mediocre I actually was. I'm not in possession of an innate curiosity, or wanderlust, or the imperial competitiveness that leads people to spend their time tallying up the places they've been, and I'm much more inclined toward the comforts of home, the profound reassurance that comes from being surrounded by familiar places, sights, sounds, smells, etc. I was always relieved when, at the end of each foreign assignment, I got to come back home. At the end of nine months spent in a state of constant confusion and helplessness, I was so physically and mentally exhausted that even the most banal exchange, like buying a bus ticket, placed an enormous strain on the limits of my comprehension, which was compounded by the psychic fatigue from forever having to translate my thoughts into another language. For weeks leading up to my flight home, I lay in my hotel bed and fantasized about being back at my apartment, back where I could take my surroundings for granted, instead of going out each day into a strange city that I could barely make sense of.

But when I finally got home from my last assignment, after a relentlessly unpleasant eighteen-hour flight, as I walked from the cab to my front door, I had the feeling that I was showing up uninvited to my own apartment. I'd been living in the same place for over a decade, even though I could afford to buy one of the upscale condos going up in the revitalized old quarter, and I could easily afford the exorbitant rent being charged for the apartments that had been carved out of the converted Anglican church downtown, and I'd have no problems taking out a mortgage on a studio in one of the refurbished warehouses that dotted the waterfront. Through a combination of laziness, sentimentality, and maybe even a bit of superstition, I held on to the cramped and rundown place that I'd moved into after university. After nine months away, the place looked the same as on the day I had left it, as if I'd only just walked out the door, but even still, I felt as if all that time I'd been away had somehow accumulated and now filled up the rooms with an atmosphere of quiet ruin. What was once so familiar suddenly looked strange. I was struck by how empty and bare the walls were. I'd never bothered to bring home the cultural artifacts or luxury items that most of my colleagues stocked up on whenever they travelled for work, and aside from state-of-the-art furniture and an impressive audio-visual setup, I hadn't added much to the place since I'd first moved in. The apartment seemed much smaller than I remembered, and even though I knew I was seeing these rooms through the prism of my recent accommodations, I couldn't help feeling unjustifiably offended, like when a restaurant I liked but hadn't been to in years turns out to have gone into steep decline and has lost all the charm and quality it once had.

When I first moved in, I thought it was a great apartment. If anything, it was more than I needed. I'd been used to sharing a place with two, sometimes three, and in one case five, roommates. For a few months, I lived in a rundown duplex with more people than I was ever able to keep track of. Throughout university, my living space was usually restricted to one room with only the most sparing use of the common areas. I was never comfortable making conversation, let alone establishing friendships with the people I lived with. You're a private person, I used to say to myself. You don't like being seen.

So I moved into my own place the moment I could afford to. It was a two-bedroom unit in a large three-story building that took up one side of a short street. I saw a FOR RENT sign in the window of one of the units, and I called the number. The Super answered and said she'd be right out to show me the apartment. Low ceilings, cheap light fixtures, a faux-wood linoleum floor that actually succeeded in fooling me the first time I saw it. I liked that it had its own entrance so I didn't have to share a common hallway with the other tenants, and I thought it was cool that the main floor had the kitchen, a small breezeway, and a living room, and the upstairs had my bedroom, the bathroom, and another bedroom that largely served as a storage space, though when I had people over and was showing them around I would refer to it as a 'study.' Twelve years later, after spending so much time in luxury hotel suites, I had become painfully aware of how small the rooms were, and the generally shabby condition of the building, but to give up the lease and find somewhere nicer would've involved forming a whole bunch of new neighbourhood relationships and local connections, and no matter how benign or even beneficial they might've been in the long run, I couldn't stand the thought of having to go through that.

In all the years I'd been living in the apartment, I had never met my landlord. Our only interaction was between the cheque I would drop off to the Super and the subsequent withdrawal of funds from my account, or the formulaic registered letter notifying me of my annual rent increase, and because we had never spoken over the phone, I sometimes wondered if my landlord really existed. Maybe the Super was the landlord and was only pretending to be the Super as a way of deflecting complaints from the tenants? But I never seriously considered this. It was much more likely that the landlord just couldn't be bothered with getting involved in the daily operations of the property.

As I opened my front door, I heard the sound of someone coming down the stairwell of the neighbouring apartment, and I waited to see if it was the shy, middle-aged woman who'd been living there for a few months before I had gone away. The people who lived in the building were mostly a mix of students and blue-collar types. They kept irregular hours and even though I was close in age to some of the students, they gave the impression of being from a different era, so it felt natural to keep our distance from one another. Whenever I got back from one of my foreign assignments there was always a new crop of tenants I'd never seen before. I would consider introducing myself, or at least nodding hello when we passed each other on the street, but since I would just be leaving on another foreign assignment soon and they would likely be gone by the time I came back, it felt unnecessary, and maybe even a waste of time and energy. I have enough going on in my life, I thought, I can't take on any more, even if I wanted to. But after spending night after night alone in a luxurious hotel suite for the last nine months, I had started to think about opening myself up a bit more, and I had told myself that when I got home I was going to make a real effort to live a more socially active life than the one I'd been living, and instead of shunning my neighbours I was going to develop strong, rewarding bonds with them. I would get to know their backgrounds, their occupations, their pastimes. I would become part of the fabric of the community, and instead of walking the streets feeling anxious and alienated, I would go around treating everyone with kindness and understanding. 'This time,' I told myself repeatedly during my last foreign assignment, as I lay alone in an enormous bed with the foreign skyline laid out before me, 'this time things will be different.' So I stood waiting, with the intention of finally introducing myself to the shy, middle-aged woman who lived next door, but nobody came out.

I went inside my apartment and called my parents, which is what I did every time I flew home from a foreign assignment, out of consideration for my mother, who could never relax when she knew I was flying until she got my phone call, even though I had pointed out to her many times that if something did happen to the plane she would no doubt hear about it almost immediately since she had the kitchen TV turned to the twenty-four-hour news channels from the moment she woke up until she finally went to sleep. And since we sometimes went for weeks without talking, it was just as likely that something terrible could happen to me during one of those intervals and it might be a while before she got the news, so it seemed almost gratuitous for me to indulge this particular neurosis of hers, but it felt equally gratuitous not to.

'When did you get in?' Mom asked. 'Just now,' I said. 'I just got in the door.' 'And the flight went okay?' she said. 'You arrived all right?' 'The plane didn't crash if that's what you're asking.' 'They found the black box,' Dad said. 'Turn that off,' Mom said. 'He's sitting there watching the news.' 'Should I be standing?' Dad said. 'Well, I just wanted to call to let you know that I arrived safe and sound,' I said. 'I'm still eight hours ahead, or behind, so I'm going to lie down on the couch and sleep.' 'You must be exhausted,' Mom said. 'Do you have anything to eat in your apartment?' 'Do they pay you for those flights?' Dad said. 'You mean do I pay for my own flights for work?' 'I mean, do you get compensated for the time you spend on these long flights?' 'I don't really know how to answer that.' 'Is there a grocery store open nearby?' Mom sounded as if she'd moved to the far side of the room. 'You need fresh food.' 'It was an eighteen-hour flight, not three days. And the food was really good. Sushi, actually. So, really fresh.' 'They certainly don't serve sushi on our flights, do they?' Mom said. 'Have you ever seen one of these black boxes?' Dad asked. 'Are you talking to me?' 'Yes,' he said. 'You fly all the time. I thought maybe you might've seen one before.' 'I don't think the black box is in a place on the plane where anyone can see it.' 'He's tired, dear,' Mom said. 'We should let him go.' 'No, that's all right,' I said. 'I find this strangely relaxing.' 'It's amazing when you think about it,' Dad said, 'that they don't break.' 'I don't like the idea of you coming back to an empty apartment,' Mom said. 'Well,' I said, 'I prefer it to coming home to an apartment full of people.' 'You know what I mean,' she said. 'They must use some pretty strong material,' Dad said. 'Why don't you get a new place?' Mom said. 'You could be living somewhere much nicer.' 'This is a pretty up-and-coming area, Mom.' 'I meant a nicer apartment. You could even move across the street. There are some beautiful houses on the other side.' 'I don't really want a whole house.' 'It would be a very good investment,' Dad said, 'and we would be willing to help.' 'That's very kind,' I said, and for a second I considered telling him that I made more in a year than he did in the best decade of his career, 'but money isn't the issue. I just haven't gotten around to it yet. I'm a busy man.' 'You're never too busy to make a smart investment,' Dad said. 'He's just full of sayings like that. A real wise man, your father.' 'Think about it,' Dad said, 'and in the meantime I'll speak with the accountant.' 'I just think you'd be happier someplace else,' Mom said. 'You're probably right,' I said. 'The best sushi I ever had,' Dad said, 'was at that restaurant in the strip mall on Campbell. Just a little place, only a few tables, but I'm telling you, the food was exquisite. I bet it was just as good as what you'd get in first class.' 'Well, I guess you'll never know.' They burst out laughing. 'No,' Dad said, 'I'll just have to live vicariously through you, I guess.' 'Maybe I'll bring you a doggie bag next time I visit.' Mom was screeching with laughter and it sounded for a second like she might have lost control of herself. 'All right, you two,' I said, 'let's settle down now.' 'Doggie bag,' Mom said. 'So, I wonder what they'll find on the black box,' Dad said. 'Is it an actual recording?' Mom asked. 'What do you mean?' Dad said. 'What else could it be?' 'Well, I don't know,' Mom said. 'Why else would I be asking the question?' 'Okay,' I said. 'I don't think it was such a stupid question to ask,' Mom said. 'I don't know what's in one of those black boxes, and neither do you.' 'Well, I know that whatever it is,' Dad said, 'it produces a recording that is used in a forensic investigation of the crash.' 'Forensic investigation,' Mom said. 'Okay, you two,' I said, 'this is no longer strangely relaxing.' 'Maybe it's some sort of transcript,' Mom said. 'Transcript?' Dad said. 'Mom,' I said, 'they'd be making the transcript from a recording. Having a transcript means there must be a recording.' 'Well, listen to the two of you,' Mom said. 'I didn't realize I was in the presence of two *forensic experts*.' 'You don't have to be an expert to read the news,' Dad said. 'Is that another one of your sayings?' I said. I went onto the balcony and lit a cigarette. 'When was the last time you read the news?' Mom said. 'You should be collecting them for a book,' I said. 'Call it the *Tao of Dad*.' 'I read on my own time,' Dad said. 'Did you read the article I sent you about the thoracic surgeon from Médecins Sans Frontières?' I said. 'Not yet,' Dad said. 'It's crazy,' I said. 'I don't understand how those people do it. Like, isn't performing chest surgery hard enough? But on top of that, the hospital is getting bombed every day, and snipers are shooting at you whenever you try to leave, and you don't have supplies or even any electricity. How do you do that for weeks, or months, or whatever, and then go back home to your wife and kids and go for dinner, or to a movie, stand in line for a coffee, with those images in your head?' 'A lot of them have nervous breakdowns,' Dad said. 'At the bare minimum I would have a nervous breakdown,' I said. 'What are you two going on about?' Mom said. 'Is this from a movie?' 'Think about the sort of person who is attracted to that sort of work, though,' Dad said. 'They tend to be a little crazy to begin with.' 'How would you know?' Mom said. 'You would have to be really tough, or a psychopath,' I said. 'I've worked with some of these guys,' Dad said. 'Who?' Mom said. 'Who have you worked with?' 'Robert Wilson,' Dad said. 'The Wilsons lived in a *gated community* in Saudi Arabia,' Mom said.

'He has done numerous stints with a variety of organizations.' 'Numerous?' Mom said. 'Variety?' 'Anyhoo,' I said. 'It's also just a really good article. Really well written.' 'Why don't you think about doing something like that?' Mom said. 'Like what?' Becoming a thoracic surgeon and volunteering to help in war-torn areas?' 'No,' Mom said. 'Journalism.' 'I have a job. One that pays very well, actually,' I said. 'But the main reason I don't think about something like journalism is that I have never once considered working as a journalist or had any interest in the journalistic profession.' 'All right, mister,' Mom said. 'I just thought you'd be good at it. You're always reading these articles.' 'Dad is always watching the news,' I said. 'Do you think he should become an anchorman?' Mom burst out laughing. 'He'd need to get his hair cut first.' 'I don't need a haircut,' Dad said. 'I just think,' Mom said, 'there's so much out there you'd be good at. You might be happier doing something else.' 'Have I told you that I was unhappy in my job? Did I say that I didn't like my profession?' 'You don't have to say anything,' Mom said. 'And even if I was unhappy,' I said, 'what's the problem with that? Plenty of people are unhappy in their jobs. At least they pay me a lot.' 'There's more to life than having nice things,' Dad said. 'I still have all the same stuff from when I first moved in,' I said. 'The point to getting paid well is that it means I have options.' 'But you've been at the same company since you graduated,' Mom said. 'How did we get on this topic in the first place?' I said. 'I thought we were talking about black boxes.' 'You two were talking about them,' Mom said. 'I'd rather watch paint dry than talk about black boxes.' 'Speaking of paint drying—' 'Sorry, Dad,' I said, 'there's somebody at the door. You'll have to tell me your paint-drying story some other time.' 'Get something to eat,' Mom said. 'I'll send it to you in an email,' Dad said.

I sat down at the little table on my balcony and lit another cigarette. It was one of those mornings where the sunlight is so warm and bright that it makes even the grimmest views seem cheery, and the whole alley was lit in the most pleasing and picturesque way. After spending so much time surrounded by the latest architectural marvels and living in the most advanced urban environments in the world, I was still impressed by the decrepit glamour of my adopted hometown. There were hardly any cars on the street, so I could hear the slight breeze moving through the leaves newly sprouted on the trees that ran along the fences. The only person outside was the lady on the other side of the alley who'd been living in her place at least as long as I'd been here, and who spent the day going in and out of her back door with her Shih Tzu. The dog would sniff around her yard while she sat on a patio chair and smoked, and just like every other time we were out there at the same time, we pretended not to notice each other, even though we were so close we could've easily engaged in some neighbourly small talk. The dog must be pretty old by now, I thought. In fact, there's no way it should still be alive since it had already seemed old when I first moved in. But it could've been a puppy back then, I thought. Of course, the old lady would've been twelve years younger when I first moved in, but from my point of view both she and the dog had always been the same age, in the way that fictional characters and dead people get stuck at a certain age. From the moment I'd landed, and for the entire cab ride from the airport to my apartment, right up until the moment I was smoking on the balcony and staring at the Shih Tzu Lady, I had the feeling that time had sped up over the nine months that I'd been away on foreign assignment, or more like it was flowing wildly through everything. 'Maybe,' I said to myself, 'it's not the same dog as before. Maybe, while you were away, her old dog got run over, or she had to put him down because his body was riddled with cancer, and she had mourned him—or her?—for a few months before finding a replacement.'

After nine months in a five-star suite with a huge wrap-around balcony that looked out onto a gleaming cityscape, it was in some ways dispiriting to return to what was essentially a fire escape on the second floor of a low-rent apartment. But while I didn't have an expansive view, and even though the balcony was so narrow that it barely fit a small table and chair, I liked to sit out there for hours while my neighbours sat out on their balconies as well and talked on the phone, or smoked, or cooked on small hibachis. My neighbours on the right side were blocked from my view by a built-in storage closet, and the ones below me were shielded by an awning, so even though many people had lived in those apartments over the years, I knew them only by the sound of their voices and often had no idea what they looked like. When I passed someone outside my building, I wondered if they might be my right-side neighbour, who I had heard the night before assembling furniture, or if they were the downstairs neighbour, who had been rehearsing for a job interview with their roommate. Unfortunately there was nothing between my small balcony and the small balcony of my left-side neighbour. I had been asking the Super to do something about this for years and even offered to pay for some sort of lattice or partition myself, but nothing had come of it and whenever the neighbours to the left of me were out on their balcony, because there was nothing obstructing our view of each other, I always wound up feeling like I should say hello or make small talk.

I sat there watching the lady and her dog out of the corner of my eye. There was a whiff of charcoal in the air. On my left-side neighbour's balcony I noticed a small hibachi with smoke wafting from the lid. Whenever something strange or out of the ordinary catches my attention—a couple in matching clothing walking a lizard, a young girl crying outside of a police station with a cat in her arms and an enormous hockey bag at her feet, an old man wearing a flak jacket slumped against the bathroom stall at the movie theatre—once the initial impulse to stare has passed, I always look away and pretend I didn't see anything. So even though a smoking, unattended hibachi struck me as a bit incongruous at nine the morning, I went back to watching the Shih Tzu Lady. I was somehow both happy and relieved to be back and angry at myself for still living here after all these years. Whatever I might have been looking forward to when I was younger, I thought, whatever I was going to accomplish in my life and career, whatever I thought was going to happen to me, had already happened, passed me by, there was nothing new on the horizon. Everything that was happening now in my life, and all that would happen to me, was simply a matter of inertia. But still, I thought, it was nice to be back home.

A man in a housecoat—not the shy, middle-aged woman, who must've moved out—came onto the balcony with the smoking hibachi. There were always people out. No matter what time of day it was, even if it was cold and raining, you could still find one of my neighbours out there taking apart an old TV set or building a picnic table out of scrap wood. 'This is what you get for staying here,' I said to myself. If I moved to a better neighbourhood then I'd never have to deal with people like the ones at the gas station where I bought my cigarettes, or the people in the coffee shop I stopped at on my way to work, not to mention the people I rode the escalator with on my way down to the subway platform. The everyday way they moved around, I thought, the grim purposelessness of everything they said, their infinite obscurity. I never missed an opportunity to bring up where I lived during small talk with my colleagues. I was proud of the neighbourhood's blue-collar bona fides. But now that I had been living here for the last twelve years the romance had worn off, and what was once authentic, charming, and culturally complex, struck me as inauthentic, cheap, and socially debased.

My next-door neighbour had lifted the lid off the hibachi and was poking at the coals with a dinner fork. The housecoat was rust-coloured. His feet were bare. His hair was so wildly askew that in another context it might have been fashionable, or at least eccentric, but on this man and in this context, it signified poverty and loneliness. He looked up from the hibachi and caught me staring at him. Instead of acting surprised or apologetic, I called to him as if I'd been waiting for him to notice me. 'Morning,' I said. 'I'm your neighbour.' He slowly raised himself from his crouched position, so slowly I had time to wonder if he'd heard me. 'You move in recently?' He nodded slightly. 'Yes.' He spoke as though I were sitting right next to him. The way he looked at me, and the virtually motionless way he was crouched while balancing on the very tips of his toes, was a little unnerving. Even though he was very still and quiet he didn't seem relaxed or at ease. In fact, I got the distinct impression that he was probably the sort of person who paced around his apartment all day with a manic energy that would have been scary to witness. He maintained a rabbit-like stillness over the hibachi, and with the defeated hunch of his shoulders, and his housecoat hanging off him like he'd been wearing it for days, I thought he must be borderline destitute. 'Yes,' he said, 'I'm new here,' and then went back to stoking the coals with the dinner fork.

As much as I can't stand making polite conversation with neighbours, or colleagues, or the people who serve me throughout the day, what I find even more excruciating is when I am stuck with someone who refuses to make small talk, but instead insists on an awkward and sometimes even unbearable silence. Even though I can't stand carrying on inane debates over whether it had rained more the previous summer, or exchanging opinions on the chances of professional sports teams, and as painful as it is to listen to someone recount in minute detail a routine surgical procedure, there is nothing more unnatural to me than not making small talk. But as I was thinking of something to say, my neighbour put the cover on the hibachi and opened the door to his apartment. 'Take care,' I said as he turned back around, picked up the hibachi with smoke pouring from its lid, and hauled it in with him, letting the door swing shut behind.

I was so tired, or jet-lagged, that at that moment, as I was slumped in the chair and smoking my third cigarette in a row, I didn't really consider how strange it was for him to bring the hibachi inside. Whether it was the guy who set up a couch and TV in the back alley so he could screen footage of a bluegrass music festival, or the guy who shot Roman candles off his balcony once a month in an oddly solemn and dutiful manner, or the lady who spent most of the daylight hours sweeping her front walk and grooming the small rectangles of grass on either side until they had the meticulous groom I associated with Japanese landscaping, the neighbourhood was full of so many strange characters that I had stopped worrying about them a long time ago.

At the beginning of each foreign assignment, I am dropped into the centre of a huge city, I thought, as the Shih Tzu Lady went inside and the alley was finally empty. My company injects me into a little bubble of corporate luxury and immediately puts me to work, and I quickly develop the ability to stay focused on something nebulous and inconsequential without being distracted by the swirl of novelty surrounding me. But everyone who has to live and work in one of the world's few megacities learns very quickly how to shut everything out. They learn that they can't afford to be curious or concerned. Just like in that recent long-form article in the *Times* about the Kitty Genovese murder, I thought. She was stalked, raped, and stabbed to death over the span of two attacks that took about an hour from the first to the last, and even though she'd apparently been screaming for help and her neighbours had heard her, nobody came to her aid, or even called the police. The police chief who oversaw the investigation was so disgusted by the callous behaviour of the victim's neighbours that he contacted a journalist at the *Times*. When the story came out it was an international scandal and a national disgrace. It was generally accepted as definitive proof of the inhumanity of urban life, and the public outrage was so intense and sustained that the government passed the first in what became a series of laws that made it illegal to stand by while a crime was being committed. But as it turned out, according to the long-form article, the story of the neighbours was completely inaccurate. A few neighbours had called the police, some had gone to their windows or went outside to look around, and one neighbour had even found Kitty Genovese huddled in a doorway after the second attack, and cradled her as she bled to death, waiting for the police to arrive. The long-form article described how the myth of the inhumane urban neighbourhood had persisted for decades, and then the journalist documented every instance of neighbourly kindness and concern on the night of the murder. But when I finished reading it, I wasn't convinced. Even if a few people tried to help Kitty Genovese, I thought, the majority of those who heard her death screams simply ignored them. The journalist of the long-form article tried to prove that the initial story had been wrong, that the victim's neighbours weren't all bad. But there is a very simple reason most of her neighbours didn't do anything to help, I thought, and it's not because they were bad people. If we stopped and listened to every stranger we passed in the street who looked as if they might be lost, confused, or in distress, if we took the time to consider every petition for charity, or to hear out every hard-luck story from our co-workers, or bothered to acknowledge the barely disguised cries for help embedded in the body language of our seatmates during our daily commutes, then it would be no exaggeration to say that our days would be taken up by the lives of others. I pass by homeless people all the time, I thought, sprawled out in the street, deranged by untreated mental disease. I tell myself that if I had the time I would stop to see it they were okay. In an ideal world, I thought, I would always be ready to offer help and support to whoever needed it, even if it was a complete stranger. But in the real world it isn't practical, and could even be dangerous, to get involved in somebody else's problems. Of course, there are some problems that are easy to fix, but most problems are much harder, if not impossible, to solve, and in my experience there's no reliable way at the outset to make this distinction. It's extremely rare to be in a position to help someone, and I'm sure that the reason so many people stand around staring at the scene of an accident has less to do with a morbid curiosity or a form of civic schadenfreude and is mostly because they desperately want to do something and they can't let go of the thought that at some point they might wind up being useful, and not completely *useless*. But most of the time, let's face it, there's usually nothing you can do to help and getting involved with other people's problems is a total waste of time.

A few years ago, I heard a couple arguing through the walls of my room in the luxury hotel where I was staying during a month-long foreign assignment. It got so bad that I considered calling the police. It was impossible to say for certain whether actual physical abuse was taking place, or if it was merely an intense non-physical fight. And even if the loud crashes and banging I was hearing were in fact the sounds of physical violence, I thought, how could I be sure that calling the cops wouldn't make the situation even more volatile? For years I'd been reading stories online about people getting shot by the police in their own homes, and while I had no idea what the cops were like in this city, I assumed they were just as bad if not worse than the ones I'd been reading about. As I was trying to decide what to do they eventually quieted down. It was nothing, I told myself, just an innocuous argument that only sounded like something worse. After a few days I heard them at it again but now it was just part of a routine.

It's never a good idea to get involved, I thought, looking down in the alley at a skunk waddling alongside the dilapidated fences. Because when we do, we usually get it all wrong. We blunder into a situation based on a misunderstanding, and in almost no time at all we offend everyone involved, creating problems where there weren't any, and introducing confusion where things were once clear. Like the time my dad called to tell me that he was giving up his dog, I thought. He'd gotten the dog a couple years before, and it had gone from being a cute puppy to an exuberant, almost wild dog, with an explosive and purposeless energy. The dog's need for attention seemed pathological, like an addiction. All of this might have been bearable if it hadn't been for the dog's shrill and incessant barking. If she was left alone, she would bark until you returned, and her voice would be cracked from the strain of going nonstop for hours on end. She would stand over her bowl or sit facing the door to the backyard and deploy her glass-cutting bark until someone fed her or let her out the back door. 'For the last year,' my dad said, 'your mother and I have been constantly fighting over this dog. We wanted a replacement for Wilbur,' he said, referring to the family dog. 'But we got something completely different.' After asking around, my father discovered that it was very difficult to give a two-year-old dog up for adoption. Once a dog has been given up or abandoned by its owners, the compassionate thing to do, his vet told him, was to destroy the animal.

'You just need a break,' I said. 'Mom is stuck at home all day with the dog while you're at work. Even if it was the most obedient and well-behaved dog, Mom would still be going out of her mind.' But my dad insisted that the dog was simply more than they had bargained for and that it was best for everyone if they gave it up. While I had no part in raising or caring for the dog, I felt as though it was up to me to save it from my father, who I believed was acting out of desperation, and would surely change his mind in a couple weeks. So, without considering the disruption to my routine, I offered to take care of the new dog. 'And if,' I said, 'after a couple of weeks, you still feel like giving her up, I promise not to say a thing.'

At this time, there was a group of girls living in an apartment on the other side of the alley who regularly held loud, raucous, all-night parties. There was hardly an hour of the day when they weren't blasting music from the blown speakers of their stereo. I would sit on my balcony and watch them dancing in cowboy boots and high heels, erupting into spontaneous chants and singalongs. One night I thought about crossing the alley and asking them to turn their music down. I held off because they were extremely attractive and even though their round-the-clock partying was annoying, I couldn't bring myself to complain because I didn't want to ruin whatever chance I might have of sleeping with one of them.

After a week of taking care of the dog all day, and then watching the hard-partying girls all night, I decided to get out of my apartment and go see a movie. Before I went out, I took the dog for a long walk and played a game of fetch with her at the park. She started in on her nails-across-a-chalkboard barking as I got ready at the door and I could still hear her while I waited at the bus stop on the corner of my street, but I told myself that she would eventually settle into her place on the couch. I don't recall exactly how long I was out for, but it couldn't have been more than a couple hours. When I turned onto my street I saw a cop car parked outside my place, and as I walked past it, two cops got out and asked if I lived there. They told me that a neighbour had complained that my dog was barking. I explained that it was a noisy dog and that I was looking after it for my parents. They said that my neighbour had said the dog sounded like it was in pain or distress. 'Yeah,' I said, 'that's just her bark. It's pretty bad. I can go get her if you want.' They told me to go get the dog. She was waiting at the door and started barking deliriously when my key hit the lock. I put her on the leash and brought her out as she continued to bark, and I thought that it did in fact sound as if she was in pain. The cops looked down at her and shrugged. 'Just try to keep her quiet,' they said. The next day I found an unmarked envelope in my mailbox and inside was a handwritten letter.

They weren't the sort of people to complain about noise, they explained, but they felt they had to do something. If they saw someone getting attacked in the street, or heard someone screaming for help, they would call the police. So why, they wrote, should this situation be any different? Any dog that sounded the way mine did was clearly in distress, and this distress, they wrote, was due to neglect and mistreatment.

As I read their letter by my balcony light, there was no doubt in my mind that their concern was a sham concern, that this supposedly principled and high-minded letter was nothing but a nasty, small-minded noise complaint. Even if they had been worried about the dog, they could've said something to me when I got home, instead of calling the cops, which I considered to be the worst thing you could do to a neighbour, and only justified in the most extreme cases.

I went over to their place the next morning. There weren't any lights on in their apartment. I rang their doorbell. I kept my finger on the bell and I could hear it ringing out in their apartment. No one answered, so I took their letter from my pocket, tore it into hundreds of little pieces, and sprinkled them in their mailbox.

You should never call the cops on your neighbours, I thought, except for the most extreme cases, because you never really know what's going on in the lives of other people, and you have only a superficial and often distorted perspective of your neighbours. Of course, that has never stopped me, I thought, from talking about people as if I know what goes on in their heads. 'She would never do something like that,' I say. 'She just doesn't have it in her.' I condemn people I've only just met, and pass judgment on others that I've known for years, basing my opinion on nothing more than a few strong impressions that, in the absence of anything more substantial, take on an exaggerated form, the way a cartoonist will seize on a single characteristic and blow it up. 'That sounds like something he would say,' I say. 'He's always talking about that sort of thing.' But the opinions I have of other people are probably misguided opinions for the most part, and if I knew the whole story, if I understood the full context, then I'm sure I would feel completely differently, so while I didn't think there was anything wrong with gossiping about other people, it seemed risky to get into making public complaints and accusations.

I lit a fourth cigarette and let my mind go slack. I wondered about whether I should keep my landline or give it up. Should I hire a cleaning service again or just take care of it myself? Should I buy a car even though I had no use for one?

At the office the next day, I was given the Mission Accomplished treatment. The time I spent in exotic locations working on huge multimillion-dollar projects that were relentlessly promoted in the company's own internal memorandums and newsletters had left my colleagues with a grossly inflated sense of my achievements. Contracts that I'd been involved in only as a formality were presented as examples of my shrewd tactical sense, while vast bureaucratic enterprises that sucked up thousands of man-hours were credited to my talent for organization and management. The almost mythical dimensions of my reputation made my colleagues feel better about their own less glamorous positions. It was more inspiring, and reassuring, they thought, to believe in a charismatic and brilliant personality who was singlehandedly managing these huge accounts, than to see me as simply a highly placed vassal in this brutal system of financial feudalism.

Despite the company's cutthroat corporate environment— the merciless performance expectations, the seasonal layoffs—I had never worried about my position. I was only ever at the home office for a few weeks before I would be sent off again on another foreign assignment, and whenever I was away I felt exempt from the office politics that seemed to govern most of my colleagues' careers. But this time, even on my first day back, I started to get the impression that the foreign assignment days were over. There were no transformative foreign initiatives in the works, Roger said to me when I stopped by his office that morning. I thought that maybe this was a sign that I was finally going to be laid off, which wouldn't have been that surprising since it was rare for someone to last as long in their position as I had. Most people at my company, no matter how valued or cherished, were usually laid off within a few years. An employee who'd been around for a decade was considered an old-timer. In the days following my return to the office, I caught up with the company gossip and went to the usual clutch of meetings (one-on-ones, town halls, debriefs, and post-mortems) but mostly I just sat at my desk and read Pulitzer Prize–winning long-form investigative articles about Donald Trump's finances, or watched previews for movies I had no intention of going to see. I came in every day dressed impeccably in one of my bespoke suits, and I went through the motions of reporting to Roger on projects that I no longer had any active role in, and going for long lunches with my colleagues, where we talked shop or spun our wheels discussing local sports, but then I would slump back into my ergonomic desk chair and start clicking through satellite images of drone strikes, or pictures of celebrities on vacation. I assumed it was only a matter of time before someone wondered what I was doing all day, but right away it seemed clear that while everybody must have known I wasn't working on anything, nobody seemed to care, not even Roger.

And even though I spent my whole day at the office doing nothing but reading long-form articles and checking my social media feeds, I came home completely drained. During my last foreign assignment, my days were full of meetings, site visits, promotional events, and award ceremonies. I would spend my morning in the back seats of taxis and town cars, slowly moving through the city from one client to the next, and then pass my afternoon responding to an exacting volume of email from the home office, until I finally curled up in my hotel bed and caught a few hours of deep, restful sleep. Any time I had on the weekends not already taken up by corporate events that my foreign clients politely insisted on was used to explore cultural landmarks and institutions, or to conduct self-guided tours through the historic neighbourhoods and city parks. I was often in a state of frenzied exhaustion, riding a slow wave of adrenaline, but I always felt ready for one more client lunch or a video conference with the partners at the home office.

But in the first few days back, menial administrative requirements that I would normally get through in the midst of a flurry of activity and professional obligations were now capable of tying me up for hours, and I still left the office with them unfinished. It wasn't uncommon for me to lose myself in one of these tasks without getting anywhere, signing up for a webinar or creating a user account on a professional forum could take all morning, and in the afternoon I might spend hours searching for a thread with a client that I was worried I'd never followed up on. At home, preparing a simple dinner could stretch so late into the evening that by the time I finished wiping down the kitchen I had to start getting my lunch together for the next day. In the span of a week, my life, which had once been so busy, had been reduced to a sparse routine that I could barely manage.

So, after a day of reading articles on Elon Musk or an in-depth analysis of the flaws in the design of the Boeing 737 MAX, the only thing I wanted to do was sit on my balcony, look at the internet, and watch my neighbours. On most nights a group of young guys in a ground-floor apartment on the other side of the alley gathered around a scrap-wood fire that they kept burning in a repurposed barbecue and forced each other to watch online clips of sporting disasters and comedy sketches. A girl in a floral print dress was usually stretched out on a lounge chair and tapping away on her phone while an enormous dog lay next to her. Through the kitchen window of the apartment directly across from me, I would watch a couple spend hours preparing food which I never got to see them eat.

I had always been upfront with my neighbours that I was only interested in being on nodding terms with them, and every one of them silently accepted these terms without complaint. Only rarely had I gone so far as to move past a nodding relationship with one of my neighbours, to a small talk relationship. But something in the way my new next-door neighbour had been tending to the coals in the hibachi, the way he had seemed both in a hurry but also unnervingly slow in his movements, left me feeling anxious about our next encounter, and more than anything I wanted to make it clear that I was a private person who wasn't interested in developing a next-door neighbour smalltalk dynamic. So I was relieved when after a few days he still hadn't come out on his balcony. A little over a week ago, I thought, I was living in a suite on the thirty-second floor of a luxurious hotel with a wraparound balcony that looked out onto the entire west side of a megacity. After a day making small talk with high-powered clients, I thought, I got to lie back on the lavishly upholstered patio furniture and stare at the skyscrapers, fantasizing about what was going on inside them. Coming back to my apartment that was nested in the centre of a drab tenement building, sitting on a small collapsible chair that barely fit on my balcony, and looking down onto the unpaved alley, which ran between the two rows of buildings like a dried-up riverbed, I felt completely exposed. It reminded me of when I'd gone on a safari as part of a corporate retreat and we had to stay in tents that had been pitched out in a wide-open field. I couldn't sleep, and spent every night thinking that all of the animals we'd seen that day were out there in the darkness that surrounded us, watching and waiting. I was terrified, even though we had armed guides.

The people in my neighbourhood, I thought, as I sat on my balcony late one night after I got back from my nine-month foreign assignment, these *alley people*, I thought, are just as elusive and strange to me as the wildlife on that safari. Just as humanity, over centuries of alienating industrial production, has been cut off from nature, I thought, I have, in a considerably shorter time frame, and without the attendant world-historical consequence, cut myself off from humanity. As I watched the Pseudo Homeless Guys throw the remains of a packing crate onto the fire they had going in their empty barbecue, I clicked on an award-winning profile of a woman who had lost her entire family during a brutal ten-year civil war. The profile started with the horrific story of how her family was suddenly wiped out in a gruesome massacre that she survived by hiding under a pile of bodies. After suffering through years on the run, enduring abject deprivation and terror, she finally managed to get a bit of money together, and with the help of a distant relative who had already immigrated a few years before, she came to the very city I live in about a year ago, and now had a job at a bakery and an apartment downtown in a neighbourhood that was only a twenty-minute walk from my front door. The idea that she was living nearby, that we rode the same buses and walked along the same streets, was fantastical to me, as if a fictional character had come to life.

I eventually got bored with the sights and sounds of the alley. I stopped watching the Pseudo Homeless Guys showing each other videos of sports riots on their phones, and I didn't even notice the Shih Tzu Lady anymore or bother to look up when a man in a motorcycle jacket walked by with a long-haired cat on a leash. I sat out there as if I were in my own living room, smoking and drinking and reading articles, watching content, or grooming my social media accounts. The alley-world faded into the background as my online-world expanded, and it seemed as if that online-world was perpetually on fire. Every day brought a fresh batch of catastrophes, a parade of spectacular horrors that I scrolled through and clicked on, poring over the minutiae of timelines, reading witness statements, flight transcripts, leaked emails. I would spend days reading every article I could find on the Seattle WTO protests in 1999, or the history of the MK-Ultra program in the CIA, chasing down information as if it mattered whether I understood the whole story, as if it were all leading to something more, an ever greater understanding of the way the world works. I watched videos of drone strikes, beheadings, mass executions, and clips of protestors being brutalized by riot police. On some nights, I was so fired up by my online activity that I felt like talking to someone about it, in real life. I used to be in the habit of talking to a couple of my old college friends over the phone once or twice a year, but it had been a long time since I'd spoken with any of them, and even though we texted every once in a while, it seemed inappropriate to blindside them with a call without giving them a day or two heads-up so they would have time to prepare, or to come up with an excuse for why they weren't available. So while I was reading an article about American Civil War monuments and drinking from my third or fourth can of IPA, I found myself looking up from my phone and then watching my next-door neighbour's balcony door in the hope that he would make an appearance. But he never came out so we could small talk about the road work going on up the street, or the current political scandal playing out in the news. His door never opened and I never once caught a glimpse of him in the kitchen window that was covered with a bedsheet. Maybe he doesn't come out on his balcony, I thought, because I'm always out here on mine.

Balcony drinking, I thought, is a way to be by myself without having to drink alone. I can spend the night watching the alley and looking at my phone and in a way my neighbours and my phone are keeping me company. On the balcony, I thought, I was a young professional enjoying the warm weather and having a few drinks, while taking in the sights and sounds of the neighbourhood. But the next day, after joylessly consuming a burger and fries for lunch at the upscale bistro on the mezzanine level of my office building, I found myself dozing off during one of the two-hour town halls, and when I jolted awake I looked up to see Roger staring back at me. So I decided to take it easy on the IPAs, and I moved from the balcony to the couch in my TV room. I continued to follow the international news cycle and monitor my social media accounts, but instead of sitting outside and drinking beer, I moved inside and started watching prestige TV and smoking weed. I read reviews and recaps of the shows I'd watched the night before, and then I read about the shows I hadn't seen yet, trying to determine whether they were good enough to add to my watch-list. I would come home with a hundred dollars' worth of takeout and watch four or five episodes while getting high and feeding straight from the sturdy plastic and styrofoam takeout containers. And while I was feeling much better now that I wasn't drinking three or four strong IPAs every night, and even though I had never done anything more than nod hello to the people I saw in the alley, once I had stopped hanging out on the balcony and moved to the couch, I felt much lonelier than I had before.

One night I was watching the first season of a new series about the McCarthy hearings and I opened the window to air out the apartment. When I sat back down on the couch I was struck by a strong offensive smell. There was something familiar about it. I leaned out the window and sniffed the air. I shut the window and sat back on the couch. The smell started to fill the room. I leaned over to sniff the couch cushions. I thought back to when I had first moved in more than a decade ago. The apartment had been infested with mice. I had tried every sort of trap on the market. Finally, I begged the Super to call an exterminator. A man in coveralls showed up at my apartment and talked for an hour about the effects of anticoagulants and how the mice would bleed out internally. 'You've got yourself a little colony here,' he said. 'So when they die it may stink up the place a bit.' The thought of a horde of mice decomposing in my apartment walls was disturbing, but after the exterminator had seeded the place with poison, and sightings of the mice dwindled and their droppings disappeared, I forgot all about the fact that they were likely rotting away somewhere, and I don't recall there being much of a smell. Earlier that day I'd been reading about the personality traits of school shooters and the effect of global warming on financial markets, so by the time I got home my mind was racing with apocalyptic images. I sat on my couch and wondered if the mice were back, imagined my walls full of tiny little corpses, packed in so tightly they resembled a grotesque form of insulation, the whole mass swarming with maggots and radiating a fetid stench that seeped through the plaster and hung over me. I fought the urge to go to a hotel. I convinced myself I was experiencing a panic attack brought on by the joint I'd smoked only a moment ago. I told myself that it was just the smell of the furniture, the carpet, and the walls. Odours that had developed over the years I'd been living in the apartment, as well as the months it had sat vacant while I was away on my extended foreign assignments. Smells that had no doubt been lingering for a while now. I wondered if it was possible that the odour was in some way related to the habit I had gotten into after moving from the balcony to the couch of passing out in my clothes in front of the TV instead of getting undressed and going to sleep in my bed. As a tiny revolt against my bachelor life, I had been sleeping on the couch. Because, for some reason, passing out on the couch in the clothes I'd worn to the office that morning felt less lonely than going to bed and falling asleep underneath my lumpy duvet. This singularly unpleasant smell, impossible for me to place, though it was maddeningly familiar, this smell that I hadn't noticed until I started spending my nights indoors, this smell that was so strong it was unsettling, this smell, I thought, was simply the accumulation of a decade of excretions and spills, fumes and smoke, steam and vaporized grease that had settled into the upholstery and was set free after I'd spent a couple of weeks sleeping on the couch. All I had to do was hire a cleaner, I thought, to get the apartment smelling just like the hotels I stayed in during my foreign assignments. I could feel the anxiety lifting as I did some online research of the city's professional cleaning services, and once I had read through the reviews of the most highly rated companies I went to my room, undressed, and went to bed.

There's nothing more satisfying than throwing money at a problem to make it go away. No matter what the problem is, or how big it might be, all I have to do is throw money at it again and again until it finally disappears. Most problems, I thought, as I lay in bed and sniffed the air, can be easily handled by relentlessly throwing money at them. My first instinct in every problematic situation is to scatter money all around me. I neutralize my problems with a money-saturation method, and it's a source of infinite comfort to me that I am paid such a high salary because I don't know how I would get through a single day without the ability to ceaselessly throw money at life's problems. I hired a trio of women to steam-clean the furniture and disinfect every surface in the apartment. I took my clothes to the dry cleaner and I bought a variety of expensive houseplants. But within a day or two the smell came back. I went through my apartment in a frenzy, smelling every surface, sticking my head in cupboards and closets, burying my face in the upholstery, sniffing the air in each room. After hours of sniffing the whole apartment like a crazed animal, I was starting to despair. The smell was everywhere and nowhere. I waited a few days to see if it might fade but it seemed to be getting stronger. What had once been offensive was now completely unbearable. I kept the front window open all day and night even though it didn't seem to help much. As I leaned out one night and tried to breathe in the early summer air, I caught a huge whiff of the odour coming from my neighbour's window.

I had thrown hundreds of dollars at a useless and ultimately demoralizing cleaning effort that only succeeded in masking the smell for as long as it took the cleaning products to wear off. Since I had first noticed the smell, I had always assumed that it was coming from my apartment, and that I must've been responsible for it. I never considered that it was actually coming from next door and had nothing to do with me. I felt like an idiot for not making the connection sooner. He's definitely the type of person, I thought, that would have problems with hygiene. All the nights I had spent out on the balcony reading and monitoring my social media account, he never came out once, and when I moved indoors and started spending my nights on the couch, I never heard a sound from the other side of the wall I shared with him. I sometimes wondered if he was even in there, though for the most part I didn't think about him, and of course I was grateful for the privacy and quiet. But now that I knew that the smell I'd been living with was coming from my neighbour's place, I spent my nights on the couch distracted by thoughts of what he was up to.

This neighbourhood is full of guys like him, I thought, scroungers who live off the rest of us, hoarders who barricade themselves into their crowded one-bedroom apartments and lurch from month to month with the money that trickles down from social assistance, all of them doing their best to drown out the screaming chaos in their minds. My neighbour was just one of the legion of shattered souls who lived out their days in solitude and poverty. But while their lives might be full of suffering, I thought, it was nothing compared to the people like the refugee woman in the long-form profile. People like that, I thought, struggle against monstrous, unstoppable, world-historical forces. Those people, I thought, serve an almost sacred role in society, like the beggars and lepers in Bible stories. Whereas people like my neighbour only have a very limited role, one that is mostly passive and definitely not sacred, that seems to consist in travelling the same downward trajectories that people like them have been travelling for thousands of years. I imagined him on the other side of my wall, hunched over a bowl of cheap meat, surrounded by schizophrenic squalor, giving off such an overwhelming stench that it was impossible for me to relax and enjoy my night of smoking weed and watching prestige TV. I may live in a rundown apartment in a shitty neighbourhood, I thought, but nobody should have to put up with this. I may not live in the trendy neighbourhoods in one of the upscale condos like all my colleagues, and maybe it is unrealistic to expect my landlord to stay on top of the upkeep of this sort of building, but there is no way I am going to keep silent while my neighbour destroys my quality of life, I thought as I put some Visine in my eyes.

'This is completely unacceptable,' I said to myself while I stood in the bathroom waiting for the Visine to take effect. 'This shit has gone on long enough,' I said, though I wasn't actually talking out loud and instead I was imagining that I was talking to the landlord. 'I know you think that just because the rent is cheap you don't have to keep the building in good shape, but if you think for one second,' I said, threatening the Imaginary Landlord, 'if you think that I am going to stand for this sort of *proprietary negligence*, then you are sorely mistaken. I'm not like the other tenants,' I said, 'I know my rights. I may let a lot slide, but there is no way I am going to tolerate living next to a biohazard.' I went downstairs and rang the Super's doorbell. I was planning on expressing myself in the exact terms I'd just been rehearsing with the Imaginary Landlord, but at the sight of the haggard look on the Super's face I decided that it didn't make sense to start with this approach. 'She just collects the rent,' I thought. 'This isn't her fault.'

She'd been the Super for as long as I'd been living there. When I first saw the place, she was the one to show me the apartment, which she'd described at the time as a 'good, quiet apartment.' Over the years we'd developed a relationship made up of the small talk exchanges we had every once in a while. It felt like just by taking the time to say hello I was performing a charitable act. From what I could tell, her days were spent sitting in her living room in the armchair that faced the front window, watching the passersby, or, when the weather was nice, sitting on her front step listening to talk radio on a battery-powered set. The brief conversational interludes she carried on with me and a couple other characters from the neighbourhood made up the entirety of her social life. So it seemed cruel to all of a sudden start speaking to her as if she worked for me.

But the only reason I hadn't moved out of this building, I thought, was so I could live anonymously and not have to get involved in situations like this. The routine, necessary, and transactional relationships that develop between neighbours, making small talk with the friendly guy who does the dry cleaning, or being on a first-name basis with the baristas at the coffee shop, were a sort of psychic tax for living in a big city, I thought. Menu banter with the server at the local diner— unbearable. Price confusion at the checkout of my grocery store—sheer agony. It wasn't because I thought I was too good for these people, though in many ways I was, or that I thought this was a shitty neighbourhood, which of course I did. I simply didn't want to waste precious free time and limited energy talking to people who were never going to be anything more to me than human obstacles that I had to figure out how to get around in my day-to-day life. Besides, I wasn't very good at making neighbourly small talk. Whatever talent I had for small talk in my professional life didn't translate when it came to my personal life. The fluency that so many people in this city exhibit as they chat confidently with drivers as they get in and out of cabs, or the obliviousness with which they ask a question outside the metro station, this inborn confidence and competency is something that I'm only able to summon with tremendous effort. Every time I order takeout, or nod hello to a neighbour, the moment I have to pick up a package at the post office, or purchase a pack of cigarettes at the store, I always feel as if I am communicating in a language I don't understand, even though I've been speaking it my entire life and it is the only one I have. The brief chats I had with the

Super were no exception. There were moments of course when I felt a patronizing warmth for her, the sort I imagine a teacher feels for their students, or a parent for their child, and, on a few occasions, instead of avoiding her, as I did with everyone else in the neighbourhood, I would wave and stop at her walkway for some harmless small talk. It wasn't until I had to complain about the smell coming from the neighbour's apartment that I realized that on account of the infrequent small talk conversations we had gone from being strangers to something more like *acquaintances*.

'Nice to see you,' she said, which I knew, for someone as painfully reserved as her, was the verbal equivalent of throwing her arms around me.

'Good to see you too,' I said.

We talked for a few minutes and took turns updating each other. I told her about the wealthy people I met on my recent foreign assignment and gave her details on some of the more outrageous instances of luxury I'd experienced, because I assumed that was what she wanted to hear. She brought me up to speed on the current tenants.

'What's the deal with the new guy living next to me?'

A meaningful look.

I was flattered that she thought we'd reached the stage where this style of silent communication could pass between us, and even though I matched her look with a meaningful one of my own, I actually had no idea what her look meant. We stood like that, looking meaningfully at each other, for an unnaturally long time, until I broke the spell. 'He's a serial killer?' I said. She made a little sound, like a snort. 'I hope not,' she said. She recited a few details. He'd been living there for almost a year, didn't go out much or have anyone over. She seemed to be expecting me to see some hidden pattern embedded within these generic facts. I was starting to get annoyed with the Super's meaningful look and I wanted to politely point out to her that while we were friendly with each other she shouldn't assume that just because we did the small talk thing that I would know what her meaningful look meant. Why won't she just tell me? I thought. What is the point of a meaningful look when she knows I was away for nine months and couldn't possibly know anything about my next-door neighbour? Maybe by this meaningful look of hers she was trying to tell me that my neighbour was a drug dealer, or maybe she was looking at me like this because of the way he sorted his recycling. With our superficial small talk dynamic it was impossible for me to know what she considered mean-ingful look material.

It's exhausting to have to draw information out of some-one. For my entire professional life I have been imploring, cajoling, seducing, and, of course, begging for people to tell me things they were inevitably going to tell me anyway but for some reason they held out until I humiliated myself trying to get it out of them. Whenever someone has something to say, I thought, as I stood there staring at the Super, they will never come straight out with it. Instead, they use it to draw you out, because as long as you are trying to get them to tell you this privileged, or private, or precious information, they have you in their power. Which is why, I thought, during meetings at the home office, everyone speaks in elaborately vague jargon, piling one clause onto another, always grasping for the latest cliché, worrying over their words as if they are saying something of substance, when they are actually talking complete nonsense, trying to keep everyone from guessing the tiny bit of useful information they have saved for the very end. I was annoyed by the Super's meaningful look, and even though by now I felt pretty certain I knew what she was trying to tell me, I was not going to give her the satisfaction of asking her anything. She wants you to guess, I thought, so she doesn't have to say it. She is trying to implicate you. I let her keep staring. I didn't lean in with a sly grin, or wink and nod to show that her message had been received. I had hoped that she might be able to tell me something useful, that she had been looking into the situation, that it was being taken care of by the landlord, but her meaningful look also meant that while she had a lot to say, she probably wasn't going to do anything about it tonight.

'What's the problem?' she said.

'Well, I'm not sure,' I said. 'But there is a really strong smell coming from somewhere in the building and I'm almost positive it's coming from his place.'

'Smell?' she said.

Yes, I said, there was a smell, and it was strong. I certainly wasn't imagining it, I said, and I was surprised that she hadn't noticed it as well.

'Can't smell anything except my own home cooking,' she said, and then laughed. One inside joke that we'd developed over our small talk conversations was that we rarely cooked and mostly ate takeout. 'He said he works on the planes. One of those flight attendants,' she said. 'You'd never get me on one of those. You heard about the plane in New York that crashed in the water after a bird flew into it? I had an aunt that went down in one of those small propeller planes. Puddle jumpers, they call them. She was on vacation in Greece. She hardly ever flew herself. She had just divorced her husband— my dad's brother—a few years before that, and I guess she had always wanted to go to Greece. Can you imagine what must've been going through her mind? It's just terrible. I can't even think about it. We used to play cards together and I don't think I ever won a game. You would think that I would get lucky at least once. But she was a demon at the card table. She just loved winning. So it's probably best I never won because she wouldn't have liked losing against me. Not one bit.'

How the fuck, I thought, does she make it through the day? When every encounter has the potential to go on indefinitely, sidelined by digressions, random observations, jarring non sequiturs, meandering reminiscences, and every other kind of conversational misdirection? Something as straightforward as purchasing a lotto ticket could wind up taking over the whole afternoon. She's never in a hurry to get to the point. In fact, she does whatever she can to avoid the point altogether. Conversation, for someone like the Super, I thought, as I listened to her recite the names of people from her hometown who had perished in violent accidents, is just a way to get through the day. She is more than happy to spend hours and hours talking in long unbroken monologues about whatever comes to her mind while those of us who may be running late, or simply in a hurry to get home, who are stuck in line, or trying to make our way down the sidewalk, all of us who don't

have the time to listen to a security guard talk about the supply chain for vending machines, or carry on a conversation
with the internet serviceman about political corruption and
conspiracy theories, those of us who don't have any time to
spare are forced to wait on these people as they jam everything up, or at least slow it down, those of us who have
somewhere to be are forever getting delayed by these people
who have nowhere to go. But after years of experience I knew
that it was pointless to try to hurry people like the Super
along. It only leads to more holdups, more conversational
longueurs. 'Did you see the news?' she might say. Or, 'That
reminds me of the time...' The only way you get anywhere
with people like the Super is to play along in the hope that
they'll eventually lose interest and set you free.

So I said that I was pretty sure her home cooking smelled
worse. She laughed and said I was probably right. The last
time she'd tried to make something *from scratch* she'd nearly
burned the place down. I made a few remarks about my own
exclusive diet of takeout food, the same remarks I always
made when we did this small talk routine about how little
cooking we did, and how inept we were in our respective
kitchens. And she asked her usual series of questions about
my opinions on the restaurants in our neighbourhood. She
asked how often I ordered from each restaurant, what I
ordered, whether I would pick up the food or have it delivered.
By now I was deeply regretting my decision to complain
about the smell. I could have just sent an email to the landlord.
Or I should never have gotten involved in the first place. It
would have been better if I had just kept silent, burned a ton

of incense, and waited for the smell to go away. Because whatever was going on next door, it couldn't go on forever. By intervening in what was ostensibly a *building issue*, I was sticking my nose where it didn't belong, getting mixed up in other people's affairs, I thought. If I had just kept out of it, the whole thing would've taken care of itself. But you had to do something, I said to myself, even though you saw him only once, and don't even know his name. I live next door to him and so I'm responsible for him, I thought, in the same way that I'm responsible for the person sitting across from me on the bus, or standing behind me in line at the checkout. If I had just stayed on the couch, I thought, I could have avoided this responsibility. I should have done what the Super did, I thought, pretended I couldn't smell anything. 'You're only paying rent here, and whatever goes on next door, or anywhere else in the building, or in any of the other buildings on this street, or any of these streets in this neighbourhood, is none of your business, and definitely not your responsibility,' I said to myself while I listened to the Super talk about the noodles and dumplings from the place on the corner of our street. All I want is to be left alone in my apartment so I can get high and watch TV, I thought, or spend my nights reading about the trial of Anders Breivik or the catastrophic bleaching of the Great Barrier Reef. I should be able to leave for work every morning without having to worry about getting drawn into a protracted small talk session, I thought. I should be able to come home at the end of the day, disappear into my apartment, and enjoy the isolation that for me is one of the most attractive features to living in a big city. But now that I'd gotten involved, now that I was assuming responsibility for the smell in my neighbour's apartment, now that I had been caught up in an eddy of small talk, now that I was speculating with the Super over how many days a flight attendant was expected to work each week, I was worried I had inadvertently forfeited my privacy and anonymity, and that I would no longer be able to count on these privileges. 'I'm glad you said something,' the Super said. 'I've been meaning to ask if you had seen him around lately.'

She said she was pretty sure his car had been towed a few days ago. It had been blocking the entrance to the alley at the end of the street, and after a week's worth of tickets had piled up under the wipers, a tow truck came and took it away. 'It was that old red hatchback,' she said, pointing down the street to where the car had been before it was towed. 'You must have noticed it,' she said. I told her that I hadn't noticed the car, even though I would've walked right by it every day on my way to and from the Metro station. 'Really?' she said. 'There were probably a dozen tickets on the windshield.' I explained to the Super that when I was on my way to work in the morning I was still in the process of waking up so I wasn't paying much attention to what cars were parked on the street or whether they had parking tickets under their windshield wipers. 'I'm so out of it first thing in the morning,' I said, 'that there could be a cruise ship parked on the street and I wouldn't even notice.' And on my way home from work, I said, I was so drained by what had gone on at the office that all I could think about was the remaining distance I had to cover before I got home and could pour myself a drink.

I said 'pour myself a drink' to the Super instead of 'smoke a joint' because, despite my daily weed habit, I actually shared in many of the prejudices that people have of potheads, and even though I knew that the Super might've had some idea of the extent of my habit, and likely didn't care how I spent my time, I had never referred to it in her presence, but when I said 'pour myself a drink' a little grin disturbed the meaningful look she was still giving me.

As she was telling me about the neighbour's car, I couldn't shake the impression that she was leading me on and watching for my reaction. My reasons for why I hadn't noticed the car, she seemed to be implying by her meaningful look, were not very convincing. I told her that when I walked to the Metro every day, things that I see all the time, such as a car blocking the entrance to the alley at the bottom of the street, were easy to ignore, or pass over without really noticing. It takes effort for me to notice stuff, I said. I have to force myself to pay attention to things. I felt myself getting irritated again with the Super's meaningful look but I still couldn't move on from the issue of the towed car since it did seem like something that I should have noticed, and I was worried that maybe all the weed smoking and prestige TV watching was starting to have an effect. The Super finally interrupted me to say that in addition to the car that had been towed, my neighbour had bounced this month's rent cheque. We had been slowly moving in tandem a few steps at a time along the short walkway that led from the Super's front door to the sidewalk, and now we were standing at the sidewalk, looking up at my next-door neighbour's windows, which were covered with bedsheets. The landlord had called yesterday to tell the Super about the bounced cheque, she said, but she'd been too busy to look into it. 'Busy?' I said. She kept looking up at my neighbour's windows. 'Doesn't look like there's anybody home,' she said. I agreed that it was unlikely, and that based on what she had said about the towed car it was reasonable to assume that he hadn't been there for at least a few days, if not longer. Maybe he'd been keeping cats, I thought, and he abandoned them in the apartment, leaving them to fend for themselves. Or maybe an animal broke into his place, and now a family of squirrels, or even racoons, was nesting in one of the rooms. By this point, I was more or less convinced that whatever was causing the smell had to be something living, or that had once been alive, but I hadn't settled on anything specific. The Super finally stopped staring up at my neighbour's windows and turned to me with another meaningful look. 'We may as well go see what's causing the big stink,' she said. 'I don't know,' I said, and then I muttered something halfheartedly about not wanting to create an awkward situation.

'Things are pretty awkward already if he's stinking you out of your own place,' she said, as she rang my neighbour's doorbell. How was it possible, I thought, that she hadn't noticed the smell before? Why hadn't she gone to see if he was home after the landlord told her that he had bounced his last rent cheque? I said it probably wasn't appropriate for me to be there, but she ignored me and pulled out a ring of keys from her jacket pocket. 'Normally I wouldn't do this,' she said, though I knew that she sometimes let herself into the apartments if she saw that someone had left their windows open during a storm, or to let the Handyman in to check on a fuse box or a leaky ceiling. 'We're supposed to give twenty-four-hours' notice,' she said. 'But these are extenuating circumstances.' I could tell she was proud of herself for using this legal jargon, and I got the impression she had been waiting for the opportunity to use this phrase from the moment I told her about the smell coming from my neighbour's apartment. I followed her inside and shut the door behind me. The darkness in the stairway was absolute. We stood there, completely still. The smell was with us, but it was different than what had been seeping through my walls. It was fuller, more textured, as if what I'd been smelling had been only a copy, and this was the original. It permeated the darkness, thickening it, and invoked a wildly unpleasant feeling of being surrounded. I could feel panic creeping in. I groped along the wall for a switch, desperate for light. When I finally found the switch, it didn't work.

'Power's probably out,' the Super said. I felt my pocket for my phone but I'd left it back at my place. We climbed the stairs in silence. At the landing, I was able to make out the outline of the doorway, and the Super, after knocking tentatively, as if she were afraid of someone knocking back, fumbled at her key ring until she eventually found the right one and unlocked and pushed the door open. A thin stream of light from a streetlamp was coming through a tear in one of the sheets covering the living-room window. The apartment was almost bare except for a layer of trash, mostly empty cans and plastic bags. I could make out something on the far wall that looked like a Metro map. The room appeared empty at first, but when I moved around I bumped into a large coffee table and a couple of plastic chairs. I heard the Super trying out light switches in the kitchen and the sound of the fridge door opening.

'Well, this might have something to do with the smell,' she said. She held out her lighter to illuminate the shelves of the fridge packed with clamshell takeout containers. The smell coming off these containers and radiating from the fridge was strong, so strong we could only stand it for a moment before the Super slammed the door shut and we ran out onto the balcony to get away from the eye-watering stench. But, I thought, it was different from the other smell.

'Maybe we should leave,' I said.

The Super lit a cigarette and leaned against the railing. She had the look of someone taking a hard-earned break. I motioned for a cigarette and leaned back against the brick wall. Standing on my neighbour's balcony with that ungodly smell mingling with our cigarette smoke, I suddenly felt at ease in a way I hadn't since I returned from my last foreign assignment. The Super and I settled into some light small talk about the tenants who used to live in the building and the ways the neighbourhood had changed over the years, as well as the ways it had stayed the same. I felt proud of myself for being able to make friends with the Super. 'No matter how far you rise at the company,' I told myself, 'regardless of the obscenely luxurious hotels you stay in during your foreign assignments, and despite your superficial and frigid relationships with your colleagues, you still haven't lost your talent for getting on the same level with regular people.'

'Pretty messy in there,' she said.

'He's got a real laid-back approach to household chores,' I said. The Super laughed.

'What sort of monkish restraint does this guy have,' I said, 'that he would leave all that delicious takeout food to rot in the fridge? I can understand saving some in the fridge for later. But there's no way I'd let takeout sit there for more than a few hours before I'd be back to finish it off. What kind of monster,' I said, 'would do such a thing?' The Super had stopped laughing. Maybe I had pushed our little inside joke about takeout food too far, I thought. I had broken the spell that had been cast over this moment on my neighbour's balcony by using our inside joke in an utterly inappropriate context. The Shih Tzu Lady came down her back step, deposited the dog on her lawn, and lit up a cigarette. The Super and I straightened up and put ours out. 'Let's check the other rooms,' the Super said.

She opened the door to the kitchen and I was about to join her when I looked over at my own balcony. This is what he saw, I thought. This is where he was, I thought. All at once I felt I'd been transported outside of myself, seeing things through the eyes of my neighbour, and seeing my balcony from his point of view, the image of the little table and folding chair was both strange and vaguely sad. It's hard for me to articulate what it was that I found so depressing about this shift in perspective, but there was definitely something revelatory going on, a terrible and exhilarating rush of understanding took hold of me. I had always seen myself—as I imagine most everyone does—as not only the hero in my own life story, but the hero in everyone else's life story as well. Not only was I the lead character, I was the *only* character, since everyone else was an extra, which is to say that they existed as filler, or background, or to give the story a feeling of verisimilitude. But what had been revealed to me as I stood there staring at the balcony where I had spent the first few weeks after I got back from my last foreign assignment, drinking expensive small-batch beer and reading about the living conditions in European refugee camps, what I saw from the perspective of my neighbour's balcony was that I wasn't even the hero of my own life story. On the morning I saw my neighbour take a smoking hibachi into his apartment the whole scene had played out in my mind as though I were a fully rounded main character while he was cast in a bit part without any lines, purely functional, a flat two-dimensional person lacking any significance outside his brief walk-on. But now I could see that in fact he was the hero in this story, and I was just a thinly sketched character, or even worse. An extra, I thought, as I watched the Super through the small window on the kitchen door. Maybe we're all extras, I thought, not heroes or protagonists or main characters. Only poorly drawn, paper-thin, one-note extras, reciting the few lines we've been given, hitting our marks and waiting for our next cue, without any idea of why we're doing what we're doing, of the larger context, or what any of it means and what the whole thing is supposed to be about. Instead of appearing in the centre of the frame, I knew that I was actually out of focus, or buried in the shadows, and that everybody saw me in the same way as I saw them, as just another face in the background that blended in with everything else.

Of course this isn't very profound, and this little epiphany on my neighbour's balcony was the sort of revelation you might expect someone to have in the late stages of adolescence, but after spending so much time by myself in foreign countries, where everyone looks the same (to me), and sounds the same (to me), I got the feeling sometimes that I was the only *real* person in the world and that everyone else was imaginary. But now that I was standing on the same spot where my neighbour, who had seemingly vanished, and, by vanishing, become more real to me than when I was in his actual presence, had been standing only a few weeks before, and now that I was looking at the chair where I'd been sitting the first and only time we had seen each other, I suddenly realized that the image I had of myself as a real person was nothing but an illusion. I was just as much a product of contingency as all the imaginary people I encountered on my foreign assignments, the people whose lives I'd always seen as determined by chance and circumstance, and what I had believed to be my unique personality was just a clutch of stereotypes and stock phrases. Now that I was seeing my balcony from the vantage point of my neighbour's I could sense my own reality dimming inside of me.

The Super shocked me out of this little epiphany by rapping her knuckles on the kitchen window. 'All the light bulbs are missing,' she said once I'd joined her inside. She held her lighter over her head but all I could see was her hand illuminated by the tiny guttering flame.

'Why would he do that?' she said.

It was obvious to me by the condition of the apartment that my neighbour had *serious mental health issues.* There weren't any bulbs in the light sockets because he probably never installed any, I thought. I could see him in the living room, hunched forward in one of the plastic chairs, sipping from a can of Coke, and trying to read a day-old newspaper by the light of the streetlamp outside his window. Music was playing, very faint, something easy listening, jazz maybe. For an instant I thought that the music was all in my head, then I realized it was playing somewhere in the apartment. Had it always been playing or did it just start up now?

'Do you hear that?' I said.

'Yeah,' the Super was standing at the foot of the stairs. 'Sounds like a radio.'

'It's coming from upstairs,' I said.

We stood together at the bottom of the stairs as modern jazz played faintly in the room just above us. For the first time since we'd entered his apartment, I wondered if my neighbour was still there. Maybe he was holed up in his room waiting for us to give up our search and leave, maybe he thought we'd broken in and he was too frightened to come out and face us. Maybe he was huddled in a corner in his room certain that we were there to rob the place and do God-knows-what to him. While we were groping around downstairs and marvelling at the abject condition of his apartment, he was up there paralyzed with fear. I was sick at the thought that he would find us here, wading through the plastic bags and empty cans that covered the floor, and as we stood at the bottom of the stairs I told myself that I should just leave before anything bad happened. Even though we had already gone this far, I thought, there was nothing stopping me from going back to my apartment and leaving the Super to handle the situation.

I didn't have any obligation to my neighbour or any of the other tenants, and my only obligation to the Super was to pay my rent on time. 'The whole point to living here for the last twelve years,' I told myself, 'was so I could keep my obligations to other people restricted to the absolute necessities,' and by following the Super to the room upstairs where the modern jazz was coming from I was throwing away the years of work that I'd put into building up this socially austere living situation.

I wasn't always this way, I thought, as I stood at the bottom of the stairs waiting for the Super to make the next move and the muffled arpeggios of an extended saxophone solo barely filled in the silence surrounding us. Back in my twenties, I thought, back when I still went out to shows or to birthday parties, or when I still got invited to weddings, or to join book clubs and trivia teams, before I moved into this apartment and started my job, I lived my life as an ambitious, personable, and outgoing young professional. But after a few years at my company I felt as if I had been reduced. Now when I clicked on a news article about a suicide bombing in the departure wing of a European airport or scanned an article about the callous polluting of a town's water supply, I no longer felt the same sympathy and outrage for the victims that I used to. And it seemed as though now my only emotional response to all the horrific stuff I read about was a feeling of grim weariness, so it was hard for me to reconcile the person I was in my twenties with who I had become.

As we stood at the bottom of the stairs, the urge to turn around and walk out was so powerful. It reminded me of when I still went out to clubs and it was impossible to carry on even the most basic small talk, and where I was relentlessly jostled, shoved aside, and crowded out by enthusiastic, aggressive, and intoxicated patrons, or of the feeling of being crammed into a subway car during rush hour and forced up against the doors, or squeezed so tightly into the crush of bodies in the centre aisle that I couldn't even raise my arm to hold my phone in front of my face so I had to spend the whole commute staring straight ahead and somehow avoiding the eyes of all the faces pressing on me. I have spent most of my life out in the world, I thought, while constantly fighting the urge to get away from the world and everyone in it. There was nobody pressing against me in my neighbour's apartment, and instead of the obnoxious din of a bar or the loud rhythms of a crowded subway car, the place was unnaturally quiet, but as we stood at the foot of the stairs I felt surrounded, shut in, and drowned out. I took the lead and climbed the stairs. As I got closer to the closed bedroom door the smell intensified, and I started to feel nauseous. For a second I thought I was going to throw up, but I kept going, not because I was worried about what the Super would think of me if I told her that I was feeling sick and had to go outside for some fresh air, at least I don't think that's what kept me going, but I kept going because I knew that if I opened up to her like that, if I exposed myself in a vulnerable way, then I would never feel comfortable around her again, and I would probably wind up having to move. 'If you don't set very clear boundaries,' I told myself, 'people will try to get as close as they can, to make friendly conversation, or to complain about their lives, to share their theories on how to improve the public transit system or solve the problem of worldwide food shortages. After tonight,' I told myself, 'the Super will expect more than a small talk relationship.'

A common complaint these days is that we no longer live in strong communities, we're no longer on friendly or even familiar terms with our neighbours, we rarely know the names of the people who live above and below us, we don't recognize them when we pass them on the street. I used to think that even though I had nothing in common with the people who lived in my building, I still understood them and could get on their level, but the truth is that I hardly ever spoke to anyone and hadn't made one friend in the last twelve years, so this belief in my capacity for sympathy and understanding was based almost entirely on the small talk I occasionally made with the Super. And now that we had gone beyond this small talk relationship, or were about to, all I could think about was how this change in our relationship threatened my balcony and couch time.

I felt along the door's edge where the knob should have been, but it had been removed and the hole had been covered over with tape. A bedsheet had been stuffed between the door and the frame. The Super kept completely still and silent behind me as I knelt down and inspected the sheet. 'That's weird,' I said. 'There's no way he's in there.' He had abandoned his lease and his car, I thought, because he was in such a desperate financial position that it made more sense for him to leave everything behind than to try to salvage something. But what if he is still here, I thought, and the apartment hasn't been abandoned at all, and is simply in this state because he has serious mental health issues. In the weeks that I had been back I had hardly ever thought about what was going on behind the sheets he had hung on his windows. I assumed that he might not have had all the best furniture, appliances, and stuff that you would expect to find in a middle-class apartment, but it had never occurred to me that he was living in total squalor, rooms completely bare and garbage everywhere. I don't know if it was because I was so terrified of what we would find that I couldn't guess at what was behind my neighbour's bedroom door, but I think it probably had more to do with the fact that even though the state of his apartment was disturbing, and the smell coming from his bedroom was overpowering, and what the Super had told me about the bounced cheque and towed car was alarming, I still didn't care how any of this ended as long as the smell went away and I could go back to spending my nights watching prestige TV on the couch.

'What is it?' the Super said. 'Locked?'

'He took the knob off.' I turned to face the Super and I could barely see the pale light of her wide-open eyes staring back at me. 'And there's a sheet stuffed in the door.'

'Can you push it open?'

'Should we be doing this?' I was whispering, though it sounded to me like I was shouting. 'Or should we maybe call the landlord?'

'Let's have a look.'

'I'm pretty sure what we're doing is against the law?'

'These are extenuating circumstances,' she said.

She reached for the door and I tried to push her arm away. 'Just wait a second,' I said, but she had already opened it a crack.

'Wait,' I said. I eased it forward with my foot until it was open enough for me to see in. Before I could get a good look the smell came at me with actual physical force, and a dull black fuzziness crowded the borders of my vision.

'Whoa there,' the Super said. I felt her hands on my back. I was irritated for a moment because I thought she was trying to push me forward, but once my vision cleared I realized she was stopping me from falling backwards. I shook my head, took a deep breath, and stepped into the room. It looked empty. The darkness was flat, uniform. There was a faint frame of moonlight bordering the sheets that hung over the window. Behind the door I could make out a mattress on the floor that looked as if it was piled up with clothes and a basketball, or at least something the same size as a basketball. I squinted into the darkness to try to understand what it was I was seeing and I thought I could see a pale yellowish film covering the clothes and basketball. I thought that maybe the dim street light filtering through the blanketed window was causing this effect, but after staring at a fixed point for a few seconds I noticed that this yellowish film was moving. Not moving—squirming. 'Go,' I said to the Super, trying to push past her so I could run down the stairs. 'Go, go, go!'

'What is it?' she said, but she was already moving ahead of me. We both ran down the stairs, back out into the street. It took me a moment before I could speak.

'There's something in there,' I said.

'What do you mean?' she said. 'What did you see?'

'I don't know,' I said. 'I couldn't tell what it was. There was a mattress, some clothes, and a basketball, maybe?'

'A basketball?'

'It was basketball-sized.'

'Basketball-sized,' she said. We both stood there, a few feet from her front door, and I waited for her to make the next move. The smell, the living, squirming, yellowish pale film that covered everything in the room, the overall degradation of the apartment, this has nothing to do with me, I thought. The Super. The landlord. This is their problem. I shouldn't even be here, I thought. I should never have gotten involved.

'Listen,' I said, 'I don't feel comfortable going into this guy's place and it's impossible to see anything in there. We don't even know what might be lying around,' I said. 'There could be used needles and that sort of thing.'

'You're probably right,' the Super said. 'Whatever is causing that smell can wait until the morning.'

'Yeah,' I said. 'Nothing we can do about it now anyway.'

PART
TWO

Whenever I am asked to vouch for someone, to provide a professional reference, or defend the reputation of an old friend against some mean-spirited small talk, I always start by talking about how long we have known each other. For five years, I say, or ten, for a long time, since forever. I speak authoritatively about what they have done in the past, or what they may say or do in the future. I have known him my whole life, I say, or since we were kids, or a little further along, when we were wild and impressionable, or hopelessly naive, or, I say, we became close later in life, because we shared the same career trajectory and socio-economic background. 'That's exactly the sort of thing she would say,' I say. Or I say, 'He hasn't done something like that in years.' I even speak on their behalf—'I'm pretty sure she wouldn't be interested' or 'He'd definitely want to meet you. I'll set it up.' I regularly and quite willingly, with hardly any encouragement or persuasion, offer up the most baseless opinions and unfounded character assessments as if they were objectively established facts, and I assure whoever I may be writing to or speaking with that all the people I've gotten to know over the years in an intimate and long-lasting way have left me with a depth of sympathy and understanding that serves as a sort of window, or lens, or even as a crystal ball that gives me a view into the lives of my colleagues, family, and friends. But maybe all this personal experience ends up making it harder to see people for who they really are. Instead of the real story of their lives, I wind up reciting a bunch of anecdotes, illustrated with a few polished scenes, and a bullet list of biographical facts. A general impersonal perspective instead of a specific and intimate one. Instead of a sympathetic understanding of the complexity behind all the people in my life I have only crude and imprecise caricatures. 'We're still getting to know each other,' I say, when I've only just met someone and can't back up my opinion and assessment with the authority of a long-standing relationship, or years of familiarity, but what I mean to say is, 'I'm still coming up with my version that will stand in for who they really are.' When I say to somebody, 'I'm looking forward to getting to know you better,' what I really mean is, 'I'm looking forward to the day when I've known you long enough that I'll stop being curious about who you really are.' What I am actually doing when I am getting to know someone, or starting a new friendship, or listening to the story of a relative stranger, is trying to categorize them, because once I've done that I won't have to think about them anymore, or worry about what they might think of me.

I told myself, after I got back from my neighbour's apartment, that I deserved to unwind on the couch by smoking a joint and watching an episode or two of the lavishly produced McCarthy-era prestige TV series. And after watching two episodes, I told myself that I deserved to smoke another joint and watch one more, even though it was two in the morning and I could hardly stay awake through the last one, which involved a protracted flashback to McCarthy's college days. At some point during the third episode I told myself that I deserved to just close my eyes and crash out on the couch. When I woke up, I was confused. It felt like I'd been asleep only for a moment, but then I panicked because I thought maybe I'd slept in. I looked at my phone and was enormously relieved to see that it was only seven. I lay there for a while, scrolling through my work emails, which were mostly from colleagues asking for restaurant recommendations or for background information on portfolios they had recently taken over from me.

When I first started going on foreign assignments, I spent a lot of time reading guidebooks and Wikipedia articles on the history and culture of the places I travelled to. I would spend all of the time I had leading up to my departure researching the local cuisine, watching the landmark films of the national cinema, and reading the canonical works of the national literature. I would study the structure of the government and the major events of the country's history, and I did my best to grasp a few basics of the spoken and written languages. I told myself that all of this preparation would demonstrate to my would-be hosts the respect I had for their traditions and way of life. And I saw all the time I spent on this research as an investment in my future self. You're expanding your cultural awareness, I thought. And you're increasing your understanding of your own culture by gaining an appreciation of the way other people see the world and live their lives.

I told myself this while I was preparing for my foreign assignments, even though I knew that deep down I didn't believe it. I wasn't curious about the people and cultures of the exotic locales I was sent to. Instead of curiosity, there was indifference. In place of admiration, there was good-natured condescension. Eventually I had to admit to myself that I never had any interest in going to these places, and that I was only interested in being able to tell other people about the places I had been. You could say the whole point to learning so much about the countries where I went on my foreign assignments was so I didn't have to bother once I got there. I struggled to master the rudiments of the language so I would never have to actually learn it. I took the trouble of educating myself on the country's struggle for independence so I would be able to nod along to political and historical small talk without having to listen to what was being said. Whenever I found out where my company was sending me, I would feel so anxious at first over how little I knew about the place, and in many cases I struggled to find the city on a world map. But after I read up a bit, the anxiety levelled off, and once I landed it took only a couple of days before I was walking the streets as if I'd been there for years. While I thought I was learning about another culture, I was really just learning how to categorize cultures, I thought, as I lay on my couch looking at an email thread with a dozen of my colleagues that had been going on for days and had devolved into an exquisitely passive-aggressive exchange between two administrative coordinators. The yearning for knowledge I had when I was in my twenties, I thought, the hunger for life that consumed me, was simply the side effect of a paralyzing fear for the world I still hadn't figured out how to classify. And now that I seem to have lost that fear, now that I have satisfied my hunger for classification and given up on the yearning for knowledge thing, all sorts of other fears have flooded in to take its place. I used to spend all my free time immersed in a variety of interests and hobbies, I thought, but now I can hardly believe I ever took any of them seriously. For years I used all of my vacation time to visit the greatest ski resorts in the world. I pushed myself to ski on the most difficult runs, to keep in excellent shape and develop my skills, but eventually I couldn't be bothered with the hassle of booking flights and schlepping my gear back and forth, spending most of the day shivering on a lift or crammed into a gondola, and paying extraordinary sums for coaching by former professional athletes, all so I could accomplish a level of ability that would only ever be considered above average, at best. So I gave it up completely, and what had once been the animating force of my life was something I hardly ever thought about anymore.

As I lay there in the same clothes I had worn to the office the day before, I thought about how I used to look down on anyone who let their passion for life go slack. People said it would happen to me too, that it was simply a product of getting older and that it was actually a sign of wisdom and maturity to never get too excited about anything. When I was in my twenties I vowed that I would never let this happen, that I would live a life of ambition, devotion, and curiosity no matter how old I was. But now, I thought, I no longer think in terms of making something of myself or doing anything with my life, and my only goal is to keep everything as it is, without any interruptions to my routines. I used to be able to read a whole book without ever looking up from the page or losing the thread of the story, I thought, but now all I can manage is to hold a book in front of my face while I think about things I said at work. Instead of reading about the colonial history of the country I'd just lived in for nine months, I watch lavishly produced *historical foolishness* on the TV every night. Instead of reading about nineteenth-century feudalism, or the great ideological shifts of the twentieth century, I thought, I obsess over an awkward exchange I had with a colleague while we were waiting for the elevator, or I consider my response to an HR memo regarding new guidelines for vacation requests. All the energy I used to devote to cultivating an appreciation for classical music is now being used for arguments with customer service representatives. Even though I see myself as a cultural person, with a wide variety of tastes in literature, music, and film, it has been years since I finished a book, or gone to a concert. All that remains of my intellectual curiosity is a voracious appetite for prestige TV. And the hours I might have once spent going to museums and concerts are now spent on my social media accounts. Which is all to say that I was a very different person from when I first moved into my apartment, or from a couple years later, when I'd taken the position that would end up sending me on foreign assignments all over the world. I can't say when exactly I started to lose interest in having a cultural life. It wasn't like I realized all of a sudden that everything that used to sustain me and move me didn't do anything for me anymore. In fact, for a long time after I stopped getting anything out of my established routines I kept buying books, and going to museums, and vacationing at the most famous ski resorts in the world, but eventually I stopped buying books when I realized I was never reading them, and when I went to a new exhibition at our city's world-class Museum of Modern Art, I couldn't even be bothered to go through every room and instead I went to the café and looked at the internet on my phone. When I went on one of my ski trips I would call it a day after a couple of runs, and some days I didn't go out at all. Throughout the years that I was reading books, going to museums, and skiing at famous ski resorts, I believed that one day in the not-so-distant future everything I was doing would lead to something greater, I had no idea what that would be exactly, but greatness of some kind, material or spiritual, I really didn't care. After a few years went by and nothing great happened I told myself that it didn't matter as long as I liked to read and go to museums and ski, and it wasn't too long after this that I stopped doing all three. There was never going to be any click, I thought, no moment of clarity, no 'This is what it's all about' or 'This is what I was meant to do.' Of course, I had always known my life had no purpose, but now I actually felt it. I could feel the purposelessness of my life in everything I did, from the simple act of opening the fridge to staring at a masterpiece on the walls of a gallery. I would like to believe that this diminishment, this thinning out that took place in every aspect of my life, wasn't simply a consequence of getting older. I'd like to believe that I was so depressed by the daily catastrophes in the news that I found it hard to concentrate on anything else, or that I'd become so frustrated at work that I simply couldn't enjoy my free time anymore. I told myself that if I stopped spending so much time agonizing over a comment I had made about an old college friend's social media post, or worrying about the exchange I had with a couple of trolls in a chat room, and instead spent more time rereading some of my books from my university days, or started playing guitar again, or got out the old Hasselblad camera I used to bring with me on all my foreign assignments, then I might recover a bit of that feeling that I was heading toward something.

As soon as I heard the sirens approaching, I started working on an email to Roger to let him know I wouldn't be coming into the office. By now I was pretty sure that my neighbour hadn't disappeared, that he'd been in his apartment this whole time, in the room I had stood on the threshold of last night, and once the full horror of what had happened, *what had been happening* since I saw my neighbour out on his balcony tending to a smoking hibachi on the day I came back from my foreign assignment, once it had finally come together in my mind, the shame over the way I had run down the stairs and gone back to my apartment to get high and watch TV surged through me like an electrical current. But in spite of the immense shame I felt over my actions, I didn't hesitate to use this incident as an excuse to work from home. I didn't need Roger's permission to work from home, but I always felt like I needed to give him a heads-up. I maintained an impeccable professional persona at the office, and I'm sure none of my colleagues would've suspected that I spent my days doing everything I could to get out of having to do any actual work. If there was a service interruption on the Metro I was thrilled. I would insist that Roger look it up online to confirm that there had in fact been a delay. 'Go ahead,' I would say, 'there should be something about it on their site.' I could tell that Roger was confused and maybe even a little disturbed over why I was always explaining myself to him. 'My internet connection in my apartment was down last night,' I would say, 'so I didn't see your email until I got in this morning.' Instead of taking responsibility in my life, instead of approaching life in an open and honest manner, instead of confronting life and all its attendant problems and challenges head-on and accepting whatever came my way, I was constantly trying to avoid responsibility. I approached life in a closed-off and paranoid fashion, and I hid from my problems in the most childish and non-confrontational ways. In every situation, every dilemma, every interaction, all I would think about was whether I might get caught saying or doing something wrong. You could sum up my whole immature approach to life as a daily struggle to stay out of trouble. The worldview I had when I was a kid was the exact same one I had as a highly paid executive.

Like everyone else working in the professional sector, I spent most of my day in front of a screen reading and writing emails, or using the inter-office chat. If I said I met with someone at work what I meant was that I exchanged an email or a message with someone. But for some reason the email I was writing to Roger was giving me a lot of trouble, and even though I typically bang out an email in a couple minutes, and can fire off a few dozen in rapid succession in under an hour, But with this email to Roger, I went over every word and scrutinized each punctuation mark as if the smallest error might open a view into what was really going on with me. I kept writing things down and immediately deleting them. Too much, I thought, and then, Not enough.

The company had a horizontal hierarchy. This meant I technically didn't have a boss, but Roger served a bosslike function for me, even though I had heard that he made considerably less than me. Roger was the one I was expected to check in with, to keep up to date, and keep in the loop, and if the company ever wanted to let me go, Roger would be the one to do it. But because of the horizontal hierarchy of the company, and despite Roger's bosslike role in my department, I found myself in the position of having to strike a balance between frequently asking for permission while also acting like I didn't need it. 'Just wanted to fill you in on the latest,' I would say. 'Thought I should let you know.' 'My apologies for the delay,' I would begin. 'Things have been crazy today.' I tried to come off as laid-back and give these emails a colloquial style, but the truth is that finding the right balance between these two positions stretched my capacity for email-writing to the limit. I would stare at the screen, cutting sentences and then pasting them back in, hovering over one word for a few minutes, or getting stuck on how to transition from the opening pleasantries to the main subject of the email. I could churn out volumes of email correspondence, but whenever I had to write one of these asking-for-permission-even-though-I-don't-need-it emails, I would come down with a bad case of email writer's block.

When I first started at the company there were a lot of phone conversations and phone meetings, but email soon took over every aspect of my work. What used to be a short phone call between two people was replaced by an email thread with at least a dozen people on it. My days were full of mix-ups, misreadings, misunderstandings, and all the other forms of miscommunication that are a consequence of the profoundly unreliable nature of email. Whenever I sent off an email that deviated from my established email persona, I would tell myself, 'They are going to misinterpret what I wrote.' A good-natured joke about someone in our department might be seen as malicious gossip and slander, or a straightforward request for more information could be taken as an outrageous insinuation. And while I obsessed over the emails I sent to my colleagues, I was even worse when it came to the emails I received from them. I came up with the most elaborate and paranoid fantasies based on unambiguous and completely innocuous emails. The longest and darkest night of my life was when I stayed up obsessing over an email that had arrived in my inbox after I'd been out with a few clients for a drink. It was an email from Roger and in many ways it was entirely ordinary, though something about it had made me certain that I was going to get fired, so I lay in the king-sized bed in my suite and replayed the same few phrases over and over, cataloguing the implications of every word. What does he mean by 'relatively soon'? What is he trying to say when he uses the term 'collaborative effort'? Even more than what was written, what caused me the most anxiety and stress was imagining what he had left out. I knew that the emails I sent were never received in the paranoid way that I imagined, and the emails that people sent me weren't written in a subtly intimidating style for the purpose of insulting and undermining me, but as I worked on my email to Roger I had a sickening feeling that he would be able to read between the lines, so to speak, and see that while I claimed to be 'deeply unsettled' over the 'discovery of my neighbour's body,' I was simply trying to avoid going into the office.

As I lay on the couch working on the email to Roger, I could hear the cops getting out of their cars and being greeted by the Super. I winced at the memory of how I had looked away from the strange misshapen heap on the bed and run out of my neighbour's apartment, but this memory didn't prevent me from wondering about whether I should go out for breakfast, or stay in and drink coffee and read a long-form article about the impact of streaming porn on adolescent boys. The image of the heap on the bed kept flashing in my mind. I replayed the balcony encounter over and over as if I might be able to discover something in my neighbour's behaviour that I hadn't picked up on at the time. The voices of the cops came through the window with perfect clarity as I worked on my email to Roger. Even during the time when I was rapidly advancing within the company and enjoying a string of successes, I thought, as I watched the cops talking to the Super, and even at the beginning, when they first started sending me on foreign assignments, I always took every opportunity to slack off and phone it in. To do the bare minimum, I thought.

As I lay there on the couch with only a thin wall between me and my neighbour's corpse, I was looking forward to spending the entire day in my apartment, even if I was now uncomfortably aware that I was breathing in the vapours coming off the body. Instead of going into the office to sit at my desk, where I would have to pretend to be busy to avoid the inane vortex of small talk that threatened to suck me in whenever I passed my assistant's desk, or on my way to the bathroom, or when I rinsed out my mug in the kitchenette, I'd be able to spend my time binge watching the McCarthy-era prestige TV series and grooming my social media accounts.

It's the small talk that makes the workday so soul-crushing, I thought, after deleting the email to Roger I'd been working on. If it had been possible to go in each day without having to talk about the dish duty schedule with Mary, or debate commuter routes with James while he changed out of his bicycle gear, if I somehow could have avoided exchanging all the Hellos! and How's it goings! that felt like so many tiny interpersonal cuts, then maybe I wouldn't have had such an aversion to the office environment. When I was away on a foreign assignment, my working relationship with my colleagues was by and large an email working relationship. Even though I had what was technically referred to as an office job, by going on so many foreign assignments I had been able to avoid the most demanding and tedious aspects of professional life. When I was away, I went for long stretches without any small talk, except for the curt and courteous exchanges I had with the hotel employees and cabbies. But, even though I avoided it whenever I could, I wouldn't have gotten as far as I had in my company if I hadn't engaged in enormous amounts of small talk while sitting around a sticky table in a crowded pub, asking colleagues about their families, their educational backgrounds, their homes, their TV-watching habits, and taking turns giving my own personal information in a confessional mode, as if we were all part of a twelve-step program, or locked up together in a cell, in a prison or asylum, where our efforts to pass the time only increased our awareness of the walls closing in. But by spending the last twelve years on extended foreign assignments, I had been spared the worst of the small talk that dominates the home office environment. Conversation with my foreign clients and colleagues was friendly and direct. When I met with clients and my fellow colleagues there didn't seem to be the same pressure that we felt back in our home offices to fill every moment with incessant, soul-killing small talk, so I rarely had to resort to it as a way to ease tension or pass the time. I had gone out for drinks with my clients and colleagues many times over years of extended foreign assignments, and of course at a certain point in the night things would devolve into passionate arguments over cultural differences, but we mostly avoided conversational cliches and would spend a lot of our time telling stories. Aside from my meetings, lunches, and drinks with my clients and colleagues, I spent the rest of my time going out at night to eat alone, or to see a movie in a language I didn't understand. I actually like this solitary and anonymous lifestyle, I thought, now working on my third draft of the email to Roger, but the problem with never spending any time with my colleagues at the office is that when I come back from a foreign assignment and see all the people I've been emailing and messaging from the other side of the world, I feel an obligation to go for lunch with them, or to join them for after-work drinks, to catch up and reconnect, and I sense an expectation that since I spend so much time away I should be making even more small talk than I normally would if I were around on a more regular basis.

I sat up on the couch and tried to focus on the email to Roger. I was writing the words 'mental health day' and trying to imagine how Roger might respond when he read them. I started to worry that it was a bad idea to use phrases like 'my neighbour's body,' or 'took his own life,' in an email with the subject line 'Working from home.' How would Roger react when he read the word 'decomposing,' or the description of my neighbour's head 'swollen up like a misshapen basketball'? I could see as I looked over the fourth draft of my email that in this professional context it was shocking and grotesque. There was no need for me to send Roger such an obscene excuse for why I was going to work from home. I could simply say I wasn't coming in today, without giving any reason. 'I'm available by phone or email. If you need me in a meeting, I'll join remotely.' All I had to say was, 'Something came up,' or 'I'm not going to be in today.' But instead of telling Roger I was under the weather, I said I had to stay *at the scene* because the cops wanted to ask me a couple questions.

The cops had double parked below my window and were blocking the traffic in both directions. One cop was standing on the sidewalk and he looked up and down the street while adjusting the heft of his equipment belt. Another cop in the driver seat of one of the double-parked cars was filling out a form. I sat on my couch trying to decide how to sign off on my email to Roger when I heard the Handyman's voice.

He'd been around for as long as I'd been a tenant, but I only ever heard him referred to as the Handyman. 'The Handyman is going to be around later today. I'll ask him to have a look,' the Super would tell me after I'd been complaining for days that I didn't have any hot water. 'The Handyman thinks he can fix it but he needs to order a special part.' The building was always in need of repairs, and the little that the Handyman did was done in a half-assed and corner-cutting way. I hardly ever saw him, but I frequently heard his loud, froglike voice sounding out in the alley. It could be early on a Saturday morning, or late on a Wednesday night, when all of a sudden he'd start shouting at someone. Usually he was shouting at somebody over the phone, but occasionally he would make small talk with one of the neighbours—the Shih Tzu Lady maybe, or one of the Pseudo Homeless Guys—and even though they would speak at a normal volume, he would continue to shout as if he was trying to be heard during a violent storm, on the deck of a freighter, over the machine noise of the ship's engine.

The Super, on the other hand, never once raised her voice in all the years I had known her. During our infrequent small talk sessions I often had to ask her to repeat herself, since whatever she was saying about the weather, or the lifestyle of one of the other tenants, was almost impossible to make out from the quiet, uninflected muddle that barely passed her lips. It wasn't uncommon for the Handyman to carry on protracted conversations with the Super in the early morning hours, when he had probably come to work on some minor task that he would end up drawing out for days, and I would listen as he carried on in his booming froglike voice, which was only occasionally interrupted by a silent gap when the Super was talking. Whenever I heard the voice of the Handyman down in the alley I would avoid my balcony, and if he was out front in the morning I would wait for him to leave, even if it meant showing up late at the office. I was constantly worried that the Handyman would trap me in one of his small talk conversations, and that he would turn my anonymous urban lifestyle into a noisy small talk hell.

I looked out my window and saw the enormous figure of the Handyman planted in his work boots. The Super was in flip-flops. They were talking to the cops, who were nodding impatiently. I listened at my window as the Handyman explained to the cops that the Super had called him this morning to look into a tenant's complaint over a smell coming from the deceased's apartment. He shouted the words *the deceased's apartment* and I sensed pride in his voice. The cops watched indifferently as cars tried to manoeuvre past the double-parked cruisers. The Handyman stood on the sidewalk with his thumbs tucked under his armpits as if they were hitched under an invisible pair of suspenders. He repeated the words 'deceased's apartment' a few more times. The cops started walking toward the door to my neighbour's place. The Handyman hurried ahead, motioning to the Super to hand over her keys. 'I hope you guys have strong stomachs,' he shouted, 'because he's pretty ripe.' He finally found the right key, and then turned back to the cops, standing in the doorway as he said something about the landlord's 'multiple properties.' I watched from my window as the Handyman held the door open for the cops, as if to say, 'This is my neighbourhood. This is my building. I should be a part of whatever you are going to do up there.' I felt embarrassed at the way he was insinuating himself into the corpse situation. It was as if I were the one down there humiliating myself in front of the cops, and not the Handyman. But even though I was ashamed of the way he was carrying on, I also felt something like envy, because if I hadn't run away, if I had gone into the room and seen the body, then maybe I would've been the one talking to the cops. 'The local guide,' I thought. 'The gracious host.'

The Handyman was still standing at the door, telling the group of cops formed in a small horseshoe under my window about another time a tenant died, though it had been a stroke, not suicide. One cop stepped forward and casually hitched his thumbs into his belt and smiled warmly at the Handyman. It was obvious that the cop was mocking the Handyman's hitched thumbs and invisible suspenders, and by hitching his thumbs under his belt the cop was saying, 'Enough is enough. You got to play out your little fantasy as the guide, or host, or interpreter, but now it's time to move along.' I doubt any of this was getting through to the Handyman, since he kept talking about the neighbour who'd had a stroke and comparing it with the experience of finding my neighbour's corpse this morning.

The sound of the cops climbing the stairs to my neighbour's apartment was so intense that I jumped up from the couch. I had never put much thought into why I didn't hear my neighbour moving around. I could hear my other neighbours who shared the wall on what I referred to as the TV *side* of my apartment, but after a few days of being back, I got used to them, since they just watched a lot of TV, or they listened to music, or played what sounded like first-person-shooter video games. I found all of this easy to tune out. They only bothered me when I could make out the sound of their murmuring voices coming through the walls. Anything was better than having to listen to the sound of people talking, I thought, especially if they were talking on the phone. So I was relieved when the guy who had moved into what I referred to as the *couch side apartment*, that had previously been occupied by a quiet middle-aged woman, seemed to never be at home, or, if he was, I never heard the sound of his voice. I didn't even think it was strange, I thought, that it hadn't just been quiet the five weeks since I saw him out on his balcony, but *completely silent*. There were times late at night when a hush settled over the building and I thought I heard faint music coming from his place, so I told myself that he was just an introvert, and a loner. I listened to the cops walk around my neighbour's apartment, their footfalls sounding like someone was emptying a bag of lead balls onto the floor.

Whenever I had fantasized about how I would respond in a life-or-death situation I always saw myself as someone with moral courage and a selfless nature, willing to sacrifice everything for a principle, a lost cause, a loved one, or a complete stranger. But I now understood that this image of myself was a false image. During World War II, I wouldn't have been the sort of person to help Jews running from the Gestapo by letting them hide in my attic or cellar. Instead, I would've joined the overwhelming majority of people who reported whatever they saw or heard to the police, who informed on one another, stole things off dead bodies, or moved into houses that had been vacated by the same people being loaded into trains and shipped to the camps. I would've stood by, I thought, and watched as people were beaten and shot. Why, when in my professional life I only ever act out of the most naked self-interest and moral cowardice, I thought, as I listened to more cops come up the stairs, would I suddenly act in the exact opposite way, even if my life and the lives of others were at stake? Why did I believe that I would somehow be able to stop being so afraid all the time? How did I think I would go from being largely indifferent to what happened to other people to someone with the moral character of a war hero? When I was standing on the threshold of my neighbour's bedroom last night, I thought, instead of feeling even a little bit of the courage or compassion that I had hoped I was capable of, all I felt was an all-consuming and selfish fear. Even though I'd lived a life that was free of life-or-death situations (aside from reading obsessively about them online), and in spite of the stability I enjoyed in my professional life, which afforded me the ability to throw money at all of my problems, I was constantly afraid. My approach to life was basically fear-based. For weeks I've been so afraid to find out what was causing the smell in my apartment, I thought, that instead of going to speak to the Super about it, I spent hundreds of dollars getting my apartment cleaned. And whenever I felt like I was coming out of this mental fog that had settled over me since I returned from my last foreign assignment, whenever I felt myself moving toward a clearing of sorts, I instinctively pulled back. It's as if I knew, I thought, that there was only one thing that could smell like that. But I had told myself that it wasn't my responsibility, that the smell coming from my neighbour's apartment had nothing to do with me. What were you supposed to do? I thought. How were you supposed to know? It was natural, I thought, to feel afraid when I was in my neighbour's apartment. I had no right to be there. It had been a good idea to wait until the morning, and to let the Super take care of it. Mind your own business, I thought. Don't get involved. Keep your nose clean. Don't make a scene. Keep a low profile, I thought. Don't draw attention to yourself.

While I was eating countless takeout meals and getting drunk on my balcony, or smoking joints in front of the TV and doing the occasional load of laundry or dishes, my next-door neighbour's body had been decomposing, I thought, as I listened to the cops' muffled voices coming through the walls as they inspected my neighbour's bedroom. I heard them going down the stairs and I watched from my window as they filed out onto the sidewalk empty-handed. That is to say, without my neighbour's body. They stood in a loose circle, chatting distractedly, ignoring the Handyman. The Super was sitting quietly on her front step. Everything was drowned out by the obnoxious sirens of an ambulance pulling onto the street, followed closely by a trio of cop cars. By now many of the other tenants in the building, as well as a lot of other people who lived on the street, had come out onto their balconies, or were standing in their doorways and leaning out their windows. Some wandered over to where the cops were standing, as if they were expecting to be asked to join in the investigation. I was finally sick of writing the email to Roger and in a few seconds I finished it. I read it over. I deleted 'cops' and wrote 'homicide detectives,' which sounded more authoritative to me. As I was coming down the stairs I caught myself whistling.

The sidewalks were dotted with groups of people swapping theories about what was going on, and somehow it had already spread around that it had likely been a suicide. Cops were going in and out of my neighbour's front door while the Handyman paced along the sidewalk in front of the building with a wide-eyed expression on his face, waiting for someone to come up and ask him what was going on. The Super was drinking from an enormous coffee mug and staring at everything going on around her.

'Well, I guess we know what was causing the smell,' I said to her.

'I guess so,' she said. 'Roman says the guy's body looked like a beached seal.'

'Roman?'

She pointed at the Handyman.

'So, he saw the body?'

'He said it didn't even look like a person.' She took a sip from her mug. 'That's probably why you didn't recognize him.'

'I couldn't tell what I was looking at,' I said. 'It could've been anything.' She sat there and looked at me. 'It was dark,' I said. 'It was late, I couldn't see, I was tired, I thought nobody was home, I wasn't expecting to find anything, it just looked like a pile of clothes.' She had been there too, I pointed out. She had seen what I had seen (and smelled what I had smelled). She had to understand that even though I had been the one to push open the door I hadn't seen anything more than she had. I had run out of the apartment, yes, but this had been more out of disgust than terror. 'It's not that I didn't recognize him,' I said. She sat there without saying a word, without nodding along in agreement, or encouragement. She held on to her mug as if she was about to take a sip. 'I have no idea what he even looked like,' I said. 'I literally saw the guy once, in the morning, on his balcony. I wouldn't be able to point him out again if he was standing right in front of me. And I definitely didn't notice there was a body on the mattress. Did you?'

'He didn't say much,' the Super said. 'Not very friendly.' There was an edge to her otherwise flat affect. Maybe she was saying this, I thought, to let me know that *she was on my side.* 'He definitely wasn't giving off a friendly vibe when I saw him on his balcony,' I said, to show her that I was on her side too. 'Don't get me wrong,' I said. 'I probably wasn't giving off a friendly vibe either. I had just gotten home after a twenty-hour flight, so it's not like I wanted him to tell me his life story. But at least acknowledge my presence when we're standing ten feet from each other, you know what I mean?'

She sat there looking up at me and said that she'd had a bad feeling about him when he came to see the apartment. 'Shifty,' she said.

I suddenly regretted everything I had just said, and felt ashamed at the way I had colluded with the Super on this rear-view characterization of my neighbour. So I said that I should probably be going, on the pretense of having to take a work call, but then the Handyman came over and started hammering me with questions.

'So, you're the one who found him?'

'When did you notice the smell?'

'Why didn't you say something before?'

When he looked at me with those intense, wide-open eyes, I felt as if he could see me for what I was. Most people, I thought, have no interest, or curiosity, or are too embarrassed or ashamed to try to see past the masks that we all wear, the screens we all hide behind, the faces we show in public that cover the private ones, our true faces, the ones we never show anyone and haven't even seen for ourselves. But, I thought, it was as though he could see through my mask, or that he didn't even see my mask in the first place. Which is maybe just an elaborate way of saying that he wasn't falling for my bullshit. I said that, no, I hadn't been the one to find my neighbour's corpse. 'As you no doubt have already heard from your esteemed colleague,' I said, 'we couldn't see the body. It was too dark.'

'Listen to this guy,' the Handyman said. He didn't look at the Super and instead kept staring at me. 'You sound like Perry Mason. You remember him? You remember Perry Mason? Probably not,' he said, sounding a bit sad. 'He's before your time.'

'I know *Perry Mason*,' I said.

'Roman loves those old lawyer shows,' the Super said. '*Matlock* too.'

I'd thought that the building had been their only connection, but now I got the impression things between them were more complex. Maybe the Handyman grew up nearby and the Super had known him ever since she was little. I had assumed that the people living on the street were like me, that they weren't born and raised here, and they all came from elsewhere, and that nobody had a shared past beyond when they'd signed their lease. But maybe there was a rich history here, a communal memory they'd been keeping quietly alive as new tenants drifted through year after year.

'You still haven't told us,' he said, 'when you first noticed the smell.'

'A couple weeks ago,' I said. 'Things have been crazy at work, so I haven't been home that much. And when I was at home,' I said, 'I was too tired to bother with a weird smell in the building. Besides, it's not really my job, is it.' While I was saying all this I was watching the Super. She probably knew, I thought, that I got home every day a little after five and hardly ever left the apartment. 'When we were in there last night I was so out of it that I honestly had no idea what was going on. And since it was too dark to see anything anyway, I figured that whatever was causing the smell could wait until the morning.'

'One more day wasn't going to kill him,' he said, and nudged me with his elbow. 'Know what I'm saying?'

'I honestly didn't think he was in there,' I said. 'Did you?' I looked to the Super, who, I thought, should've been backing me up. She was *the Super* after all, and if she had thought my neighbour's body was rotting on a mattress and hadn't done anything about it until the next day, then wasn't that worse than if I didn't do anything about it? Is the Super more guilty than me? I thought. But even though it's common to speak in terms of degrees of guilt, and the entire legal system is based on the presumption that you can accurately measure just how guilty a person is, it struck me in that moment as utter nonsense.

'No,' the Super said. 'There's no way I would've slept one more night in the same building if I had known.'

'Well,' the Handyman said, as if he were responding to a question neither of us had asked, 'I knew right away. When Karen called, before she even said anything, I knew. I said to myself, He finally did it. I could tell he was headed for it. It was only a matter of time.'

'Karen?' I said.

'You could see it in his eyes,' the Handyman said.

'Tell him about the barbecue,' the Super said.

'What about the barbecue?' I said.

'Suffocated himself,' the Handyman stood there with a smile on his face.

'Like he—'

'Sealed himself in with a lit barbecue,' he said. 'The smoke eats up all the oxygen and chokes you out.'

'Jesus,' I sat down next to the Super. 'That sounds awful.' I'm not sure how, exactly, I had thought he had done it, but once I found out about the hibachi, the brief moment I'd had with my neighbour on the morning I got back from my foreign assignment appeared to me in extremely vivid detail, and I could see that he had been in a hurry to get inside, and that he'd avoided looking me in the eye, and that I had probably caught him in the moment right before he went to his room and sealed himself in.

'Not necessarily,' the Handyman said. 'He probably took a bunch of sleeping pills too. That's what I would do. You drift off and that's it. It's a really common way to do it where he's from. One minute you're dreaming, next minute you're not.' He was projecting his froglike voice as though he were teaching a roomful of rowdy children and needed to shout to get his message across. He is the sort of person, I thought, who would explain to a mother what it feels like to give birth, or tell a pilot how to fly a plane. He's going to be out here all day, I thought, in the role of resident expert, talking about the ways that suicide methods vary across cultures, something he likely only found out about today, and is now going on about as if it was something he'd been studying for years.

As I was sitting on the Super's front step, I realized that it had been a mistake to send that email to Roger. It would be impossible to hide out in my apartment and get high all day while binge-watching prestige TV if all these cops were hanging around. A crowd had gathered on each side of the street—on my side was a mix of the customer service and low-level administrative types, as well as little groups of students, while the other side was made up of older long-term residents or upwardly mobile professionals. My side of the street rented. The other side owned. But both sides were wondering, I thought, when the cops were going to bring out the body.

An enormous police officer with a fauxhawk hairstyle came up and interrupted the Handyman's lecture.

'Are you the neighbour?'

'Yeah,' I said. 'That's me.'

'You were with Ms. Leblanc last night in Mr. Elhassan's apartment?'

'Ms. Leblanc?' I said. 'I mean, yes, I noticed a smell. But I didn't know what it was.'

'A smell,' he said.

I expected him to take out a notepad and start writing down what I was telling him, but he just kept staring at me. 'Yeah,' I said. 'I noticed it a couple of weeks ago, maybe. It wasn't that bad at first.'

'Okay,' he said. The sides of his head were shaved into an elaborate calligraphic design and the hair on top was sculpted into a sharp ridge. 'And last night you searched his apartment and didn't see the body.'

'I didn't really look,' I said. 'It was dark. I couldn't see. I had no idea what I was looking at.' I looked to the Super and the Handyman. They were looking away.

'So when you were in Mr. Elhassan's room last night you didn't see his body lying on the mattress?'

Why wasn't he writing anything down? Maybe, I thought, he wasn't even supposed to be questioning me. Maybe he was just fucking with me, killing time while the cops up in my neighbour's apartment finished their examination, or whatever it was they had to do before they could finally take the body away. 'It was impossible to see anything.' I said. I wondered if the cop's hairstyle was controversial among the other cops, or if they simply overlooked his affectation. 'I don't know what a corpse smells like, and it never occurred to me that he might be dead. I thought he might've been hoarding something, storing trash in his place, that sort of thing.'

'It's Simon, right?' Now he took out a notepad.

'Yes,' I said. 'Well, no, actually. It's Peter. My last name is Simons.'

'Okay,' he said. 'Simons?'

'Yes,' I said. 'That's right.'

He looked out from his pad and frowned, 'Two first names?'

'Not really,' I said. 'Simons isn't a first name. Simon, yes. Not Simons. Simons is actually a pretty common last name. Peters is also a common last name. So you could say I have two last names. Or that I have a last name for a first name.'

'Okay,' he said. 'You going to be home today?'

'Not really,' I said. 'I have to go into the office.'

'Not really,' he said, stuffing his pad into the pocket of his bulletproof vest.

'I mean, I can stick around for a while if you need me to, but I have to go in at some point.'

'It'd be good if you stayed here,' he said. 'The detectives will want to speak to you.'

'The detectives?'

'The detectives,' he said. 'They should be here soon.'

He went back to the other cops standing in front of my neighbour's front door, and now I noticed that a few of them also styled their hair in variations on the fauxhawk theme, while others opted for the shaved look. The women kept their hair in severe ponytails, or wore it short in elaborate asymmetrical styles. There was something about this stylistic fastidiousness that irritated me. I stood there and watched the cops sip from their coffee cups as I fantasized about confronting them. 'Is all this really necessary?' I would say. 'Do so many of you really need to be here?' 'These guys are so corrupt,' I said to the Super and the Handyman. 'I read somewhere that we have the most corrupt police force in the country.' They nodded along to what I was saying but the Handyman had a skeptical look on his face and he said that he didn't know how people measured that sort of thing, but every cop he'd ever had to deal with had always been thoroughly decent and respectful. As the Handyman was defending the cops, a woman who'd been living in the building for at least as long as I had came up and asked him for a cigarette. For at least as long as I'd been living in the neighbourhood this woman had been spending her days standing in the doorway of her ground-floor apartment, and even though I walked by her all the time I'd never once said hello to her—which didn't stop me from coming up with a private nickname for her.

'What a shit show,' the Grim Reaper said. She turned to me. 'You found him, right?'

The Handyman answered for me, and explained to the Grim Reaper that while I had been in the apartment with the Super the night before, he had been the one to actually find the body. 'They didn't see it,' he said. 'Too dark, he says.'

I rent this apartment instead of buying a place, I thought, so I won't have to get involved in this sort of thing. I don't want to be part of a community, I thought, I don't want to have to look out for other people, and I don't want other people looking out for me. I don't want to get caught up in the weird relationship the Super, the Handyman, and the Grim Reaper have with each other. At this point in my life, I thought, I am totally fine with the fact that most of my interactions with other people are customer service interactions, and as far as I am concerned, I thought as I watched the Grim Reaper ash her cigarette into the empty flowerpot on the Super's front step, my life has been almost completely reduced to customer service experiences. Deeply personal situations that had to do with my parents, or problems related to friendly misunderstandings with my colleagues, had begun to take on the form of customer service encounters. I even applied a customer service logic to my sexual relationships (though it'd been a while since I'd had one of those), and just like in a customer service relationship, I was singularly focused on whether I was satisfied or not, and regularly offered up feedback and comments about how the overall experience could be improved. My overall worldview was that of a customer, and I behaved as though life was nothing more than a collection of customer service-like transactions. Which is why, even though it was the first time in the twelve years I'd been living there that anything like this had ever happened, and there was no way my landlord could have anticipated it, and certainly couldn't have prevented it, this didn't stop me while I was standing there with the Super, the Handyman, and the Grim Reaper from having yet another customer service fantasy where I confronted my landlord. I told my Imaginary Landlord that I shouldn't be expected to investigate building incidents on my own, or with the Super. It shouldn't be my responsibility to check in on tenants who don't appear to have any family or friends, or to be employed, or to ever go out for that matter, and who pose a risk of having an accident and winding up injured or—God forbid—dead. It's just luck that I happened to be back from my foreign assignment, I said to my Imaginary Landlord. I could just as easily not have been around to notice the smell, in which case it could've taken much longer before anyone would've said something since apparently I was the only one who had even noticed a smell coming from his apartment.

How is it possible, I thought, that in one of the richest countries on the planet, with a welfare state and medical system that is the envy of the entire world, in a city that has been steadily bureaucratized within an inch of its life, where not even a square foot of property hasn't been bought and sold at least a thousand times over, how is it possible for a body to rot in a modest tenement building on a partially gentrified street, and for it to take weeks before it is finally discovered? I sat there, listening to the Grim Reaper list off all the people she knew who'd committed suicide, and I felt the same surge of irritation I get during bad customer service experiences. I was disappointed over this conversation in the same way I would be if a waiter got my order wrong, or the room I had reserved wasn't ready, or the Wi-Fi in my apartment wasn't working.

'It's not very considerate if you ask me,' the Handyman said. 'Leaving everyone to clean up after you. Polite thing to do is to jump off a bridge.'

'It's not like you're the one who has to clean it up,' the Super said.

'I may not have to get my hands dirty.' He seemed genuinely offended. 'But I'm still here when I should be at the garage.' The way he said this seemed to call up something from their past, and even if I didn't know the details, it was clear that the *garage* was a powerful thing that the Handyman had over the Super.

The crowd gathering on the sidewalks kept getting bigger and louder. I could still make it in to work on time for the directors' meeting at eleven, I thought. 'They said that it was a pretty open-and-shut case,' I would tell Roger, using an expression I had heard countless times during my marathon sessions of prestige TV watching. At the top of the meeting I'd tell them about my neighbour, and my colleagues would be happy for the diversion. Of course I wouldn't tell them that I had avoided checking on my neighbour for weeks, and I wouldn't tell them that I had run away and hid out in my apartment until the Handyman came the next day, or that the Handyman was the one who discovered the body and called 911. Instead I would tell them that I had complained to the Super, that I had discovered the body and called the police, and I would imply that throughout the whole ordeal I had exhibited the sober decisiveness that the situation had called for.

But if you actually do go in to work, I thought, you'll probably wind up telling them everything. You'll tell them about the hibachi and you'll tell them about how you ran from your neighbour's apartment. You'll make a full confession in the hope that your colleagues will tell you that you didn't do anything wrong, I thought. I am always asking other people to excuse things I have done that they have no way of excusing— for them to forgive me for things I have said that it's not their place to forgive. In my customer service world view I believe that what matters most is the opinion of other people. You would think that since I had given up on my so-called personal life, I would also have given up on my public reputation, and that I wouldn't worry so much about how I was perceived by my colleagues, or what my neighbours thought of me. But it turned out that the more I withdrew from the *outside world*, the more I became concerned with what the outside world thought of me. I often found myself wondering what the guy at the convenience store thought of me, or how I came off to the woman who worked at the ticket booth in the Metro station. And so I was desperate to know what the Super, the Handyman, the Cop with the Fauxhawk, and the Grim Reaper thought of me for failing to identify the smell in my apartment as the smell of my neighbour's corpse, and then running from the corpse, and then, instead of calling 911, watching prestige TV for a couple of hours before passing out on the couch. I fought the urge to call my parents and ask them whether they thought what I did was wrong, even though I knew they would be a sympathetic audience, and that they would share my customer service world view. It would be better to just go into the office, I thought. Unlike the Handyman, or the Super, or the Grim Reaper, my colleagues at the office spoke my language, and they knew where I was coming from, even if I wasn't close with any of them. I knew they would reassure me by saying things like, 'There wasn't anything you could have done,' and 'I would have done the same thing.' I felt lonely there on the stoop, surrounded by people who didn't know me as a highly paid professional responsible for a multimillion-dollar portfolio, but as the guy who had watched TV while his neighbour's body decomposed for five weeks. I was about to excuse myself and go back to my apartment to shower and change for work when I got a text from Roger.

'Sorry,' I said, interrupting the Handyman's story about an *Arab guy* he knew who had committed suicide. 'I've got to call the office.'

'It's a free country,' the Grim Reaper said. 'You don't need our permission.'

But I felt as though I did. Even though I had arranged my life so I was accountable to only a couple people, and took every opportunity with them to try to reduce even further my small share of responsibility, and even though I was doing everything required of a citizen with a midrange six-figure salary, I thought, I still felt an obligation to these three. My day-to-day life is nothing but an unrelenting series of obligations, I thought, an insurmountable mountain of expectations, a preposterous series of requirements. It never ends, I thought. In fact, these obligations seemed to increase exponentially every year. The longer I lived, the further away I got from the freedom that had been my lifelong goal. I was free, but only in the most impoverished and morally corrupt sense of the term. The freedom I wanted was less the typical retirement that an upper-middle-class professional like me usually hoped for, and more a form of obsolescence, a blessed uselessness, a sort of personal and professional living death. I envisioned a time in some not-so-distant future, when I had finally paid my dues and settled my accounts, said my goodbyes and made my peace, so that the rest of my days would flow by in a frictionless existence and living would be an act as subconscious and effortless as breathing. Of course, when people asked me about my life plan, which was actually a very common topic of conversation in my social and professional circles, I never put it in these terms, and instead I said things like *cottage*, or *semi-retirement*, I would say, *combined assets*, or *passion project*, but always at the back of my mind was this freedom-fantasy I had organized my life around, and still believed I could somehow achieve. You are a thirty-five-year-old man with an enormous amount of professional responsibility and power, I thought. But you behave like a prisoner waiting in line at the cafeteria.

The Handyman had resumed his anecdote about the *Arab guy* while the Super and the Grim Reaper took synchronized drags off their cigarettes. The three of them were talking to each other as if I had already left. It occurred to me that maybe they had been waiting for me to leave this whole time, that I was keeping them from talking about my neighbour as freely as they would have liked. They're probably uncomfortable talking openly in front of someone like me, I thought. Or maybe they want me to leave so they can gossip about me.

I often imagine that people are talking about me when I'm not around, that they wait for me to turn my back and then start tearing me down. I take it for granted that my colleagues are thinking about me, but it's far more likely that they hardly ever think about me, or talk about me with each other. Most of us have only a handful of people whom we think about and discuss among friends and family, while the majority of people we encounter throughout our lives leave an impression that lasts only as long as we are in their presence. Maybe we get fired in the most disgraceful way, seen to the door by security while carrying a cardboard box containing family photos and some other personal items, and when we're at home, weeks later, we can hardly stand the thought of what people must be thinking about us back at the office, the terrible, mean-spirited things they must be saying about us, fired for reasons that weren't explained and they can only speculate on. But the truth is that the moment we were fired they already started forgetting us, and that nobody even mentions our name anymore, let alone bothers to say anything nasty or kind about us. I want to believe I'm as real to other people as I am to myself, but I probably only exist for them as a two-dimensional walk-on, an extra, blending into the background scenery like a minor character from a book they read a long time ago. So even though, aside from my neighbour, I felt like I was the central character in the incident involving my neighbour's body, I knew that the Handyman probably didn't see it that way, and neither did the Super, and certainly not the Grim Reaper. I probably wasn't holding them back from talking about me, or preventing them from saying anything at all for that matter.

After getting the text from Roger, I could feel panic rising and infecting my thoughts. The Handyman was saying something about the *Arab guy* that I didn't understand, much like when I find myself lost in the midst of an episode of prestige TV after having drifted off for a couple minutes, missing out on crucial scenes and dialogue, so that later on in the episode nothing makes any sense to me.

Don't worry about Roger, I thought. Aside from the fact that it had the form and tone of a court summons, there is nothing wrong with his text, I thought. But I was worried all the same that there was something in my email that had given me away.

I took up a position on the other side of the street. The cops outside my neighbour's front door looked bored and aside from occasionally disappearing up the front stairway and then wandering back down a few minutes later, they mostly stood around and sipped from coffee cups that were apparently bottomless. Standing on the sidewalk a few feet away from me was a woman in top-of-the-line athleisure wear, offset by some very expensive-looking jewelry. I called Roger, and as I stood there listening to the phone ring, the woman looked over at me, and gestured rudely at the cops. I smiled back to show her that I was on her side.

'So you're having quite an interesting morning,' Roger said. He sounded annoyed.

'Sorry,' I said. 'Obviously this is not how I would've chosen to spend my day.' I waited for him to say something. 'But I don't think my neighbour was thinking about the inconvenience he was going to be causing me when he decided to kill himself.'

'No,' Roger said, 'I imagine he had other things on his mind.' I could hear the sound of his fingers tapping rapidly on his keyboard. 'So, how'd he do it?'

'Well, I'm not exactly sure,' I said, 'but the rumour is that he did it with a barbecue.'

'Good God,' he said, without letting up on the keyboard. 'He set himself on fire?'

'Jesus, no,' I said. 'He shut himself in his room with a barbecue. It sucks all the oxygen out of the room. Suffocates you.'

'Ah,' he said. 'Never heard of that method.'

'Yeah, it's a cultural thing,' I said, watching as the Fauxhawk Cop flirted with one of the paramedics. The paramedic, to my surprise, took a pack of cigarettes from her cargo pants and lit up. 'I guess that's how they do it where he's from.'

'I see,' he said. 'Makes sense. So why do they need to talk to you?' Roger asked, pausing on his keyboard. 'What do you have to do with it?'

'I was the one who found the body,' I said. 'The building superintendent asked me to come with her this morning. My neighbour was overdue on his rent and nobody had seen him for days. I went in with the Super this morning and found the body.'

'Oh,' he said. 'That must've been unpleasant.'

It would've been better to tell the truth—that I hadn't actually discovered the body, that I had searched my neighbour's apartment and had run away at the crucial moment—but I felt like maybe I wasn't being very convincing, and the temptation to put myself at the centre of my story was too powerful. I wanted Roger to think that I had risen to the occasion. Maybe I should tell him that I was injured in some slight way, I thought, or that I was being treated for shock. But even though the story I had told Roger was full of lies, it corresponded to how I felt. If it hadn't been for the nagging fear that he would somehow find me out, I might have told Roger that I had been friends with my neighbour, that we chatted from time to time, and had drinks together every once in a while. The story I told Roger was just as plausible as what had actually happened, I thought. I had been tired, and irritable, when I went to complain to the Super about the smell. You weren't in the right frame of mind, I thought. If it had been any other night, you would've definitely gone into the room, I thought, you would've seen the body, and you would've called the cops.

While I was telling Roger my fabricated and self-serving story, I kept watch over the cops gathered at my neighbour's walkway as they made small talk, joked around, and carried on in the same way most people do when there's downtime at work. I imagined what it would be like to be a cop, to keep calm as you pushed open a door that had been sealed up with a bedsheet. Courage, I thought to myself at the same time as I was recounting to Roger the 911 call I had never made, is just a matter of getting used to things. Once we have seen a terrible thing, I thought, it begins to look normal to us. I often fantasize about what I would do in a home invasion by narco kidnappers, or what it would be like to fight in an insurrection, or how it would feel to live through a natural disaster. I imagine terrible car crashes involving my parents, and heroic rescues of children from burning buildings. I put myself in the place of those refugees making the suicidal Mediterranean crossing in an overladen and unseaworthy fishing boat, carrying a newborn baby in my arms. So when I thought about how I had behaved during each stage of the incident with my neighbour's body, right up to this shame-lessly distorted account I was giving to Roger over the phone, I was horrified that those actions might signify a rule, and not a deviation. That's not who I am, I thought. I wasn't myself.

As I stood there, describing the condition my neighbour's apartment had been in to Roger, I experienced a sudden and vivid recollection of Joseph Conrad's novel *Lord Jim*, a book I read for English class in university, and then again on my last foreign assignment when I picked up a copy at the airport bookstore, and although I had read it twice, something I've done with only a couple other books, I felt ambivalent after rereading it, unsure if it was really as great as it was supposed to be, and before that day on the sidewalk outside my neighbour's apartment, I really hadn't given it much thought. It's about Jim, who as a boy dreams of becoming a sailor after reading stories about the glorious sea battles of the Napoleonic Wars. And when he's not much older, still more a child than a man, he manages to become a seaman, but instead of serving on a warship to fight foreign tyrants he winds up on a merchant ship transporting human cargo—pilgrims from Singapore to Mecca. Instead of taking orders from a heroic and battle-scarred captain, and serving in a great naval order, he enlists with a shipping company that is more or less a criminal trading operation, where he's bossed around by a stereotypically unscrupulous and cowardly German. When the ship has an accident at sea and it's clear that it's going to sink, Jim doesn't do the honourable thing and evacuate the human cargo they are transporting. Instead he jumps into a lifeboat with the captain and first mate and they row to safety, leaving all the pilgrims on board to drown. But a few days later, the news arrives that the ship didn't sink—the pilgrims managed to keep it afloat by pumping water out until they were rescued by a passing frigate.

What struck me about the book, when I first read it for a university class fifteen years ago, is that it took the first hundred pages to get through the events I just related above. The story is told in a convoluted style, and Jim spends the first half of the book giving his confession to another sailor, Marlow. Jim is ashamed of what he has done, and disgusted with himself for failing to live up to the romantic notions of honour he'd been dreaming of his whole life, and he can't understand how he ended up jumping ship when he'd always thought he was the sort of person who was simply waiting on a moment to prove how heroic he actually was. He's convinced that there must be something hidden among the details of his story, and only by a thorough and painstaking recounting of everything he saw, everything he felt, as well as his thoughts on these feelings, and his interpretation and opinion on his own thoughts, would he be able to convey to Marlow (and uncover for himself) what had really happened on the night he found himself fleeing a sinking ship. Even though the facts are a matter of public record, Jim is desperate to tell his side of the story to Marlow, to plead his case, to convince at least one other person, a fellow seaman (*one of us*) that while he may be guilty, he is also innocent. If the facts are given enough context, Jim thinks, it will be possible to see his actions in an entirely different light. A soft, sympathetic light. And, as it happens, by the end of Jim's protracted and anguished confession, he succeeds in bringing Marlow around to his way of seeing things.

One point that Jim is pretty emphatic on is that he wasn't afraid and that his decision to jump ship could in no way be considered a failure of courage. Jim tells Marlow that his thoughts were of the human cargo, and how there weren't enough lifeboats to save even half of them. But if he wasn't afraid of death, Marlow wonders, and hadn't been thinking of saving himself, then why did he wind up in one of the lifeboats with the rest of the ship's crew while the pilgrims were left behind to drown? So Jim contextualizes every moment leading up to his decision to jump ship, and is so careful to recount every tiny fluctuation in his thoughts that it becomes impossible for Marlow to condemn him. 'He was not afraid of death,' Marlow explains, 'he was afraid of the emergency.… He might have been resigned to die, but I suspect he wanted to die without added terrors, quietly, in a sort of peaceful trance.' And not, Marlow thinks, amid 'all the horrors of panic, the trampling rush, the pitiful screams.'

Jim isn't afraid of the idea of death, Marlow thinks, at least not the sort of death he'd been fantasizing about ever since he was a child reading stories of Napoleonic seamen travelling the world in the name of liberty, equality, and brotherhood, who gladly sacrifice themselves for their naval brethren, the sort of death that only arrives when the moment is right, after destiny has been fulfilled and his story can be safely passed down through the ages, never to be forgotten. Not only is he not afraid, Marlow thinks, Jim even craves this sort of death, and has spent his whole life in search of it. But what Jim hadn't been searching for, and what terrified him when he encountered it, was the specific form that death took in the practice of his profession, drowning on a merchant ship with a degenerate crew and hundreds of pilgrims, his body lost at sea and his short, unremarkable career ending in oblivion.

For his whole life, Jim had looked forward to the day when he would face the ultimate test, the moment when the greatness he believed he was capable of, his fate, as it were, would finally be revealed. But when he found himself in an actual life-or-death situation it turned out all wrong. The incongruity with his past fantasies of heroism and the horror of this real catastrophe left him with the feeling that he was exempt from any sort of responsibility. After spending hours recounting every little detail leading up to that moment—as if the sheer bulk of information proved that he'd had no other choice, that it hadn't even been a matter of choice—after scrupulously avoiding anything approximating an admission throughout their whole night together, he finally concedes to Marlow that he had in fact jumped ship, and abandoned his post, leaving hundreds of passengers, though they were technically cargo, behind to drown. But then he seems to immediately regret his confession. 'I had jumped,' he says, refusing to look at Marlow. 'It *seems*.'

The latter half of the book is taken up by Jim's adventures with an indigenous tribe in Polynesia, where he lives the rest of his short life in the most recklessly heroic fashion, hellbent on proving that he is actually what he'd always imagined himself to be. He is eventually killed by the very people he had come to save. Marlow relates this part of Jim's story as if he is trying to correct the record, and introduce nuance to the crude impression of Jim in the public after a widely reported and scandalous trial, to prove that there was something more to what happened, something that would end up if not exonerating Jim, then at least casting his actions in a more sympathetic light. Ever since he was a boy, Marlow thinks, Jim had been waiting on the day when he would fulfill his destiny. But when the moment finally arrived it caught him off guard. Jim was surprised, Marlow thinks, by how unremarkable the fateful day turned out to be, and so instead of the heroic self-lessness he expected of himself there was nothing but fear and confusion, and he acted in a way he regretted, and spent the last years of his life trying to redeem.

'It's actually pretty sad,' I said to Roger as I watched the cops drink from fresh coffees that one of the EMTs had handed out. 'He came here from Libya, apparently, or was it Lebanon? Anyway, he didn't have any family here, so ...'

'Poor guy,' Roger said. 'There's a lot of hurt out there in the world.' He was at his keyboard again and I wasn't sure he'd been listening. 'Don't worry about the meeting with Inner-zone. We'll tell them something came up.'

It took me a moment to realize that Roger was referring to a meeting with one of our biggest clients that had been sched-uled last week. The fact that I had forgotten about this meeting, I thought, and that it would've been obvious to Roger that I had forgotten about this meeting, was very alarming both for Roger and for me, although for different reasons. Since I'd got-ten back from my last foreign assignment, I'd been spending my days at the office reading long-form journalism at my desk, sending an email every once in a while, and showing up to meetings. If I went too long without sending an email, I started to feel insecure, and if I went a few days without attending a meeting, I felt like I didn't exist. And now, five weeks into this routine, I was starting to lose track of time and my surroundings. I would be sitting at my desk, or staring at one of my colleagues during a meeting, and all of a sudden I would get the uncanny feeling of not knowing where I was, and why I was there. But just as quickly I would recollect myself, so to speak, and I would remember that I was at my office, in my home city, that I was a well-paid executive in a large company, living in the same apartment I'd been in for the last twelve years. I would take an hour to compose an email that a client had already been waiting on for over a week, and that I had promised to send by the end of the day, but then I would leave for the day without sending it. Only a few days earlier, I had asked my assistant to book a meeting with the communications director, and then when the meeting came up in my calendar I couldn't remember why I'd asked for it. So because of this meeting with Innerzone, one of the only meetings in the last few weeks where my presence was essential and not just procedural, and where the meeting itself was enormously significant and not one of the catch-ups, debriefs, strategy sessions, reviews, or presentations that typically clogged up my schedule, as well as the offhand way that Roger brought it up that was somehow both casual and menacing—this was the first time in over twelve years that I was genuinely scared I might lose my high-paying position at the company. I had always assumed that I'd coast along until it was time to trade up and take a position somewhere else. But the sound of Roger's voice on the other end of the line made me worry that I had ruined everything. 'I have lost control,' I was essentially saying to Roger when it became clear that I'd completely forgotten about the Innerzone meeting. 'My nights are leaking into my days. I can't maintain the boundary anymore. I can't be trusted. I no longer have my eye on the ball, I'm not in the game. We're not on the same page. My priorities are all out of whack,' I said, not out loud, but through my conspicuous silence. And the email I had sent to him earlier, I thought, after agonizing over every word, and struggling to find the right tone to tell him that I had to work from home because I had been a witness to my neighbour's tragic suicide, instead of coming off as professionally casual and wholly unremarkable, which is what I'd been going for, probably read like a thinly veiled confession of my dark and unbalanced mental state.

I assured Roger that I would make it to the Innerzone meeting later this afternoon. 'Sorry,' I said. 'I should have been clearer in my email this morning.' Instead of admitting that I had forgotten about the important client meeting, I came up with this lame and preposterous lie about poor communication. This was a go-to for me, my favoured professional alibi, and by now Roger was used to hearing me explain away even the most glaring fuck-up on poor communication skills. I obviously hadn't remembered about the Innerzone meeting, and for me to tell Roger that it was because of poor communication was an insult to his professional character, and his personal dignity. This compulsion I have for lying, and for forcing people to go along with my lies no matter how humiliating and obvious the lie may be, this behavioural tic, something I only used to do infrequently, had grown into a full-on pathological condition, this lying-disease, I thought, was the source of all of my professional insecurity. If it weren't for this reckless reflex to lie about even the most banal incidents, it's possible I might have enjoyed my time in the office. Maybe I would've gotten to know some of my colleagues a little better, or I might have struck up a friendship outside of work. But every time I claimed I had left a voice mail for someone that they must've accidentally deleted, or when I suggested that an email they should've already received might have wound up in their junk folder, I was adding another lie onto the series of lies that I had built up around me and that kept me walled off from my colleagues.

'Well, I'm glad we cleared that up,' Roger said. 'I must've misread what you wrote because I could've sworn you said you were going to work from home for the day.' I was still surprised when he challenged me in this passive-aggressive way. The lie I was asking Roger to go along with was so obvious, and it was offensive to him and humiliating for me, but it was cruel to explicitly call me out, I thought. To say to me, 'You're lying. And while in the past, I've been willing to go along with your little lies, this time I'm not going to let you get away with it.'

'I had a pretty crazy morning,' I said. 'But I will be there for the meeting. Things look like they're wrapping up here.'

'Glad to hear it,' Roger said.

I stood there with my phone up to my ear even though Roger had already ended the call. It's not that I'm a materialistic person, at least not in comparison to my colleagues, I thought, who spend most of their time either planning what they are going to buy, or discussing what they have recently bought. I pride myself on getting by with the essentials, without going in for the extravagances that I can easily afford. But in spite of my relatively austere lifestyle, I felt as if I couldn't get by on anything less than an enormous executive salary. When I was in my twenties, I thought, I never had aspirations for this sort of professional success and financial security. I didn't seek out this life so much as I drifted into it. People like me, I thought, who have my particular socioeconomic background, can wind up advancing in their career and making a lot of money just by showing up every day and being ready and willing to do whatever the company asks of you. Because I am capable of carrying on a conversation with someone I've only just met, because I am exactly what people expect, because I look the part and deliver my lines reasonably well, I thought, I've been given an extraordinary amount of money, almost all of which I have put into investment accounts that I never pay any attention to. Nobody is more aware than I am of how little I deserve this financial success, I thought, still holding the phone up to my ear. For as long as I can remember I have had a visceral distaste for hard work, and, like many lazy people, I have always tried to do the least amount of work for the largest amount of money. I had expected that once I finally finished university my laziness would lead me toward a do-nothing position with zero responsibility where I could wait out the days between vacations while collecting a decent salary. But instead I wound up getting promoted to what was considered in my industry to be a very prestigious position. The money was nice to have, I thought, but I'd only ever had a functional relationship with it, which is to say I liked what money could do for me, but I didn't care for money in and of itself. Among my colleagues, I thought, this was considered naive and immature.

I stood on the other side of the street watching the Handyman small talk with a group of cops eating croissants off the hood of one of their cruisers. I should've minded my own business, I told myself. Just like when I got the urge to volunteer for one of the charity drives at the office, or when I got the impulse to offer advice to a colleague who was going through a series of medical tragedies that had plagued her family for years and consumed all her time and energy outside of work, or any time I thought about getting involved in or supporting a political cause I was reminded that whenever I did help, or advise, or get involved, it was invariably a disappointing and sometimes infuriating experience. Whenever I got caught up in the drama of other people's lives, I always regretted it later on. I never said to myself, 'That was a worthwhile and fulfilling experience,' or 'Even if it didn't make a difference, it was still worth it to try.' Instead I thought, That was a waste of time, and What's the point? As much as I tried to blame other people for inconveniencing me, and filling up my life with their problems, I knew that ultimately it was my fault for getting involved in the first place. 'I should've stayed in my apartment,' I said to myself. 'Eventually someone else would've complained.'

People drifted from one walkway to the next and gathered into small cliques. Renters huddled together in one group, new homeowners in another, and a gang of old-timers stood on the corner and stared at the cops. The old-timers had bought into the market at an unbelievably low price back in the sixties and now spent their retirement keeping watch over the comings and goings in the neighbourhood. The new homeowners had bought up the nicer homes on the side of the street that faced my building. They had paid what they considered to be bargain prices to get in early on a part of town that was still pretty rundown but would no doubt be transformed within the next couple of years. Just a few feet away from me, the Athleisure Wear Woman was talking to another woman in almost identical athleisure wear. At first I thought they were standing there silently, watching the crowd of cops drink from their bottomless cups of coffee, but then I noticed they were talking ever so slightly from the corners of their mouths, and for a paranoid moment I wondered if the reason they were being so discreet was because they were talking about me. There was a group of good-looking young people crowded onto the tiny front yard of one of the nicer homes, no doubt part of the burgeoning restaurant and bar scene that the neighbourhood was becoming known for. They were dressed like celebrities and drinking Caesars, all of them wearing expensive-looking sunglasses. They held on to their phones and some of them smoked cigarettes or vaped, spewing plumes into the air. And they talked to each other all at once with regular upswells of exaggerated, insincere laughter. They looked wasted, as if they'd all just spilled from the doors of a dance club. The discovery of my neighbour's body, I thought, and the outsized police response must've felt to them as if the whole thing had been staged for their amusement.

When I was in university, I went to a lot of parties, although I rarely felt like going, and only went to them because of my friends at the time, who seemed to want to go to as many parties as they could manage. With few exceptions, parties were events I endured rather than enjoyed. And just like all the other joyless obligations in my life, whether it was Sunday school or little league hockey, I comforted myself with the thought that when I was older I wouldn't be obliged anymore, and that I would be able to do whatever I wanted. But now that I was standing only a few feet away from these attractive and intoxicated young people who looked as if they weren't much younger than me (though they seemed to be from another era), I felt an urge to join them, and laugh along with them in the same over-the-top way. After spending every night since I'd returned from my foreign assignment either out on my balcony getting drunk and reading about North Korea's nuclear program, or getting high on my couch and watching award-winning prestige TV, I was feeling a little bored with myself. 'Maybe it would be good for you to chat with the neighbours,' I thought, 'to actually speak with someone outside of your personal and professional spheres.' I stood there watching these young, good-looking people, trying to decide whether I should introduce myself or go back to my apartment and get ready for the Innerzone meeting. Isolated moments from the last five weeks kept flashing in my mind. I saw myself lying on the couch at 3:00 a.m. surrounded by cold takeout, a thick layer of weed dust covering the coffee table, reaching for the controller every time there was a loud scene in the show I was watching, and worried the sound might be bothering my neighbour. There I was, sitting out on the balcony and watching the Pseudo Homeless Guys break down furniture to feed the fire they had going in their barbecue. And there I was again, this time reading an article about a group of child soldiers, occasionally getting up as if to stretch, although I was really just trying to get a better look at the tiny gap between the window frame and the bedsheet my neighbour had hung over the kitchen window, that had bluebottle bugs crawling up and down the pane. I saw myself at my kitchen table in the morning, drinking a latté made from the espresso machine the company gave me after the Christmas I spent in Italy on foreign assignment, scrolling through the headlines and deleting spam from my personal email account. And in all of these scenes, I would've remarked to myself at some point, *He must sleep all day*, since I never heard him moving around.

Why not jump off a bridge or an overpass? I thought. What was the point of sealing himself in his room? Who did he think was going to find him? When I saw my neighbour hunched over the hibachi, his robe practically dangling in the coals, was there something in his eyes or in his body language that might've indicated what he was planning? If I hadn't been so self-absorbed would I have picked up on this? While everything else from our encounter was vivid in my mind— the light above his kitchen door, the cheap plastic flip-flops on his feet, the ordinary kitchen fork he was using to turn the coals—I couldn't recall his face. 'There was no way you could've guessed what he was up to,' I told myself. Although now I suspected it probably wasn't a coincidence that on the same morning I came back from my foreign assignment my neighbour had decided to kill himself. He had been waiting for me to get back from my foreign assignment, I thought, and had already decided, without having even met me, that I was going to be the one to find him. This hadn't been a fit of passion, I thought, or a tragic onset of despair he had been powerless to resist. This plan had been worked out months before, maybe longer, and he started to get impatient for my return. On my first day back, he heard me through his wall and came onto his balcony to get a good look at me, I thought, to judge whether I was the right sort of person, the sort who would notice the conspicuous absence of any signs of life in his apartment, who, after the slightest inclination that something wasn't right, such as the faint whiff of rot emanating from a closed kitchen window, would take it upon himself to promptly inform the building superintendent of his suspicions. On account of my bland good looks, the inordinate attention I pay to personal hygiene, and the aura of authority that emanates from my fashionable and expensive clothing, he probably thought I would catch on right away to what he had done and discover his body within a few days. Instead I spent weeks out on the balcony reading long-form journalism, or on the couch watching morally complex TV series about doctors and lawyers, drug dealers and politicians, and sad, unremarkable people from all walks of life, and all of these shows were deeply realized with fastidious attention to detail, whether they were set in pristine professional spaces, depraved inner-city ghettos, listless suburban sprawl, apocalyptic war-ravaged countrysides, or domestic interiors of bygone and fondly remembered eras, while only a few feet away from me, separated by a paper-thin wall, my neighbour's body continued its steady, inexorable decay. In the same time it took me to scan the Wikipedia entry on the Chinese dynastic order, or read an oral history of the first successful cloning of a sheep, a few million cells would have disintegrated, his body would've swollen even more, its colour deepened and darkened. Until I stood at the threshold of his bedroom, I thought, I never considered the possibility that the smell was coming from a dead person. But instead of going into the room and confirming what I must've known by then, or at least suspected, I ran away and left the body for someone else to find. I was so uninterested in my neighbour, I thought, that I never wondered about what he was doing in his apartment. I wasn't curious. I didn't care. I did not see him, in the same way I didn't see the people pressed up against me on the Metro, or the people who sat across from me at the food court. I had taken one look at him in his bathrobe, and I had decided, not consciously, that he didn't matter to me. He would never be anything more than background, just part of the landscape of my everyday life. I would never think about him, wonder what his story was, and would most likely never remember his name. He was the sort of person I wouldn't bother saying hello to, not out of mean-spiritedness, but because it didn't seem necessary. And maybe I had noticed, not consciously, that my neighbour was in a tremendous amount of psychological pain, and his dishevelled appearance and bizarre behaviour were proof, if it was needed, of the precarious state he was in. In the same way that I might dismiss a strange noise at night just so I don't have to get out of bed and go investigate, I probably dismissed the smell just so I wouldn't have to get involved in whatever my neighbour was obviously going through.

The Handyman was talking to the two Althleisure Wear Women, and even though they had friendly and concerned looks on their faces, they were ever-so-slightly backing away from him, and seemed almost to be recoiling in discomfort. Whenever I am caught, like these women were, by someone like the Handyman, someone always ready to tell people what they think they know about the world, someone who can go on and on without a break so there is never a chance to interrupt, to excuse yourself, to get away, or if I'm not directly trapped but still find myself waiting behind a Handyman-type in line at a store, or stuck at a bus stop while a Handyman-type lectures some unlucky commuter about conspiracy theories involving municipal politics, or rambles on about a lurid piece of neighbourhood folklore, whenever I am held hostage by one of these Handyman-types I am overcome with irritation that quickly develops into full-blown rage. Except in those rare moments when I'm not in the midst of doing something, or going somewhere in a hurry, and instead I'm meandering through an alley or side street on my way back from an errand that hadn't been necessary but served as an excuse to get out of the apartment, in those moments I sometimes feel so generous with my time that I even indulge one of these Handyman-types. But as I listen to their interminable stories I inevitably start to wonder how these Handyman-types ever get anything done. A trip to the grocery store could turn into a prolonged discussion with the cashiers and store managers, one that ranged from online privacy to the legality of modern surveillance systems, or a subway ride could devolve into a series of debates over the efficacy of the new ticketing system.

These Athleisure Wear Women, who I usually only ever saw as they made their bag-laden way between their apartments

and their SUVs, stood on the sidewalk listening to the Handyman as he described the gruesome discovery of my neighbour's
body. It looked as though he was just getting started and was
planning on talking to them for a while, even though the
women were practically screaming at him through their
shared body language to cut things short. He either didn't
notice or ignored them, and carried on with such force and
purpose that he came off as mildly threatening. How can
someone like this hold on to a job, I thought, let alone get
through the most basic interactions, like ordering takeout
food, or signing up for a phone plan? The Handyman-type has
no sense of proportion, I thought. He has none of the natural
discretion necessary to civic life, and of course he intrudes on
people's personal space with impunity. But more than anything else, I thought, these Handyman-types have no regard
for time, whether it be the time of day, or the small bit of time
alone someone gets on their commute to work, which is to
say these Handyman-types are indifferent, or insensitive, to
professional time, and it is this that makes the Handyman-
types so infuriating to a bachelor like myself, whose sole wish
is to be able to make it to work and back again every day without getting stuck listening to somebody's hard-luck story or
paranoid fantasy.

The Athleisure Wear Women managed to get free of the
Handyman by taking shelter inside one of their SUVs, and
now he was looking around for someone else to talk to. I
moved closer to the good-looking group of young people
drinking Caesars. 'Aren't you the guy who found him?' said a
blonde girl wearing a bathing suit. I pretended I hadn't heard

her, or that I had heard her but thought she'd been talking to someone else. After she repeated her question, I even pointed at myself and mouthed the words, 'Who? Me?'

'Yes, you,' she said. 'I heard that you were the one.'

'No,' I said. 'Sorry. That wasn't me.' I snuck a look to see where the Handyman was and was relieved to see that he'd drifted back to the Super's front step.

'Weird,' she said. 'That guy over there told me you found the body.' Her friends looked at their phones, a couple of them laughed awkwardly. I tried to put them at ease and remarked as nonchalantly as possible that he must've made a mistake. I told them that I'd never set foot in my neighbour's apartment.

I saw that they didn't believe me, and this bothered me as much as if I had actually been telling the truth. When the Bathing Suit Girl asked me if I was the one who found him, I thought, it was as if she was accusing me of something. If I had said, 'Yes, I was the one who noticed the smell. Yes, for weeks I didn't do anything about it. And yes, I went into the apartment with the Super and we opened the door to the room where the body was. But no, it's not accurate to say that I found him. It was the Handyman who went in this morning and made the actual discovery'—if I told her what had really happened, I thought, then she would have been repulsed, and seen me as a coward, and while that may have been a fair assessment in this specific instance, I still believed that on the whole, in the core of my being, and at the end of the day, I was a good person. I may be lying to the Bathing Suit Girl and to her circle of attractive and fashionable friends, I thought, but this lie is a more accurate reflection of who I am. It wasn't only that I was worried about my reputation in the neighbour-hood, or that I was ashamed for how I had run away from my neighbour's corpse. Of course I was very worried and deeply ashamed, and those feelings certainly influenced the lies that I told, but the reason I lied to the Bathing Suit Girl and her friends was entirely pragmatic. If I told the truth, this girl, who was more or less covered in elegant tattoos, would lose inter-est in me and start talking to someone else. I tried to keep her attention so she wouldn't say, 'Have a nice day,' and that she had to 'go inside for a second,' that I should 'take care,' and that she would 'see me around.' But it didn't seem to be working because she was constantly looking down at her phone and then looking up to smile at me in the same way that I smile during customer service encounters when I am no longer listening. I was painfully aware of my lack of tattoos.

'Who was he?' she asked.

'No idea,' I said. 'I think he was from Libya or Lebanon. Something like that.' I panicked for a second and searched their faces because I was worried that my remark could be taken as racist. Thankfully, everyone looked white.

'Yeah,' said a guy with an ostentatiously groomed beard, 'I think you're right. I'm pretty sure I've seen him around. He drove that old-school Chevette.'

'That guy?' the Bathing Suit Girl said. 'He was kind of hot.' They nodded solemnly, as if she had delivered a micro-eulogy. How was it possible that I had never seen these beautiful people before? I must've passed them on my way back from work, I thought, or on one of my frequent trips to the store, or to pick up some takeout. While I had been sitting on my balcony, or lying on my couch, while my neighbour's body had been rotting in his bed, I thought, these beautiful people had been here this whole time, living out their rich, dynamic, and interesting lives. Just moments ago, I had been worried about getting questioned by the detectives, and whether I was going to get in trouble at work for missing the Innerzone meeting, but now all I could think about was getting to hang out with these gorgeous people. I wanted to do what they were doing. I want to get fucked up, right there in the street in front of everyone, at ten in the morning.

'Do you think I could have a hit off that?' An enormous joint had been lingering at one end of the circle. A red-haired guy with an expression of permanent surprise—the effect of a wide, unblinking stare—was talking about a friend who had just returned from Lebanon. 'Apparently it's beautiful,' he said. The girl standing next to him, wearing an old-fashioned jumpsuit, agreed, and she said that while she had never made it to Lebanon, she had lived in Israel for two months and it definitely ranked in the top five most beautiful places she had ever been. The cops were sipping from their coffee cups. Some of them were chatting with a couple of paramedics who were packing away their gear in an ambulance, and then drove slowly down the street with their sirens off and disappeared around the corner. Within minutes, more cop cruisers and two large armoured vans took their place at the curb, disgorging at least another half-dozen beefy cops. It was impossible to keep track of them all streaming in and out of my neighbour's apartment. The scene on the sidewalk now included the staff from the bagel shop around the corner, half a dozen transit workers, the construction crew that had been renovating the brick facade of one of the buildings on the nicer side of the street, and two old men who usually spent the day sitting on the stoop of their building but today were stretched out on lawn chairs as if they were watching a parade. Despite the heavy police presence, people were openly sipping on bottles of beer or sharing joints, and the attractive customer service personnel I was hanging out with were in the midst of a full-on debauch. I saw the Handyman and the Grim Reaper, now back with the Super on her front step, looking over at our group. The Handyman got up and I was worried he was coming over to talk to us, but he stopped at the old men in the lawn chairs and crouched down next to them, gesturing for a beer from the six-pack at their feet. I should go to the Innerzone meeting, I thought. It was happening in an hour. Roger would be expecting me to show up at least half an hour in advance so we could get on the same page, strategy-wise. The Bathing Suit Girl had introduced herself by now, although I'd been too distracted when she did, so I still didn't know her name. I lit a cigarette and waited for an opening in the trivia session on municipal bylaws for burial and cremation. 'It's actually super illegal to just bury someone outside of a cemetery,' the Guy with the Surprised Look said. 'You're not even technically allowed to spread someone's ashes,' the Pseudo Paratrooper said. 'Like when you spread your grandparents' ashes on a beach or whatever—that's against the law.' Before I had a chance to give my opinion, they had moved on to whether or not it was a criminal offence to commit suicide.

It was hard to believe that all these cops were here just for a suicide. How many of them would be dispatched to the scene of a triple homicide, I thought, or a ten-car pileup? Was there a crime so terrible that there could never be enough cops to handle it? I stood there sipping my Caesar. I knew that if I didn't show for the meeting there was a good chance that Roger would never forgive me for it. Even if it took years, I thought, he would do everything he could to get me fired. But how could he possibly expect me to come in to work when, as far as he knew, I had just been traumatized by the discovery of my neighbour's body in a state of advanced decay? I was the lead on the Innerzone file and had been shepherding the clients for three years, but the meeting could run smoothly without me. Roger just wanted me there, I thought, because we were going to be reporting on some crappy numbers. He had insisted in advance of the meeting that we would have all hands on deck, as a sign of our commitment, he said, which would hopefully reassure our clients about their fairly heavy losses in the previous quarter. At this point in my career, at least ninety percent of what I did at my job was just for show, without any real substance to it, and this meeting, although crucial to our continued relationship with Innerzone, was no exception. We could have simply sent them this information in an email, I thought, and if necessary, maybe even set up a conference call, but instead we set up a full lunch meeting with every senior staff member, as well as some midlevel employees who were only implicated in the most nebulous administrative capacity. For three hours we would have to sit and stare at each other throughout interminable slide presentations full of warmed-over statistics and hyperbolic business-speak. I should just text Roger, I thought, to let him know *I'm not going to be able to make it for the Innerzone meeting after all*. The Surprised Look Guy was showing around a picture on his phone of a mountain bike he was thinking of buying. The Pseudo Paratrooper had unzipped the top half of her jumpsuit, letting it hang down so she could show off a scar from a high school car accident. Everyone seemed full of nervous energy, frantic almost. They disappeared in pairs to do lines, or share some pills. I was determined to get in on that too. I wondered if the Bathing Suit Girl was flirting with me or just being nice.

Since I started working at my company, I thought, I have been moving steadily through the upper echelons of the so-called horizontal executive hierarchy. I have a reputation for being competent, reliable, consistent, upbeat, results-oriented, and an all-around asset to the company. But I realized now as I stood there getting high with these attractive customer service personnel, that I had undermined this reputation through thousands if not hundreds of thousands of discrete actions over the last few weeks, so that anybody I worked with knew, without having to take even a cursory look at what I was up to at my desk back at the home office, that I was unproductive, dishonest, hypocritical, lazy, and ultimately a liability to the company. Every morning I told myself that I was going to get it together, go in with my best foot forward, buckle down and finally get some real work done, instead of just going through the motions, doing the bare minimum to keep up appearances. But after making these promises to myself I would invariably drift into a long-form journalism reverie, and then back at my apartment, after having watched countless hours of god-knows-what, I woke up the next day, hungover and nervy, and told myself I was in no shape to start making big changes, to turn things around and show everyone that I really wasn't a lazy and dishonest liability, that I was actually a trustworthy asset, so I put it off for another day, for when I didn't feel so tired. But I promised myself that I wouldn't keep putting it off, because I knew I had to make a change before it was too late (as it had been too late for my colleagues Sharon, and Dan, and Kevin, and Gio). I was amazed that nobody had taken me aside yet, and I assumed the reason they didn't say anything was because keeping me on as a glorified mascot who read long-form articles about the growing anti-vaccination movement was somehow in my company's best interests. For reasons I didn't understand, keeping me in my salaried position was preferable to letting me go. It probably helped that I never crossed any lines. I showed up to work in presentable, non-food-stained clothing. I made passable small talk. Occasionally I bought pastries for the admin staff. But the strain of slacking off for at least eight hours a day and spending all of my time in my office reading the internet and tending to my social media accounts was starting to wear me down and I had the urge to throw it all away.

I was watching two very hairy guys who had been either repairing or dismantling a vintage bike and were now taking a break. They joined the circle and openly stared at me. I waited for them to ask me about my neighbour, but it turned out they just wanted to ask me about the road bike I kept locked out front of my apartment. They couldn't believe I kept such an expensive and world-class racing bike locked up to an old wrought-iron fence with a cheap lock that anyone with a crowbar or hammer could break open in under a minute. I told them that I was pretty ambivalent about the bike since every time I passed it it reminded me that I had spent thousands of dollars on bikes and biking equipment with the intention of becoming an avid cyclist, and in the end I only went out a handful of times before I admitted to myself that I found long-distance cycling extremely boring. I told them they were welcome to it as long as they promised to keep it out of my sight.

The construction crew had moved on. The Athleisure Wear Women were vaping inside their SUV. One of the old-timers on the lawn chairs had gone off to relieve himself or get more beer. The Handyman was leaning against the driver side of a police cruiser and chatting with a cop who had the face of a teenager and the body of a competitive weightlifter. The scrum of cops had split off into loose little groups, some stood by their cruisers and stared at their phones, while others continued to chat and sip mindlessly from their coffee cups. The group of attractive customer service personnel treated me with the sort of kind indulgence you might show a dog that had wandered into your yard. I couldn't understand why it was taking so long for the cops to remove my neighbour's body. Were they sweeping the surfaces for prints, or using special lights to look for hair and fibres? Checking for signs of forced entry? Taking blood samples and examining the body for defensive wounds? Did they have to wait for the detectives to arrive and make a procedural call that the cops didn't have the authority to make?

For weeks I had been watching, in addition to the McCarthy-era prestige TV series, a violently forensic show about serial killers, images of bodies torn to pieces, crushed and mangled, or laid out on gleaming steel trays, splayed open and dismembered—while only a few feet away a body was decomposing in an airless room. I had literally breathed him in. And despite the nauseating smell, which, I must have known, somewhere deep down, or at least suspected, could only have come from the rotting carcass of a very big animal (bigger than a squirrel or raccoon), despite the fact that the smell was obviously coming from my neighbour's apartment, I thought, I never went to his door to see if everything was okay.

I imagined what was happening at the Innerzone meeting. I wondered what Roger would tell our clients about me not being there. I thought about who would be annoyed and maybe even alarmed at my absence. I stood there surrounded by these down-to-earth, fun-loving, and drop-dead gorgeous customer service personnel, and while I listened to them discuss the political economy behind tipping I was fantasizing about how I would confront Roger once I went back to the office, how I would call him out for his cold, corporate demeanour, for the insulting and callous way he had dismissed my neighbour's tragic suicide. I imagined sending a terse text message. 'Apologies,' it would say, 'I couldn't swing it.' I fantasized that I would send another text saying, 'In fact, I've been dealing with some serious health and family issues since I returned from my last foreign assignment and I'm afraid I'm going to have to take some time off to deal with them.' By graciously accepting a third Caesar, as well as a pill from a small silver case one of the bike enthusiasts had been passing around, I was turning my back on a lucrative, prestigious, and altogether undemanding position. I told myself that I was finally seeing things clearly, even though I knew that the pill I had taken had something to do with the clarity and intensity of my feelings. But even taking the pill into account, as well as the weed and the Caesars, and the high I was getting from talking to the Bathing Suit Girl, I was sure that at least some of my confidence was genuine, and I was certain that everything was about to change, and that it was probably the first time in the whole history of my professional career that I wasn't afraid of getting in trouble.

From my very first day at the company, I had been terrified of getting caught doing or saying something that I wasn't supposed to be doing or saying. Whenever I had to make a tough call that was certain to have implications for my career, as well as not insignificant effects on the health and well-being of potentially thousands of poor strangers, I always used the fear of getting caught to guide me. My behaviour during meetings, the friendly yet curt way I handled myself around admin staff, even my conduct in the executive washrooms, all of this was determined by a number of intense and interrelated fears that included everything from screwing up a client relationship and costing the company millions in lost revenue, to mild humiliation over an obnoxious comment I made about a recent political sex scandal. I was terrified of getting found out, busted, exposed, and for everyone to see what I really was and what I'd been up to all these years. My entire professional life had been nothing more than a series of banal deceptions that added up to a colossal con. I was giddy at the thought of finally dropping the act.

'Your phone is ringing.' The Bathing Suit Girl (who I heard someone refer to as Sarah) was pointing at the phone in my hand. It was Roger. I declined the call.

I should've answered, I thought. I should've explained to Roger that it was simply impossible for me to get away, that the cops had been questioning me for the last two hours, that they had taken my phone and only returned it to me just now. Roger should have heard me say that I was *devastated* over not being able to make the meeting. He should have even felt a little guilty for giving me such a hard time earlier. 'After all,' he should've thought after getting off the phone with me, 'he just had a traumatic experience. I don't know what the procedures are for this sort of thing. It's entirely possible that he has to sit around all day and wait to be questioned by the detectives, instead of just leaving them his number.' I was waiting my turn in the arm-wrestling contest that had inevitably started up among the largely shirtless customer service personnel. As I stared at my phone, all the hazy fantasizing I'd been indulging in was swept away in one great gust of fear. I saw at once, with the enhanced clarity of the skin-crawling high I was getting from the mystery pill, that I hadn't been serious about leaving the company. I was terrified of giving up my life of easy employment. There's no way I'll get a reference from Roger after today, I thought, and since they're the only company I've ever worked for I'm going to have to start over from the bottom. Worse. No references at my age, I thought, you might as well have a face tattoo. How, in the span of a few hours, I thought, did I go from a place of complete security to the brink of total disaster? I found myself getting angry about my neighbour again. As I held the phone in front of me in a frozen, stroke-like posture, the certainty that he was to blame for all this started to take hold.

'You look all serious,' the Bathing Suit Girl said. She threw her arm around my waist and I had the odd sensation of getting turned on and off all at once. The turnoff was the shame I felt for using my neighbour's suicide as an excuse to get all messed up with these fun-loving, impossibly hip, and supremely attractive customer service personnel, and this very same depraved behaviour, this nihilistic daytime debauch, I thought, was also what was turning me on.

'We should see if the cops want to arm wrestle,' I said.

'I'm worried they would take it too seriously,' she said.

'They do have a long history of taking things too seriously,' I said.

'Nothing against your neighbour,' she said, 'but I think they're taking this one a little too seriously.'

'They have to go through the motions,' I said. 'They have to treat the apartment like a potential murder scene. Suicide is legally a crime,' I said, 'so they have to preserve the chain of evidence. There's probably a bunch of boxes that they have to tick before they can remove the body.' I felt an urge to keep talking even though I could hear how obnoxious I sounded. I told her an anecdote that I'd heard from a colleague a long time ago, except now that I was telling it I made it sound as if it had actually happened to me. I told her about a trip I had never taken, to a city I had never been to, and how I witnessed someone hit the pavement after jumping from the roof of a hotel, when in actual fact it wasn't until last night, I thought, that I'd seen a dead body outside of a coffin. In the wild, I thought.

'That's crazy,' she said.

'I know.'

'I just got back from there,' she said.

I asked her what she had been doing there. It wasn't a common tourist destination, and I thought by pretending I was genuinely interested she wouldn't think to ask me about my own time there, since I was now worried she was going to catch me in my lie. She told me that she was there for a conference where she had presented a paper. I nodded along as if I knew what she was talking about and it took a minute before I finally realized that the Bathing Suit Girl and her friends were not just customer service personnel, they were also graduate students. I asked her what year she was in and she leaned forward as if she didn't want her friends to hear.

'I'm in the third year of my PhD.'

I shouldn't have been so surprised. It was, after all, a university town, and young, good-looking people like them, I thought, were never satisfied with working in customer service jobs, even if they were at the most popular and lucrative bars and restaurants in the city. They worked in customer service jobs, I thought, to supplement their academic careers. The whole time I'd been with them I'd been treating them as if they were working in customer service jobs for a living, and it was shocking to realize that everybody there was only working in customer service jobs as a stopgap while they completed their PhDs. I had thought I'd been at a customer service party, that I'd been partying with customer service personnel, when the whole time I'd actually been at a PhD party and was drinking and getting high with PhD students. This whole time, I thought, I've been telling myself I was at a working-class party, and that the conversations I was having were working-class conversations, but I was totally wrong about this. It was actually an intellectual party, and, without even realizing it, I'd been having intellectual conversations. The arm-wrestling contest wasn't a natural custom that had long ago been woven into the fabric of their working-class lives, I thought. It was an eccentric, self-conscious game that these PhD students had come up with as an ironic comment on patriarchal culture. I thought I'd been flirting with a bold and curious working-class girl, when I'd actually been engaged in an unequal battle of wits with a brilliant young woman whose eyes blazed with an intelligence I had completely overlooked. I tried to hide my surprise by asking what she and her friends were studying.

'You make it sound like we're all working on a class project together,' she laughed.

'Papier mâché volcanos?' I said. 'Bridges made with popsicle sticks?'

'Exactly,' she said. 'Dissecting frogs. Experiments with static electricity. That sort of thing.'

She lay down on the little square of lawn that was pockmarked with bald patches of dry, hard ground. It looked uncomfortable, but when she patted the spot next to her I lay down obediently. The white-knuckle high from the mystery pill brought with it a powerful sensation of helplessness. 'All this time,' I said to myself, 'you thought you were talking to an average working-class girl, and without realizing it, you made all sorts of working-class assumptions. The things you said were intended for a working-class audience, but instead, you were talking to an intellectual.' I would have never said the things that I'd said, or at least I would've said them in an entirely different way, if I'd known from the beginning I was dealing with PhDs, and not with customer service personnel. We lay there on the cold, hard ground while some of her friends stood over us and talked about their shared enthusiasm for a prestige TV series I'd never heard of. I fantasized about what my life might have been like if I had done a PhD.

'So, what do you do?' she said.

Something about the way she asked this question made me think she was hoping that I was also a PhD student, and that she'd be disappointed with an account executive, even if I told her about all of my foreign assignments. But I told myself that I was being paranoid, that I was probably feeling a bit isolated now that I knew she was in her third year of a PhD and that she travelled halfway around the world to give talks at prestigious conferences. It's highly unlikely, I thought, that this laid-back, beautiful, and unpretentious PhD candidate would look down on non-PhD people. Maybe it was nothing, just a banal question, standard small talk, and I was projecting my non-PhD insecurities on to her. But it was already too late. In every friendship I've ever had, whether it was with someone

I'd known my whole life, or a fleeting encounter like this one, there was always a moment when the other person did something I couldn't forgive—an ignorant remark, an innocent gesture—and our connection, our *rapport*, was completely ruined. No matter how close or friendly we had been with each other, once they said or did the thing that I couldn't forgive, then everything from that point on was just a matter of keeping up appearances, and what might've once been a genuine and trusting friendship became nothing more than a sham relationship. Even if, as was the case with the PhD candidate I was lying next to, I didn't want our connection, or rapport, to be spoiled by an offhand question, there didn't seem to be anything I could do to avoid it, I was incapable of moving on, getting over it, putting it behind me, letting go. I lay on the hard, dusty ground, the grass so stiff it stuck through my shirt like thorns, and the high from the mystery pill so powerful it felt as though my body had seized up and I was frozen to that spot. I thought about my neighbour, lying in his bed, his body rigid from rigor mortis, the room cordoned off, a couple of forensic analysts busy collecting evidence while the coroner took samples. Or maybe nobody was in the room right now and while they were waiting to take my neighbour away they were observing a respectful distance, gathering in front of my building, or sitting in their vehicles and drinking from their coffee cups. It was a perfectly innocent question, I thought. She was simply being polite by asking it. But I knew then that I would never forgive her for it.

'I work for a huge company,' I said. 'I have one of those jobs that is basically impossible to describe.'

'I see.' We lay there on our backs, staring straight up at the cloudless spring sky.

'Well,' I said, 'I should probably go to work.'

I didn't pay attention to what she said as I picked myself off the ground, but when I thought about it later, I was pretty sure that I had heard her say, 'I know it was you.' I crossed the street and walked past the two drunks sitting in their lawn chairs, gripping the armrests and staring at the cops as if it was their job to keep watch. I wondered if I should go into the office. 'No,' I told myself, 'it's too late.' All it takes, I thought, is one meeting, or email, a remark during after-work drinks, or a tiny screw-up that wastes time and energy that could've been used more profitably, just one question during a compulsory staff meeting, or an awkward exchange on the elevator, and your career and professional future can be totally destroyed. It is tempting to believe that if we can destroy our career, I thought, it's also possible to rebuild it, to believe that we always have the opportunity to correct our past mistakes, to make up for them, or redeem them. We talk about do-overs, or hitting restart. You're being tested, I thought. This thing with your neighbour is a test. I stood there on the sidewalk watching the Fauxhawk Cop show the Handyman something on his phone. I had ruined my quiet, anonymous life, where everybody left me alone. From now on, I thought, you'll be known as the Guy Who Found His Neighbour's Body, or didn't find it, or found it and ran away, who went back to his apartment and stayed up all night watching TV. For a second I even fantasized that maybe none of this was really happening. All a bad dream, I thought. When something bad happens there's always part of me that feels like it's not real. What I mean is that the bad thing seems like an outlier, or not part of the official version of my reality. The things that feel real to me are the things that I am always dreaming of, fantasizing about, and hoping for. The only reality that I've ever been willing to accept is the one where I am who I think I am. 'This isn't really happening,' I say. 'It wasn't supposed to be like this. That's not who I really am,' I say. 'I would never do that,' I say.

I was standing on the sidewalk, a cigarette in my hand, swaying from side to side without being fully aware that I was swaying. I was still trying to come up with what I was going to say to Roger about the Innerzone meeting. Missing the meeting was totally out of character for me, I would say to Roger. It simply wasn't my style to go around missing meetings, and if I did end up missing something as important as this afternoon's meeting, it could only be because of things completely beyond my control. The real me would never do something like that. 'It's like when you're on the subway, and out of nowhere you imagine attacking another passenger. You dismiss this thought as a random impulse, right? A gut reaction likely related to stress and fatigue?' I would say to Roger, 'You would never consider that these dark thoughts are representative of who you really are. When you flirt with the barista at your local café, or make a spontaneous donation to disaster relief, these actions could just as easily be considered a reflex, or a reaction to a string of nice weather. When you reflect on things you have done in the past, you can accept whatever shows up in the reflection that makes you look good, and you feel as though what you're seeing is right and true,' I would say, 'but all the other stuff that shows up in this reflection that makes you look bad is a mistake, or at least that's what you tell yourself. An aberration. False.'

The weeks I'd been wasting away in my office, maintaining my social media accounts and keeping up to date on online conspiracy theories about school shootings, could be attributed to the traumatic effect the smell of my neighbour's body had had on me, I thought. As a small challenge to myself, I tried to keep the leaning pillar of ash on my cigarette from falling. A car pulled up and a man and a woman, impeccably dressed, in flashy and nearly matching suits, threw open their respective doors the instant the engine cut and made their way toward the cops standing around my neighbour's stoop. The detectives, I thought. Seconds later I wondered if I hadn't actually said it out loud.

I was surprised by how much they corresponded to the image I had in my mind of what detectives should look like. He was blandly handsome, with the effortful build of a male comic book character, while she had the good looks and humourless hair and makeup of a white-collar criminal. There was a whiff of a sibling resemblance. The clichéd quality of their appearance was a bit ridiculous, actually, and I wondered if they were aware of the effect the look had on people, if this was part of a strategy, to play off the rich lineage of film and TV detectives everyone was so familiar with, or were they just going along unthinkingly with the stereotypical presentation because they felt obliged to follow the trends in TV detective fashion. Or maybe the nice suits that so obviously set them apart from the other cops were simply standard departmental issue. Maybe the generic quality of their features, the same sort of features that get criticized in TV and film for being unrealistic, was just a matter of good genes and scrupulous hygiene and not a deliberate imitation of the clichéd TV detective. In the same way that celebrities, even the minor ones, create a field of gravity that draws people to them wherever they go, everyone on the street drew closer to the detectives as they talked with the cops gathered outside my neighbour's front door.

I walked over to join the Handyman, the Super, and the Grim Reaper, who were still holding their ground on the Super's front step. They were talking to the Fauxhawk Cop about professional sports statistics. I pretended to follow along for a bit, but eventually I interrupted them and told the Fauxhawk Cop that I couldn't wait around much longer. 'Important clients,' I said, and I said, 'Billion-dollar portfolio,' I said, 'My rights,' and kept on repeating the phrase 'Time is money.' The Handyman turned to an enormous cop with the facial features of a twelve-year-old, and tried to keep the exchange of professional sports statistics alive. The Grim Reaper said something about 'terrorism' and 'radical Islam' to the Super, who was staring at the detectives and aggressively smoking a cigarette. The men in the lawn chairs were cackling and pointing at one of the PhDs, who was throwing up in the empty flower bed that stretched along the sidewalk. 'I can't stick around any longer,' I said, loud enough for the detectives, who were only a few feet away. 'This has nothing to do with me. I'm hardly ever here. Most of the time I'm travelling for work.' For appearance's sake, I was saying all of this to the

Fauxhawk Cop and the Super and the Grim Reaper, but of course it was actually intended for the two detectives, who didn't appear to be listening. I wasn't really *saying* it either, more like shouting it with a steadily increasing intensity. The detectives kept on chatting with the other cops while the Fauxhawk Cop was slowly pushing me back to the sidewalk and ordering me to calm down, although each time he said the words *calm down* he seemed to get even more irritated and aggressive. 'Sir,' he said, 'you need to *calm down* right now. I need you to step back and *calm down*.'

I should apologize, I thought. I should step back and calm down. But I felt a rush standing there chest to chest with him, and while I had no idea what was going to happen next, I believed I was ready for anything. Then he suddenly snapped and shouted, 'Get back!' and all of my boozy courage flushed out of me. 'You told me to stick around,' I said. 'Sir,' he said. 'Go back to your apartment. Now.' The Handyman called something out to me but as I pushed through my front door I didn't bother turning around.

Once I was back on my couch, in the same position I'd been in that morning, I became aware of how fucked up I was. Out on the street, I'd been focused on what was going on around me, though *focused* probably isn't the right word, more like overwhelmed, so it wasn't until I was back on my couch that I finally calmed down long enough to notice that my vision was doubled, my thoughts were swirling, and I had to brace my arm on the coffee table in front of me to stop the room from spinning. When I'm surrounded by people I don't know, or put in situations I don't understand, I can go for hours without noticing that I'm cold, or hungry, and it's only once I've returned to normal, to my familiar surroundings, and my everyday activities, that I become aware of myself again. It's only when I'm surrounded by all of my old things, and insulated by the thoughts and memories they conjure up, that I have any clarity about how I am feeling from one moment to the next.

'Idiot,' I said out loud. 'You're a fucking idiot.'

I slid down on the couch but kept one foot on the floor, and for a long second the room held still. I imagined that Roger was in the room with me. He wasn't saying anything, just staring at me with a look of disappointment on his face. 'I know what you're thinking,' I said to Imaginary Roger. 'You think that I used my neighbour's suicide as an excuse to work from home. I may have lied about discovering the body and calling 911, but I was telling the truth when I said I couldn't make it into the office. I never lied about needing to work from home,' I said. 'I can look you straight in the eye and say with complete sincerity that I have always been honest and above board with you about professional matters, and when I said I had to work from home, I was telling the truth.' I looked Imaginary Roger in the eyes and told him how sorry I was for missing the important client meeting, but that it had been out of my hands. 'I know what it must look like,' I said to Imaginary Roger. 'I'm fully aware of what you must be thinking. *How could he put up with the smell for so long?* I can only say that as bad as it was, I assumed it would eventually go away, and even though it was so strong it sometimes made my eyes water, I still got used to it in a weird way.'

I could hear the detectives talking to the cops in my neighbour's apartment. I prayed they would leave without bothering to question me. I put my other foot on the floor and lightened my grip on the coffee table.

'Fucking idiot,' I said.

It was hard to hear what the detectives were saying to each other. Even though the walls were paper-thin, their voices were drowned out by the blood pulsing in my ears. I lay on the couch and tried to recall everything I had said while I was outside, agonizing over every evasive answer I had given, the flat-out denials and the outright lies. The mystery pill wasn't wearing off. If anything, since I had come in from the street and lain down on the couch, things were only getting worse. I tried to come up with a remedy. Something to eat will make things better, I thought. But I couldn't decide on anything. Maybe watching prestige TV will make me feel better, I thought. But I couldn't decide on a show. A nap might be the best idea, I thought. But I didn't want to be asleep if the detectives came to my door.

I gripped the coffee table. I forced myself to drink some water. I considered putting on music, not because I felt like listening to it, but because it seemed like I should be doing something, and not just lying on the couch with only the sounds of the people outside coming through my window. The blood surging in my ears finally died down. I didn't hear the detectives anymore. I imagined them in my neighbour's bedroom, the hibachi in the middle of the room, the heap on the mattress. I thought back to the night before, when I had run down the stairs and out of the apartment. Aside from the shock I had gotten at the sight of what turned out to be my neighbour's body, I think that what really freaked me out was the feeling that I was walking into a problem that I wouldn't be able to throw money at. A problem that simply wouldn't respond to my money-throwing method. If I had gone into the room and confirmed that the heap on the mattress was my neighbour's body, I thought, then I would've been obligated to call the police. I wouldn't have been able to smoke the joint I had planned on smoking, or watch the prestige TV I'd planned on watching. Maybe I was scared of not being able to get fucked up all by myself while watching huge volumes of streaming content, I thought.

I remembered the expression, or more like the lack of expression, on his face as he brought the still-smoking hibachi into his apartment. What I had noticed then but only appreciated now, I thought, was how he had the look of somebody who had been alone for a long time. As I lay on my couch and took my pulse to see if it was going as fast as it felt like it was going, I remembered that on the day I saw my neighbour bring the hibachi into his apartment the impression he gave off, while I was on my balcony only ten feet away, was that he didn't really see me, or that he didn't see anyone really, and he didn't seem to be aware of anything beyond *his immediate surroundings*. I had picked up on all of this in that moment on the balcony right before he killed himself, I thought. He had obviously been in distress, and on some level I must've known at that moment what he was planning, even though his eyes appeared calm as he kept focused on the coals of the hibachi, but the only thing I had been worried about was that he might introduce himself, try to strike up a conversation, or ask me over for a coffee.

As I was lying on the couch, I couldn't decide whether it was better to have my eyes open or shut. Open, the room was blurred and out of alignment. Shut, it felt like my body was going into free fall. After I'd had my eyes closed for a long time, I opened them to see the detectives standing at the threshold of my living room, as if they were waiting to be invited in.

I must've passed out, I thought. I tried to piece together an unbroken sequence—from my experiment with opening and closing my eyes to the detectives' sudden appearance at the threshold of my TV room—but everything was mixed up in my mind and I didn't even know if I'd been on my couch for only a few minutes or if it had been hours since I'd come in off the street. They entered and I watched as they surveyed the room and poked at the bags of weed on my coffee table, glancing disapprovingly at the remains of takeout food from the night before. You're definitely not dreaming, I thought. This feels too real. Even if you are dreaming, I thought, it is probably best to act as though the detectives are really in the room, just in case.

'You left your front door open. I hope you don't mind. We let ourselves in. We were told you might have some information about what happened.'

'I was just resting my eyes,' I said. 'There's something wrong with the door. I've been meaning to ask the Super to have it fixed. Sorry about the mess.'

The Female Detective moved to the corner across from me and looked out the window while the Male Detective stayed standing by my coffee table. They were radiating impatience.

'I'm almost never here,' I said, finally sitting upright on the couch and addressing the Male Detective. 'I travel a lot for work. Just finished a nine-month stint abroad. I'm never here long enough to get to know the neighbours.'

'And what do you do for work?' he said.

I told him about my position and the company I worked for.

'And you live here?' the Female Detective said.

'I know,' I said. 'I've been here since I was in university. I'm away so much and just never got around to moving to a better place.'

'We're in a bit of a hurry,' the Male Detective said.

I have always justified my self-destructive behaviour with complicated forms of compensation. I might spend the night drinking and reading long-form articles until my vision blurs and I pass out on the couch, and then spend the next day hiding in my office and reading about the global refugee crisis and waiting out the clock, but I would tell myself that my self-destructive after-work routines were retroactively compensated by reading about these refugees, since I was expanding my sympathy for, and knowledge of, the *global situation*. I had compensated for my shameless treatment of customer service personnel by having once worked in the customer service industry myself. When I spent night after night eating takeout, getting high, and watching the McCarthy-era TV series, I compensated the next day by doing two sets of ten push-ups. Whenever I bought an expensive watch or a seven-thousand-dollar suit, or dropped twelve thousand dollars on a Japanese kitchen knife, I retroactively compensated for these luxuries by all the money I had saved in rent at this apartment instead of what I'd be paying for a high-priced condo. I avoided the people in my neighbourhood and saw them as nothing more than obstacles and inconveniences. They existed for me in the most broad, unsympathetic stereotypes. I saw the women in my neighbourhood in the most crass gender stereotypes, and the blue-collar workers in outdated class stereotypes. But I considered my foreign assignments as compensation for all of this since, when I was preparing for a trip, I spent so much time learning about other cultures and places. So, I started to explain why I had waited weeks before doing anything about the smell. I was desperate to tell the detectives my side of the story. If I could get a word of sympathy or understanding from them, I thought, it might compensate, or at least mitigate some of the regret I was feeling for ruining my professional reputation and throwing away a well-paying position at a world-class company.

'I saw him the day it happened,' I said.

The Male Detective gave me an annoyed look. The Female Detective was standing at the door. 'The officer you gave your statement to said you'd never met your neighbour,' she said.

'Well, that's true, because we didn't really meet. I just saw him out on his balcony.' I felt foolish for the way I was sunk into my couch looking up at them. 'I'm pretty sure that's the day he did it.' I told them what I saw. The Female Detective listened to me from her spot at the window, while the Male Detective stood next to the coffee table and stared down at me.

'That's it?' he said.

'Yeah,' I said. 'I feel like maybe there was something I could've done.'

'Maybe,' he said. 'But there's nothing to do now, is there?'

PART THREE

When I moved into my apartment over twelve years ago, the rooms were bare, the floors immaculate, the holes from all the nails and screws that had once held up family photos, posters, shelves, and other art objects and decorations were plastered over, and the walls freshly painted. I had looked at other apartments but in many of them the landlords hadn't bothered to efface the traces of the previous tenants. I could still make out where the pictures had hung, or the floors retained the pale impressions from where the furniture once stood. Sometimes there were a few items of clothing left hanging in one of the closets, or cans of food in the kitchen cupboards. These mementos gave off an aura, or conjured up images of what the previous tenants had been like, how they had lived and what these rooms had been used for, the company they'd kept or the time they'd spent alone, what they'd talked about, and also the things they didn't talk about. So there was a risk that even after I painted the walls and scrubbed the floors, and after I changed the appliances and the locks, I might not be able to fully get rid of these traces, to exorcise the aura and purge the images so that when I looked around each room all I would see was my own life reflected back at me.

Whenever I checked into a hotel suite or condo I always did a thorough inspection of every surface, each piece of furniture, the bathrooms, the closets, and especially the bed. If I found any evidence of the previous guests, even if it was something as benign as a slightly depleted toilet paper roll rather than a fresh one, I would fall into a listless depression that might go on for days. I don't think I'm a clean freak, or that I suffer from some form of undiagnosed neurosis, and I'm not the sort of person who lies awake at night wondering about the last time the bedspread was cleaned, or whether the remote had been sterilized. And the depression wasn't caused by feelings of inadequacy or low self-esteem, brought on by these small, yet significant lapses by the cleaning staff, even though it betrayed a troubling lack of respect at the highest levels of hotel management for the enormous sums of money that my company had spent there over the years, not to mention all the extra business we sent their way. I think that what really got me down and why I let these small flaws in otherwise impeccable service take on so much meaning is because each time the service in these world-class hotels and accommodations fell below my impossible standards I felt as if it was a sign of a larger problem and what I saw as a global decline in high standards.

It may seem outrageous to consider a small lapse by the housekeeping staff at one of the best hotels in the world as proof of the decline of civilization, but I have spent so much time in these hotels, which are among the most famous symbols of the greatest cities in the world, and I'm almost certain that these lapses are part of the widespread phenomenon of nobody giving a shit about anything anymore that is threatening the very core of humanity. Everything is half-assed, from the bottom all the way to the highest level. There is this myth of refinement, this story of excellence, this tale of absolute perfection. We talk in the most exaggerated and unrealistic terms, exalting the mediocre, praising the good enough as though it were the best, when the truth is that nothing is ever done well, or well made, and most of us are just phoning it in. We speak about an actor's performance in a film as being transformative, an instant classic, when in reality it is only a passable performance and no more remarkable than the other performances turned in that year by actors who do not represent so much the pinnacle of accomplishment but are simply all we have, and for that reason we say that they are the greatest performers of their generation and one of a kind, which is true in a very limited sense. It's not that I'm nostalgic for a time I never experienced, the truth is that I wouldn't want to live at any other point in time in history, but it's hard not to think that maybe back when things weren't so disposable and cheap, when things weren't breaking down all the time, when people did their jobs with dignity and skill, that it must have been nice to feel proud of the made world, to be able to hold our heads high instead of hanging them in shame.

But to be honest, I'm not sure I even believe in this conventional theory of production, the theory that objects, which were once made with care and precision and designed to last for generations, are now produced in the most careless fashion and rarely last for a few months before they break. I think that there never really was a time when things were made in a masterful and flawless fashion and since the dawn of civilization we've been building disposable items that typically break after a couple of uses. Maybe the history of human productivity can be boiled down to a bunch of people passing off a weak effort as if it were world-class. One of the most luxurious hotels I've ever stayed at was in the news recently for feeding their guests horse meat instead of beef. The customers never noticed. The restaurant was exposed only after a disgruntled waiter posted something online. Last year, windows were flying off a world-renowned luxury high-rise apartment building where I had once spent six months for one of my foreign assignments. The building managers blamed the company that had supplied the windows. The window company blamed the construction firm for botching the installation. If only they had done this, they said. Next time they'll do that, they said. It's not that I'm outraged over the morally vacuous capitalist culture of these hotel companies and condo developers. What I can't stand is the way these hotels and high-rise condos are represented everywhere in our culture as the *ideal*, when they are actually *second-rate*.

I will occasionally spot one of these famous hotels in a movie or prestige TV show. Film and TV producers are constantly exploiting these powerful icons of the world's megacities, and at the sight of them on screen I always get the urge to go back, to see if the luxury and glamour will still work on me. But on the handful of occasions that I returned to one of the hotels I stayed at on a foreign assignment, I was always struck by the cheap novelty or the kitschy shabbiness of my surroundings. The rooms seemed either cramped, or vast and empty, the lights were dim instead of sparkling, the corridors narrow and lifeless instead of elegant and bustling. I wound up irritated with the bad service at the hotel bar, and the concierge who couldn't find my reservation *in the system* and kept asking me to repeat my name, as well as the air conditioning in my room that turned on and off all night long. The illusion that the world is a place full of highly functioning people and well-made things has been irrevocably spoiled for me. All I see now is a sort of low-functioning disorder, and after years of disappointing customer service experiences I have become acutely sensitive to even the most benign, unintended slights.

A few days after my neighbour's body had been discovered, the apartment was disinfected. Two guys in white overalls came to my door to warn me that they were going to be using chemicals to clean the apartment. 'We kill everything in the air,' the Short One said. He told me about the machine they used and how it emitted ozone, or that it did something to the air in the room that turned it into ozone, which, he explained, was essentially a form of atmospheric bleach, in that it killed off every molecule it came in contact with, including oxygen, he said, clearly proud of the destructive force of the machine he was about to start up next door. 'So, if you smell anything, if you notice a weird smell, you need to call us right away,' he said. 'It's really rare but if there is a leak or something like that then it might kill off all the oxygen in your place, and trust me, you don't want that.' The Tall One must've noticed that I was afraid an invisible gas would be seeping through the very same gaps and seams that had previously let in the smell of my neighbour's corpse, suffocating me by way of a chemical reaction I didn't understand. The Tall One assured me that this wasn't going to happen. 'It's not dangerous,' he said. 'There's nothing to worry about. Just call us if you smell anything.' But I'd already been completely taken in by the Short One's eerie description of the ozone machine, so the half-hearted attempt by the Tall One to calm me down didn't work. 'But this place is full of cracks and holes,' I said. And then I told them that I had discovered the body precisely because the smell had been unbearable, and if the smell could find its way into my apartment, I said, then why wouldn't the ozone leak in here as well. The Short One didn't even bother addressing my concerns and instead asked me to tell them more about the discovery of my neighbour's body.

I had recited my story so many times by then that I'd developed a rigorously scripted routine, with the pace and shape of a scandalous dinner party anecdote. In my routine, I would exaggerate the grotesque smell of my neighbour's body, while doing my best to downplay the timeline from the first time I noticed the smell to the night the Super and I went into my neighbour's apartment. I told these two professional cleaners, who looked like they'd probably smoked up right before coming to my door, and who were now trying to appear sober in a way that was kind of funny, and kind of sad, that I immediately phoned 911. After finally convincing the Super, I said, to let me into my neighbour's apartment to see what was causing the smell that I had been complaining about for weeks. I told them that I was shocked by the laid-back tone of the 911 operator, who in my opinion seemed way too informal and unhurried, and even a bit rude. Because I thought the professional cleaners looked like the sort of guys who would be up for a little male bonding, I told them that the first cops on the scene were a pair of extremely attractive women. 'I don't know about you guys,' I said, 'but there's just something about a woman in uniform.' But, as it turned out, I had totally misread the cleaners. The Tall One politely and delicately explained to me that, while they were certainly no strangers to the effect that a uniform had on someone's sexual attractiveness, he and his much shorter colleague were gay, and while this didn't mean they didn't appreciate the beauty of the female form, he said, it didn't really do it for them in that way.

Whenever I humiliate myself with someone in such an obvious and shameful fashion, my first instinct is to turn away and never look at them again. So I tried to rush through my story, but the Short One had a puzzled look on his face and said that he was confused because he had been told by the Super that it was the Handyman who had called 911. As I've already mentioned, I am constantly afraid of getting into trouble at work, and of course in my day-to-day life I was just as afraid of getting caught for doing or saying something wrong, like telling a lie to a couple of professional cleaners I had only just met. So even though I had been blatantly exposed, I didn't admit to the lie. I suggested that they must've misheard the Super, or maybe she'd been confused (she was very old after all), I didn't invent the maddening call to the 911 operator, I said, and I definitely didn't imagine the two athletic and attractive cops who had come to my door. They smiled and said that they had met countless building superintendents over the two years they had been working for the professional cleaning company, and every one they met loved to talk. I felt like they were just saying that so I'd let it go and they could leave, since what had started out for them as a routine professional courtesy had devolved into a sad display of dishonesty. As much as I wanted them to go, I was also desperate to redeem myself, to maybe even convince them that I was telling the truth, so in the hope that they'd find my curiosity flattering I started asking them questions about their work.

It turned out this wasn't the first time they'd heard of someone committing suicide by this method. 'They all do it,' the Tall One said. By 'they,' he went on to explain, he meant North African men, and by 'do it' he hadn't meant the act of committing suicide, something which he was hardly an authority on as far as demographics went, and in his own professional experience he hadn't noticed any glaring racial disparities among the people they cleaned up after—he was only commenting on the way my neighbour had killed himself, and that both he and his colleague had seen this method used before by other North African suicides in the two years they'd been doing this job. I was enormously relieved that we'd taken up this topic and that we'd moved on from the 911 lie, not least because pseudointellectual discussions are my specialty. I can talk about national health policy or water security—it doesn't really matter what the topic is as long as it is an important issue that has already been exhaustively covered in the media. I like arguing a position I haven't thought about and have no interest in, and I have a flair for citing, with convincing authority, facts that are often inaccurate, or just made up, though hardly anyone ever challenges me. I love making sweeping generalizations and blunt assessments, or analyzing a cultural or political event as though my opinion was of great consequence, and not just the confused expression of a fairly ignorant person. I can't stand small talk, I thought, as I listened to the Tall One talk about all the suicides they'd cleaned up after over the last two years, but sometimes I don't mind shooting the shit.

'North African,' I said. 'I thought he was Lebanese.' They looked confused and for a second I wondered if I'd made a mistake, maybe Lebanon was in North Africa. 'I'm pretty sure the lady said he was Libyan,' the Short One said. 'Definitely Libyan,' the Tall One continued. 'People from North African countries always do it this way. It's a cultural thing.' He started listing various suicide methods and the cultures and nationalities that practised them. It's almost perversely beautiful, I thought, that there are so many ways to kill yourself. 'Don't forget suicide bombing,' the Short One said, interrupting the Tall One as he was speculating on the reason behind the preference Irish people had for hanging themselves. Throughout our conversation the Tall One had kept a sombre, almost severe tone, but now he responded to the Short One's interruption with an obscene string of jokes about suicide bombing. I'd never heard any of these jokes before, but they were obviously examples of a whole genre. I consider myself to be a relatively well-informed and cynical citizen of the world and not so easily shocked or offended. There is no form of human depravity that I'm not at least passingly familiar with after years of reading the internet, not to mention my experience in the system of global finance, but I was initially thrown off by how thoroughly nihilistic and sadistic these suicide-bomber jokes were. Since the cleaners were both young and gay I had assumed they wouldn't go in for that sort of thing.

'How many suicide bombers does it take to screw in a light bulb?' the Short One asked. 'A rabbi, a priest, and a suicide bomber walk into a bar,' the Tall One said. 'A suicide bomber goes to the doctor and the doctor says, Well, do you want the good news first, or the bad news?' 'A suicide bomber catches his wife in bed with his best friend.' 'A suicide bomber blows himself up, and when he gets to St. Peter's gate, the angel asks, why should we let you in?' They shouted the punchlines and then burst out laughing. I eventually figured out the tune, so to speak, and came up with a couple of my own ('Knock, knock.' 'Who's there?' 'BOOM!'). They kept it going until the knock-knock theme had been exhausted. The Short One took the opportunity, as we stood silently in my doorway, grinning at each other, to start telling a third-hand anecdote about a friend of a friend whose father had been killed on 9/11. As I listened to him recite the heartrending details of his friend's father's final moments, I felt bad for my part in the suicide-bomber knock-knock joke cycle, in the same way that I used to feel ashamed as a boy when I had joined in on a schoolyard beating, or took part in some grotesque act of suburban sadism, torturing a neighbourhood cat and that sort of thing. But I also felt as though I had redeemed myself in their eyes for the lie I had told about discovering my neighbour's corpse and my insensitive remarks about the sexually attractive cops, and I even got the impression that they liked me. There is little that I won't do or say in order to get people to like me. When I'm not consumed with anxiety over getting in trouble for something I did or did not do at work, then I am entirely focused on doing and saying things that will make other people like me, even people I don't like or respect, or people that I don't care about. I will express opinions that aren't my own, or invent a past that never happened, claim beliefs that I don't believe in, or share enthusiasm for something I have no affection for, all so that people—often people I have only just met, like the professional cleaners—will have no choice but to like me.

After the apartment was disinfected, it sat vacant for three months before new tenants moved in. The Super told me that the landlord had taken the opportunity at the unexpected vacancy to renovate the apartment. I occasionally saw two guys unloading tools from a white van when I left for work in the morning, but they were always gone before I got back, and I sometimes thought of what was happening next door as a form of real estate chrysalis. I remember this as a period of long unremarkable days. The fear that I had on the day my neighbour's body was discovered, that my position at the company was at risk, and that I had ruined my career in a spasm of reckless self-destruction, was, as it turned out, entirely unwarranted. It would have been completely understandable, given my declining status at the company, for Roger to take the opportunity to cut me loose, set me up with a generous severance package, a stellar referral, and toss me back into the white-collar job market, where it would only take a moment for someone like me to rebound into another high-paying executive position. Instead, they kept me on and there were no repercussions. When I came in the next day and finally worked up the courage to stick my head into Roger's office, he said that the Innerzone meeting had gone well, and he seemed genuinely uninterested in my abject apology. 'I managed to keep them happy,' he said. 'But I'd rather not have to go through that again.' He even laughed when I told him about being questioned by the detectives. I wasn't sure why he thought it was so funny, but I laughed along with him.

So it seemed like my position was safe, though instead of sending me away on another foreign assignment, they kept me at the home office, where I literally had nothing to do. Roger said the company was restructuring the foreign offices and I could expect a new assignment in the *near short term* once the *market stabilized*. The company seemed to have been perpetually restructuring over the last few years, so I wasn't sure what he meant. I could never make any sense of what was going on in the global economy, even though, like everyone else I worked with, I spoke about it incessantly. According to the news, we were experiencing a worldwide recession, which was supposedly the greatest economic calamity to happen in the last fifty years, but it would be a lie to say that I, or any of my friends, family, and colleagues, were affected in our day-to-day lives by this so-called *historically unprecedented crisis*. We were all wealthy, or well off at least, and it didn't seem to matter how many crises or crashes took place, everything around us stayed the same. But the company was certainly affected. Our liquidity had dried up. There weren't many placements at the exotic locales they typically sent me to, and when there *was* one, it went to one of the younger guys. Though, in spite of this overwhelmingly dreadful financial state, the dismal forecasts, the anemic figures, the grim march of low and midlevel layoffs, despite the enormous debt—or, as we called it, leverage—the company was carrying, I was still being paid a tremendous amount of money to sit around all day and read a deeply researched long-form article on the origins of Wikileaks. I scanned news sites for hours, catching up on the latest catastrophes. Entire cultures were being destroyed. In China, Uyghurs were sent to live in camps that were run in the most fantastically brutal fashion. Hundreds of millions of people around the world were being subjected to perverse forms of economic sadism, tortured on a daily basis by ever newer and crueller financial instruments. But you don't have anything to worry about, I thought. None of this affects you.

So I spent the vacancy period, which lasted throughout an unusually hot and dry summer, getting fat off takeout and watching the world burn in fine-grained journalistic detail. I would pass my time at the office sitting at my desk, and then wait for my colleagues to leave at the end of the day so they would see me sitting there on their way out. When I got home, I would be buzzing with nervous energy and I often started drinking and smoking weed as soon as I got in the door. I wasn't a complete recluse during the vacancy period. I went out with my colleagues occasionally, but I was becoming increasingly overwhelmed by the surfaces of social scenarios and could hardly listen to what anyone said. I would drink too much out of nervousness, black out, and wake up the next day completely blank. Even though I still had a few friends from my college years who I spoke with during the vacancy period, and with whom I used to have long, wide-ranging, and intense conversations, sharing the most personal stories and feelings, I felt like we no longer had anything worthwhile to say to each other, and this left me feeling lonelier than if I had just stayed home. I went out for drinks one night with an old college friend and I wound up telling an anecdote about a ski trip I'd been on without realizing he had been there with me. Even after he politely reminded me that he'd been staying in the room next to mine on the ski trip, I still couldn't summon the memory. Maybe the reason I forgot about him, I thought, is because he doesn't mean anything to me anymore. And on another night during the vacancy period, I went to the movies with another old college friend, and the movie was one of those comedies that starts off funny but then turns serious, one of those movies that lasts for two hours of maudlin blandness until it limps to a vacuous finale. We stood outside the theatre afterward and commiserated over how terrible it had been. 'I couldn't believe the dialogue,' I said to him. I told him that in my opinion the absolute worst scene in the movie was the one where the main character has a deathbed heart-to-heart with their older sister, who started off the film as a wild child before being punished with a cancer storyline in the third act. But my friend said that the only scene in the whole film that wasn't offensively bad was the scene with the dying sister, because, in his opinion, they had done a good job of showing how brutal that disease can be. I disagreed with him and said that, in my experience, people with a fatal cancer prognosis didn't act that way, but on my way home I remembered that his sister had died of cancer only a few years ago—I had even been at the funeral. And maybe the most glaring instance of this absent-minded ambivalence was when I got together with a colleague, someone I only ever hung out with one on one, drinking a lot and carrying on the same conversation we'd been having for years about the seemingly ongoing worldwide political crisis. We were doing a bit of macho flirting at the end of the night by arguing over who should pick up the tab, and when he threw his credit card on the bar I glanced down and realized that until that moment I hadn't known his last name.

During the vacancy period I spent the first half of the day sitting at the office and the second half on my balcony. The nights were clear and warm and I felt completely relaxed now that I knew there was no risk of having to make small talk with my next-door neighbour. I embraced this more subdued lifestyle. After so many foreign assignments in vibrant and spectacularly beautiful cities, among people whom I never got to know except in the most fleeting and superficial way, I was happy to spend my time in my sad, rundown apartment, where I felt completely at home. After years of never being able to fully relax, because, even when I was alone in my hotel room and I was fixing myself a snack or lying on the couch reading, I could never get over the feeling that someone was watching me, it was nice to finally feel invisible again, which is how I felt when I was on my balcony overlooking the alley. It was only after I got home from my last foreign assignment, I thought, that I noticed how everything I did was a bit *off*. The way I opened doors wasn't the way I usually opened doors. The way I stood in line wasn't how I would normally stand in line. And even the way I slept in bed was not how a person typically goes to sleep.

I could sense how far I had fallen in the opinions of my colleagues. Whatever prestige I had once enjoyed as one of the company's success stories had pretty much worn off. I was obsolete, already past my prime, out of date, old news, etc., etc. At the end of the day, I thought, I'm not part of the company's global restructuring strategy. Nothing but a drain on the company's bottom line. Since I got back from my last foreign assignment, I had gone from being a results-oriented team player to a loner who slacked off all day. In the weeks leading up to the Innerzone meeting debacle, I might have been slacking off a lot, but I still bothered to keep up appearances. But during the vacancy period I couldn't even be bothered to pretend I was doing any real work. I came into the office every day and put in a solid eight hours of slacking off without even pausing for a break. I got in every morning, poured myself a coffee, fired up my computer, and got right down to slacking off without even saying good morning to my colleagues. When they did pop by my office to say hi, or to make an inappropriate comment, or to remark on the latest terrorist attack/mass shooting/natural catastrophe, I put out a friendly but ultimately unwelcoming vibe. I was impatient to get back to slacking off. If my phone rang, which it rarely did, I usually let it go to voice mail, but if the call was coming from someone I couldn't ignore I'd answer in an exasperated voice and end the call as soon as possible, furious over the interruption in what had been until that point an uninterrupted slacking-off session. Occasionally all this slacking started to get to me, and to relax I would do fifteen minutes of actual work, which was all I needed to refresh myself and get back to slacking off at a frenzied pace. You might think that not doing any work every day for eight to ten hours is easy, that it takes very little effort or energy to slack off while everyone around you is working (more or less). But you would be wrong. Slacking off—like actual work—is an unending and undifferentiated activity that can contract or expand, like gas, to fill up whatever time and space it is given, and since I really do have a strong work ethic, as well as a surprising level of discipline and stamina, I felt compelled through the vacancy period to do as much slacking off as possible. Personal emails, power bill payments, full symphonies on YouTube, investment banking, online chess, taking care of my dry-cleaning, personality quizzes, maintaining my social media accounts, throwing out receipts, reading customer reviews of restaurants I'd never been to, doing my taxes, and of course countless long-form articles about the fast-fashion clothing industry. I would get started on a twelve-thousand-word piece on denim production, but before long I would switch to watching videos on how to mount a widescreen TV, which somehow led me to an exchange on the social media feed of a friend who I no longer spoke to.

'Not only do I spend my day not doing any work,' I said to myself as I climbed the steps to my apartment after another day of slacking off, 'but my time is doubly wasted because I am always terrified that I am going to get in trouble, so while

I am endlessly scanning articles and creeping around social media, or sending messages and emails full of business speak and techno babble and simultaneously indulging in and avoiding small talk with my colleagues, I am never able to enjoy myself and just relax.' And the only way to salvage something from the ruins of the day, I thought, was to spend the night getting high and watching prestige TV. With all of my economic and social privilege, I thought, the surplus of freedom and opportunity, not to mention the world-class education, the greatest life I could envision for myself was a well-funded drug habit and prestige-TV routine. Every once in a while I'd drift off from whatever it was I was watching and think back to all those nights I was out on the balcony, or on the couch, while my neighbour's body was on a mattress only a few feet away. I would think about the morning I saw him in his housecoat crouched over the hibachi and I had said hello, or waved. I tried to recall what I did the rest of that day, but I couldn't remember. I probably stayed out on the balcony and looked at my phone. I must've gone out to get something to eat at some point. I tried to envision what my apartment looked like that morning, hoping to conjure up the spectre of myself on the balcony. But everything I came up with lacked the authenticity of a real memory. I was just making stuff up.

It's impossible to remember now what I had done on any given day during the vacancy period. It's difficult to say with any certainty how I might have felt on a Tuesday in June, or what I had for lunch on a Thursday in mid-July, or who I spoke to at work during the whole month of August, or what I watched when I got home, or what I ordered for dinner. But I do recall how throughout the vacancy period I sometimes fantasized about getting framed for my neighbour's death. The two attractive detectives would interrogate me for hours, refusing to believe me when I told them I had no memory of my activities on the day in question. They would charge me and throw me in one of those solitary confinement cells like I had read about in countless long-form articles on the U.S. prison industry. And one evening, as I was elaborating on this fantasy and I was just at the point of embarking on a deep philosophical discussion with a child killer in the neighbouring cell, my doorbell rang.

Two girls were standing on my front step. They asked if I was the Super. They were probably students, I thought, maybe at a business school, and they looked Middle Eastern, or maybe Indian, I couldn't say for sure. In the instant after I opened the door, I had already sketched out a life for the girls—friends from childhood who came here together and were focused on doing their parents proud. They spent most of the time at the library. Drinking was forbidden, or they just didn't like alcohol. They rarely had friends over, and when they did, they usually studied together or at most they might watch a movie. 'We have an appointment to see the apartment,' one of them said. 'But nobody's answering.' They were both wearing immaculately black tights and jerseys. Their eyes were cartoonishly large and they both had their hair pulled back in jaunty ponytails. I thought they looked a little too wealthy for the sort of students who lived around here. These sorts of girls, I thought, live in condos downtown, not in buildings like this one. Nobody like them, I thought, has ever lived in this place.

According to my colleagues and the creative talent behind my favourite TV shows, sex is a powerful force and a bottomless need that people are constantly trying to resist and satisfy, but according to my personal experience, sex is only a dim concern and usually an afterthought. I can go for a long time living off the scraps of my sexual past without ever feeling the urge to go out and make new memories. But if these girls move in next door, I thought, and we end up becoming friends, then it's probably only a matter of time before I hook up with one of them. They will invite me over for a delicious, home-cooked meal, I thought, some sort of traditional dish that they used to have back home on special occasions. I will bring a couple bottles of wine, and we will all wind up getting drunk. It will be natural to wind up in bed with one of them, I thought. They stared at me while pressing on the Super's doorbell. I was mildly offended that they took me for the building-superintendent type, and I wanted to come up with a reason to mention that I was actually a very well-paid executive in a large multinational company, but they rang the Super's doorbell again and this time I could hear her coming to the door. I felt like I should say something else. I couldn't think of anything. So I ended up uttering an inarticulate and elaborate goodbye while clumsily doffing an invisible hat.

The next time I saw them was a couple weeks later on the day they moved in. I was sitting at my little balcony table drinking and smoking, my finger marking the place in the book I was reading, when they literally burst through their back door. The Thin One asked if she could bum a smoke and then immediately launched into a monologue that ranged across family history, career ambitions, health issues, and included a few indiscreet remarks about 'street people.' There is nothing worse than being trapped by a monologist and forced to listen as they describe the most mundane aspects of their life, a protracted bureaucratic war they've been waging with their internet provider, or the history behind their purchase of an electric car. Whether I am commuting to work, or grabbing breakfast at my local café, I am always on the lookout for anyone who has the look of a monologist, and whenever I encounter one I have an unfailing instinct for when they are about to launch into the story of their appendectomy, or how they used to own a horse. Most of the time you can see them coming because of a needy look in their eye and the way their mouth is always just a little bit open, but I still get caught off guard occasionally. Just recently, a security guard at the local liquor store told me all about his theories on cryptocurrencies. 'You should've seen him coming,' I told myself as I stood outside the door with a box of booze threatening to slip from my grip. 'Now you're stuck here listening to an epic monologue.' Of course, living in a dense urban environment means that from the moment I wake up until I finally pass out, I am bombarded by the voices of people telling me who they are and what they want in long, dramatic speeches, delivered as though they aren't really talking to me and more like they are talking to themselves. There's really no way to escape, aside from shutting myself up in my apartment. So every day I go out into the world and risk getting stuck with a monologist, and what I absolutely cannot stand about these people is that I always know exactly what they are going to say. This, more than anything, is the source of my profound disgust for monologists—when I'm stuck having to listen to one of my colleagues' monologues about their kids' summer camp schedule, or when I'm listening to the typical bus passenger monologist lay out their plan for a lasting peace between Israel and Palestine, I can see, as though it's a future projection, what they will say and then how I'll react. As I sat on my balcony listening to my new neighbour tell me the most intimate details of her parents' lives, I knew that every time I went out on my balcony she would be out on hers waiting to continue her monologue right where she had left off. A large portion of everyone's life, I thought, is spent listening to the hushed confessions of casual acquaintances, the brazen disclosures of coworkers, sordid anecdotes from cab drivers, hurried asides from waiters, as well as shocking pronouncements from complete strangers. Spending a portion of the day listening to the fears and anxieties of other people, I thought, as the Thin One told me about her grandfather's funeral, was my way of giving back to the community. The emotional-labour equivalent, I thought, to shovelling the snow on the sidewalk in front of my apartment, or helping a friend move a large appliance. When I sat out on my balcony and listened to my neighbour explain why she decided to stop using refined sugar I felt as if I was performing my civic duty.

I've always considered myself an excellent judge of character. I have a talent for guessing at the hidden motives and secret urges that people try so hard to keep from one another. I won't hesitate to speculate on the unspoken feelings in an email from a colleague, or the reasons behind a celebrity divorce. I will speak with authority on the mental health of an old college friend, and while I might not have spoken with them for months, I am confident that my diagnosis is spot-on. I can talk for hours about someone I met at a crowded party, who I didn't even speak to directly but only overheard while they were telling their story to their circle of friends. Without any family background or social context I will come up with all sorts of theories of who this person is, not just the role they play in public, but their true nature. Because my judgments are based entirely on clichés from prestige TV and long-form journalism, the personas I imagine for other people are broadly stereotypical clichéd personas, and when I talk about someone it always sounds like I am describing a fictional character instead of a real person.

So I imagined that Judith, the Thin One, spent most of her day anxious over the mundane circumstances of her life. And that Mahdi, the Quiet One, spent her days studying for a law degree and looking forward to the day she would no longer have to share an apartment with Judith. It was only a matter of time, I thought, before they got sick of each other and moved out.

But until that happened I was going to have to put up with some relentless small talk from Judith. 'Have you seen the bus stands?' she would start off, and within minutes she would have moved on from buses to what she referred to as her problems with addiction. Instead of the soft-spoken international student I had envisioned the first time we met, it turned out that she was a dropout who had been fighting a debilitating dependence on hard drugs for the last two years. Judith stared at me with wide-open eyes as she chain-smoked my cigarettes and told me about the time she was committed to a psychiatric institution by her mother. It looked as if she was experiencing the whole thing again. She recalled her time there with a vivid level of detail, telling me all about the volatile relationship she had with one of the nurses, and the disorienting effect of the algae-green walls and fluorescent lighting. 'It's because of how I was raised,' Judith said to me on a night when I had waited until it was close to midnight before sneaking out onto my balcony, only to have her come out *within seconds* as if she'd been waiting for me. She insisted that she didn't really smoke, though she appeared to enjoy it much more than I did. She refused to buy cigarettes, she said, because by leaving her habit to chance she could keep up the illusion that she didn't really need them.

'My mother didn't have time for me,' she said, 'so my sisters had to raise me, but they didn't know what they were doing, so they just treated me like I was the same age, even though they were all at least ten years older than me.' I'd thought that Judith had a foreign accent on the day they came to see the apartment, but after a few of our balcony encounters I found out that she'd been born and raised in a suburb just outside of the city. She told me about her mother's extended family, and the tragic death of a childhood friend, and her record of small car accidents, including the very first, which happened during the parallel-parking portion of her driving exam.

In my experience, people are always desperate to tell someone their life story. If they think you might be a sympathetic listener, or at least willing to hear them out, they will spend hours telling you about the most humiliating and painful moments of their lives. People have confessed the most degrading things to me while I've been waiting at a café counter for my drink. There is no end to what people are willing to tell you as long as you sit there and give some slight indication that you're listening. 'Don't stop,' you say. 'I'm interested. Tell me what happened next. Tell me more.' It's as if all people do is spend their day trying to find somebody who will listen to them. Unless you shut people down, avoid eye contact, show nothing but hostility toward anyone who asks you if you have a second, or tells you that they need to run something by you, or tries to draw you in by asking you how you are doing, or what you are up to, unless you close yourself off from your friends and colleagues, then you should expect to spend a significant portion of your life listening to heartfelt confessions. If we let people in, if we show that we're up for it and that we're not in any rush, that we have nowhere to go and nothing to do, then they will pull up a chair and never leave. They will talk for hours until you're too tired to think and you can't even make sense of what they are saying anymore. They will ask to spend the night just so they can keep talking and when they get up the next day they will start right back up where they left off.

Judith told me about her family, but more specifically, she told me about the fucked-up dynamic she had with her family. She also told me about a series of events in her life that she described variously as either crazy coincidences, fate, weird luck, or completely random, and how these events were all related to her decision to drop out and move in with Mahdi.

Each time I went out on the balcony she would come out within minutes and start in on another family saga or personal struggle. 'I used to be really fat,' Judith said to me one night only minutes after joining me outside. She would lean over her railing as I sat there with my phone, or a magazine, or maybe even a book, and without considering whether I was up for hearing about her anxiety disorder and body dysmorphia, she would start in on one of her protracted monologues. And once she started talking about her childhood pet's agonizing final moments, or her traumatic experience earlier that day at a meeting with a bank manager, it was as though she fell into a mild trance, and her eyes, which I thought of in only the most clichéd terms (piercing, brilliant, dazzling) got that faraway look that people get when they aren't just remembering something, but are actually reliving an experience. She would go on and on without a break for me to excuse myself, without a pause where I could say that while I would love to keep chatting with her, I had to go in and catch up on my email. It was obvious that Judith was in some sort of distress or pain, but she could have been talking to anybody—it didn't have to be me. This has nothing to do with me, I thought. She is like this with everybody.

'You have a way with people,' my dad used to say to me when I was younger. At that time, I was a popular kid with a large circle of friends, and he had noticed how I functioned as a sort of emotional hub for the group, playing the role of counsellor and peacemaker. So for a long time I saw myself the way he had described me, as someone who was *good with people*. In my twenties, I spent hours on the phone with my friends and the whole time I thought that the reason they were so open and comfortable as they told me things that normally would have humiliated or at least embarrassed them was because of my particular blend of empathy and intelligence. I became convinced that I should try to exploit this somehow, to professionalize it by going into therapeutic practice, or marketing. It seemed like a waste not to profit from it in some way.

'You should be a model,' we say to beautiful people, since it strikes us as an unconscionable waste that they wouldn't try to make money off their appearance. 'I bet that would make a really good movie,' we say to someone who has just told us of their parents' immigration experience. It's as though the only stories worth telling are the ones that can be sold, so it's hard not to see every moment of our lives as a chance to make money. We hear about people who get paid to watch TV as part of consumer focus groups, rumours of medical experiments that pay people to get high all day, programs that will comp your travel if you promote their services to your friends. It seems like people everywhere are cashing in, and when I spent my whole afternoon texting with an old high school friend about his recent divorce, or a colleague invited me to lunch and spent an hour gossiping savagely about their admin assistant, I couldn't help thinking that listening to them was a form of emotional labour for which I wasn't getting paid. It was hard for me to hang out with people without feeling like I was getting ripped off.

Maybe you still have a talent for connecting with people, I thought, a way of putting them at ease, or quickly building up trust, so that after only one or two encounters they feel free to open up, and so even though in social situations I may give off a cold, unwelcoming vibe, people nonetheless seem to feel a compulsion to confess when I'm around. But as I listened to Judith describe her weekly meal plan, I thought, no, there's nothing special about me. There's nothing particular that I say or do that puts people at ease or leads them to trust me over someone else. In fact, the only reason that so many people were eager to tell me their life stories, I thought, was simply because I never cut them off, or interrupted to say I didn't have time. I never said, 'We'll have to catch up later,' or 'I'd love to hear more but I have to go.' Instead I said, 'Oh, yeah?' and 'Really?' and 'That's terrible.' I sat patiently and listened while they talked, and they were only too happy to keep going.

I came home every night feeling emptied out after slacking off for ten hours. I would sit at my little balcony table with a drink and smoke a cigarette and pray that Judith wouldn't come outside so I could enjoy some time alone. But she was always at home, and a couple of minutes after I sat down she would usually come out to her balcony and start up at the point she had left off the last time we'd talked. Judith sucked up all of the time I spent out on the balcony and fed off my grudging participation in our one-sided conversations. As I sat there listening to her get increasingly worked up over how many dogs and cats are abandoned every year by people who move out of apartments and leave their pets behind, I thought back to the time I had spent on foreign assignments, working out of hotels, filling my days with maddeningly pointless meetings, infuriating conference calls, and humiliating dinner parties and working lunches. The only thing I looked forward to when I was on these foreign assignments was the moment when I would be able to spend a night on my balcony completely free from interruptions. And now that I was back home, I had to spend the whole night listening to Judith's opinions, essentially forcing herself on me and insisting that I pay close attention to the uninterrupted flow of her mind. It seemed impossible for me to excuse myself, and I always left her feeling completely drained. 'You're a pretty quiet guy, aren't you?' Judith said to me one night as I was trying to read a long-form article about offshore tax havens. She had started talking about the ongoing difficulties she'd been having with her boss. After recounting an email exchange almost line by line, she seemed suddenly irritated with me. 'You probably just want to be alone,' she said. 'No,' I said. 'I'm glad for the company.' She laughed as if what I'd said had been extremely funny. I was going to take this opportunity to go inside and wait in my kitchen until it was safe to go back out, but she stopped me by insisting that I come over to her apartment for a drink. 'We're neighbours,' she said.

Until that point, I had refused the invitation, which she made almost every time I saw her, but just then I was somehow unprepared. Judith was extremely good-looking, and I suppose that something about the way she was leaning over the railing and smiling at me could have led to my slight hesitation, which she took as a yes. Even though many people would consider a man of my age and circumstances to be in the prime of his life, I initially didn't think she was coming on to me. Many of my friends and colleagues appear to have robust sex lives, or at least the desire for a robust sex life, and

I regularly hear about their scandalous affairs, ruinous separations, and other sexual entanglements that they somehow find time for while working ninety hours a week, and even if their robust sex lives often caused them a lot of pain, I envied my friends and colleagues. It had been a very long time since I was preoccupied by who I wanted to sleep with, and, perhaps more importantly, who wanted to sleep with me. There was a time of course when all of my waking life was devoted to convincing people to sleep with me, or finding people who might even want to sleep with me without having to be convinced. I spent years solely focused on this one thing, but I was never very good at it. I often made the mistake of thinking that people who were nice to me were being that way because they wanted to sleep with me. When I indicated that I was looking forward to sleeping with them, I usually discovered that they had no intention of sleeping with me, and many times they were surprised and offended. But when someone actually wanted to sleep with me without needing me to convince them, and we ended up actually having sex, it was usually a small-scale disaster. I was always so grateful when somebody wanted to sleep with me that I never turned anyone down. And if they were willing to sleep with me repeatedly, over an extended period of time, then I would stay with them for as long as that lasted. But for a while I had hardly even thought about people I wanted to sleep with and I spent even less time wondering about who wanted to sleep with me. I guess it's possible that one of my colleagues wanted to sleep with me, and every time we talked on the phone, or exchanged emails, or passed each other in the hallway, they were preoccupied with how they could use these brief encounters to facilitate a full-blown affair. But I hadn't seen any sign of it. I don't think this somewhat celibate period had anything to do with lack of confidence, low self-esteem, or the depressive state I'd been keeping myself in over the last year. I can't remember when I lost interest in sleeping with other people, but at some point this powerful force no longer had any effect, and where I once saw people who I wanted to sleep with, or who wanted to sleep with me, I now saw people who I needed something from, or who needed something from me. So even though Judith was good-looking in a way that could be described as *striking*, and there were days when I felt like laughing at the sight of her since she could be so beautiful at times that it was frankly ridiculous, whenever she invited me over for a drink I wasn't thinking about whether she wanted to sleep with me as much as I was worried that she wanted something from me, aside from cigarettes.

But it seemed necessary to go over once and get it out of the way. Whenever I meet somebody new and they ask me to go for a drink, or to come to their place for a little get-together, or maybe just grab a coffee sometime, I feel obliged to accept their invitation at least once. After that, I never accept another. They may think I am unfriendly, or awkward, but nobody can accuse me of being rude or uncivil if at least on one occasion I give in and say, 'Sure. Sounds great. Why not?' I'd been planning on spending only five to ten minutes in Judith's apartment, but when she offered to give me a tour I felt as though I couldn't refuse. As she was showing me around her apartment it seemed impossible to hurry along her exhaustive explanations of the origins of each item of furniture. I stood there helplessly as she subjected me to a thorough summary of the rigorous research that she had conducted before each purchase. 'I'm the one who does all the decorating,' she explained, gesturing toward a wall in the TV room covered in framed black-and-white snapshots. 'Mahdi doesn't care what the place looks like. She'd be happy living out of a cardboard box.' I said it didn't seem like Mahdi spent much time at their apartment. Why didn't she join Judith on the balcony more often? 'She's doing her PhD,' Judith said, surprised, as well as notably irritated, that I hadn't known this about Mahdi. 'Her supervisor wants her to present a paper at a really important conference next month, and she's teaching two classes this semester, and she's finishing the last section of her dissertation, so she basically wakes up in the morning and goes to her office and doesn't come home until like midnight every night.' Judith appeared to be waiting on a sympathetic remark, or gesture, as if Mahdi's academic obligations were a burden for her as well. 'That sucks,' I said. 'It really does,' she said, leading me upstairs. 'Like, if I knew she was never going to be home...'

She showed me her bedroom, bright and well organized. Judith explained she had furnished it entirely with second-hand furniture she had found online. 'Except for this,' she said, taking a seat on the bed and launching into the story of how she'd decided on what sort of mattress to buy. And in that moment, even though it had been so long I couldn't be sure if I would recognize the signs, I wondered if she was trying to tell me that she wanted to sleep with me. I wondered if she was hoping I would join her on the bed, and whether she had been planning this moment with me since the day she moved in. I wondered if the reason she had been spending most of her nights out on the balcony, and smoking my cigarettes, even though according to her she wasn't much of a smoker, was because she was waiting for when she knew Mahdi wasn't going to be home to invite me over so she could sleep with me. Judith has wanted to sleep with me since the first time we met, I thought. If I hadn't been so distressed over the way she had invaded my privacy, then I would've noticed that everything she's said to me, and everything she's done, were the words and actions of someone who wants to sleep with me.

'So, I heard the guy who used to live here had a heart attack,' she said, patting the spot next to her on the bed.

I had thought about what I would tell Judith and Mahdi when the subject eventually came up, though I'd always envisioned it taking place on the balcony and no matter how often I rehearsed the scene, I could never decide whether I would tell them what had happened. I knew there was no way the Super would have told Judith that the previous occupant had killed himself in her bedroom, and then rotted on a mattress for five weeks before his body was finally discovered, and I imagined the satisfaction I would get from doing the right thing, as well as the morbid excitement that would come from recounting the grotesque image of the darkened room with a mattress on the floor and a hibachi in the centre, surrounded by ash in what was now a clean and meticulously decorated bedroom. I should tell Judith the truth, I thought, not because she deserved to know, or from a sense of solidarity with a fellow tenant, and not because it was obviously the right thing to do, but because I thought that if I told her the truth about what happened to my neighbour it would compensate somehow for all the lies I had told to my colleagues. But when Judith said that my neighbour had died from a heart attack, I didn't correct her. At the moment when I should have told Judith that no, the previous tenant hadn't died from a heart attack, and that he had committed suicide by asphyxiating himself with a hibachi in the room we were sitting in, I decided to keep quiet and let her believe the story the Super had told her.

When I lie to somebody to spare them some pain and embarrassment, or discomfort and inconvenience, I always tell myself it's for their own good. I lie constantly to my friends and co-workers, as well as to the people I meet in my daily customer service experiences, I thought, while I was listening to Judith explain her preference for blinds over curtains. But I only lie when the truth doesn't really matter, I thought. I can tell when being honest is the right thing to do. In principle, telling the truth is always the right thing to do, but for most of my life, both in a personal as well as in a professional context, it was usually more pragmatic to lie. 'It's not the right time,' I would say. 'Telling the truth will only make things worse.' There is always a good reason for lying to someone, I thought, but there's hardly ever one for telling them the truth. But it's more likely, I thought, that the only reason I lie so much is to spare myself pain and embarrassment, as well as discomfort and inconvenience.

'I was on a business trip when it happened,' I said, sitting down next to her on the bed. 'I never met him, but from what I heard he was a pretty solitary guy.' Until that moment I only ever saw Judith as a source of annoyance and disruption, but now, looking at her sitting on her single bed, which was so pristinely made it looked as though it had never been slept in, I was so powerfully attracted to her I hardly noticed what I was saying. 'Apparently he used to be a flight attendant,' I said, 'but he went on disability or something like that, and I guess that was when things started to go downhill.' Judith told me that she had thought about becoming a flight attendant last summer, and it was only then that she realized she had developed a fear of flying. We shared stories about our first experiences of going on a plane and as we were talking she leaned back on the bed so she was resting on her elbows. This is it, I thought. How could I have guessed that while she was always bumming my cigarettes, and talking about everything from the death of her childhood friend to her history of losing cellphones, that she had been flirting with me the whole time, and the reason she came out on her balcony every time I was outside wasn't because she was too cheap to buy her own cigarettes, but because she wanted to sleep with me. But I thought it seemed pretty clear to me now, as she was basically lying down on the bed and smiling up at me, that this was exactly what had been going on and I simply hadn't recognized the signs.

Although I was aware of people at my office and in my circle of friends who were having affairs with each other, the thought of sleeping with someone I worked with, or with one of the few women I knew outside of work, or even starting up something with one of my married friends, seemed ludicrous to me. When I left the office at the same time as Louise, Roger's assistant—whom I had been working with for years and whom I rarely spoke to outside of the office, and who, by all conventional standards was ideally suited for someone like me, and who, if our lives had been governed by the logic of sitcoms and date movies, I would have hooked up with long ago—there was never a moment as I walked a few paces behind her when I felt compelled to catch up with her and try out a little flirtatious small talk. If she asked me to go for a drink, I thought, if she said that she didn't feel like going home since it was such a *beautiful night*, if she said that it seemed literally insane to hurry back to her apartment to spend the night sitting inside all by herself on her couch watching TV, it still would never have occurred to me that she might be interested in sleeping with me, and that the invitation to join her for a drink was a pretense for a sexual relationship. Maybe people were trying to tell me they were interested in sleeping with me, I thought, and I just never picked up on it. Maybe these signals were being sent out at a frequency I couldn't see or hear. Maybe I'd been going through life casually rejecting or flat-out ignoring the earnest and even desperate attempts people had been making over the years, and this transparent effort by Judith was simply the most recent in a long line of similar attempts. Maybe what I had always interpreted as friendliness, collegiality, or common courtesy had in fact been open displays of naked lust and desire. But, I thought, this seemed extremely unlikely. I couldn't even remember the last time someone had looked at me the way

Judith was looking at me. I could, however, remember that every time I'd seen this look in the past I had turned away and acted like I didn't notice, but now, I thought, here I am staring at Judith and not looking away, as she lay on the bed and told me about her experiences with airplane turbulence.

I sat there on the bed, observing the curve of Judith's hip, her flat belly, the dark hair on her arms, still not convinced she was actually hitting on me. There were moments when it seemed obvious that she wanted to sleep with me. Why else would she invite me to her room, and to join her on her bed? Why would she lie back as if she was waiting for me to make a move? Though technically, I thought, there is nothing about what she is saying or doing that is even remotely flirtatious. Her position next to me on the bed was completely natural. How is it possible, I thought, to be so deeply confused about whether someone lying only a few inches away from you wants to sleep with you? Judith adjusted her position, shifting to one elbow and curling her legs underneath her in a way that struck me as uncommonly graceful. Maybe, I thought, my solitary personal life, my frenzied social media activity, along with my insular and increasingly surreal professional experience, has made it impossible for me to have a normal, straightforward, uncomplicated, and emotionally coherent relationship, as if I have lost a language I used to speak fluently, I thought, or forgotten how to play an instrument I used to play beautifully. Except that I never really knew how to speak the language, I thought, and I never played beautifully or even all that well on any instrument, so to speak. So it felt like I had lost something that I never had in the first place.

I stretched out my legs so they nearly brushed up against Judith's. I have never understood what people want from me, I thought, but I'm even more confused over what I want from them, which is why I have spent my whole life trying to set things up so I have as little to do with other people as possible. It must feel great to be able to clearly see what someone is trying to show you, to understand what they are trying to say. It must be wonderful to be able to trust your instincts, and know that your feelings come from a place within you that is reliable and true. But all my relationships with other people, even my so-called closest friendships, I thought, are murky instead of clear, full of suspicion instead of trust, and wholly unreliable and false. Instead of treating people with genuine affection, I thought, I simply reenacted the behaviour of the friends and colleagues I considered to be authentic people. Whenever I told my assistant she'd done an excellent job, it wasn't because I believed that her work had been in fact excellent (although it usually was), it was just that I had felt at that particular moment that it was the sort of thing that a good boss would say. I told my dad that I loved him at the end of our phone conversations not because of the real affection I had for him and wanted to share through these simple and still powerful words, but because, according to my analysis of the situation, not telling my dad at the end of a phone call that I loved him would have seemed odd, or strange, especially after he had just said that he loved me. Which is all to say that I relied pretty heavily on social conventions and didn't have much confidence in my emotions or instincts when it came to inter-acting with other people. With people who observed different social conventions, or who responded to my social conventions in a nonconventional way, I was completely helpless. Maybe Judith's way of talking was the sort of thing that had been passed down from her parents, or her extended family and friends, and what I thought was physical intimacy was nothing more than a cultural reflex. Maybe this behaviour was common to the community her parents had left when they came here to start a new life, and so it was just as common now, in the expatriate community I assumed they lived in, and where Judith would have picked up this instinct for intimacy. Isn't this one of the main features of immigrant culture? I thought. The closeness, the connection to traditional values, to cultural convention, to familial bonds, to social norms, instead of the moral free-for-all that characterizes my so-called culture? Maybe what I thought were signs that Judith wanted to sleep with me were nothing more than the customary signs of friendship in her community.

I gave her a look and she looked right back at me with an open and friendly expression. It's disgraceful to go around thinking someone wants to sleep with you when in fact they don't, I thought. When in fact they've never considered it, and even if they had, it would have been only so they could dismiss the possibility. It's true, I thought as I lay back on the bed, listening to Judith talk about her stint as a dogwalker, that in my personal and professional lives I hardly ever think about sleeping with other people or whether they want to sleep with me, and so all the humiliation I used to experience because of my lack of sexual confidence was now completely gone, and even my memories of those feelings of shame and impotence were very faint. But I still manage to disgrace myself in nonsexual ways pretty frequently, I thought. Like when I did that interview with a headhunter to see what was out there, and also to keep up my self-presentation skills, and I left convinced that I had won over the interviewers, but I didn't even get a call back, and later I heard through my professional grapevine that one of the interviewers had described my performance as *underwhelming*. Or like the time I went for dinner at an old friend's place and talked all night in a way that felt intimate and significant, and I woke up the next day feeling as if our relationship had entered a new stage. But then weeks went by, and I didn't hear anything from him, and he didn't reply to my messages. I looked at Judith and wondered if she might somehow be picking up on my thoughts and that any moment she would sit up or even get up off the bed and put a little distance between us. Maybe give me a look as if to say, 'Some other time.' But she didn't move.

And then I heard the door open downstairs, and it suddenly occurred to me that maybe this had all been planned by Mahdi and Judith. Maybe Judith had invited me over not because she wanted to sleep with me when Mahdi was off working on her dissertation, but because they wanted to have a threesome with me, which they no doubt had been planning since the first day we met. I listened to Mahdi come up the stairs and thought back over the last few weeks. Judith had been coming outside every night to bum cigarettes and complain about the way she was treated at the call centre where she occasionally picked up shifts, but what she had really been doing was feeling me out to see whether I'd be up for having sex with two people at the same time. Maybe they did this sort of thing all the time, and it was part of the special bond they shared, or I assumed they shared. Two girls, both from insular and conservative backgrounds, all of a sudden free to act out the most extreme taboos. I should have seen this coming, I thought. When Mahdi came into the room, I expected her to climb into bed with us.

Instead she said hello. She was warm and polite, but I could tell that she wasn't happy to see me. She looked tired. 'The guy who died was a flight attendant,' Judith said. 'How depressing is that?' 'Why is that depressing?' Mahdi said, as if she really was curious. 'I don't know,' Judith said. 'I just picture him all alone in the kitchen with his uniform still on. I can see him eating one of those microwave dinners, and it breaks my heart.' 'Yes,' Mahdi said, 'that is sad.' She looked at me, 'Had you met him?' She asked this in such a direct way that I almost answered honestly before I caught myself and remembered the lie I'd already told Judith. 'No,' I said. 'I travel a lot for work. Or, I used to. I was away when he moved in. He was gone before I came back.' 'I wonder which room he died in,' Judith said, and looked around as if there might be a commemorative plaque or sign pointing out the spot where the neighbour collapsed from the heart attack. 'I hope it wasn't in my room,' and then turned to me. 'I insisted we have separate rooms. I think it's important to have your own space.'

In that moment, the shame and humiliation I was feeling was so powerful that I actually considered hiding underneath the bedcover. I thought of myself as a *worldly individual*, and like I said earlier, I felt like I still might have a talent for *sympathetic understanding*, but I hadn't even considered that Mahdi and Judith might be in a relationship. I hadn't noticed the way they spoke to each other or their body language. Nothing sparked my interest or curiosity or made me wonder, 'What's their story?' or 'What's going on between them?' Until now, I realized, I had only ever seen them as an obstacle to enjoying my free time on the balcony in the way I had grown accustomed to during the vacancy period.

'What do you do for work?' Mahdi asked. I told her about my company, and unlike almost every other time someone asked that question, I could tell that Mahdi was listening to everything I said. Instead of being upfront and honest, I made evasive generalizations about the precise nature of my work and even lied about my job title, adding 'Global' to make the position sound more impressive. And as I kept babbling on about my career, the disgraceful conditions of my employment finally became clear to me with the force of a low-level revelation. There's something fundamentally wrong about getting paid for nothing, I thought. There was no way that someone like Mahdi, who for some reason I believed to be a person of rigorous decency, could respect anyone who would stay in a position, no matter how lucrative, where they had nothing to do all day.

Ever since I'd gotten back from my last foreign assignment, I thought, I'd been stuck in a sort of professional purgatory while my entire foreign portfolio had been given away to the pool of new hires hungry for the road work, for a chance to distinguish themselves the same way I had. At first I was worried I was going to get fired, but it turned out that while my colleagues no longer had any faith in me, and all future opportunities were closed to me, the company had no plans to get rid of me, and nobody, including Roger, had any interest in how I spent my time in the office. So I wasn't worried about getting fired anymore and I was free to come and go as I pleased. And while Roger checked in on me occasionally, he never seemed bothered that for months now I hadn't done any actual work. Spending my days in my office and doing absolutely nothing while avoiding my colleagues, I thought, and then spending my nights getting drunk on my balcony or smoking joints on my couch while consuming hours of prestige TV should have sunk me into a depression by now, but I was so focused on my daily routine that it hadn't occurred to me until this moment on Judith's bed that it might be possible to feel a little bit happier, or a little less angry.

'Finance,' I said. 'I'm primarily involved in areas of financial risk.' The shame I felt for how I'd been spending my time since I got back from my last foreign assignment, combined with the shame I was feeling for thinking that Judith had invited me to her apartment and taken me to her room because she wanted to sleep with me, and then shame from thinking that Mahdi came home because she wanted to sleep with me too, and that they had planned this all out over the weeks since they'd been living next door, the shame I felt while I was now sitting next to Judith on her bed (which might've also been Mahdi's bed, since one of the beds would've served as their bed) and Mahdi asked me what I did for work, this tremendously overwhelming glut of shame was so disorienting that all I could think about was how this would all be over soon and

I could go back to watching prestige TV and getting high on my couch, and how I would never speak to Mahdi and Judith again except in cases where it would be rude not to. Judith started talking about the prevalence of suicide among dentists, but I interrupted her and said I had to make a work call. 'Thanks for the tour,' I said. 'Next time I'll show you mine.'

A few weeks later, after Mahdi had presented her thesis defence, they started hosting large gatherings of their friends at least a couple times a week and in between these get-togethers there was a constant stream of drop-ins, pop-bys, stopovers, and hangouts. The initial impression I had of Judith and Mahdi as being studious, conservative, and more inclined to chocolate cake and chick flicks than vodka cocktails and methamphetamine, turned out to be wrong. They spent a lot of time out on the balcony playing their music through their phones and shouting over one another about everything from identity politics to pop music to pet grooming and the best place to buy fresh vegetables. It's impossible to exaggerate the depths of my disappointment when I came home from work to find them already set up on the balcony with three or four of their friends, somehow managing to all fit comfortably around their tiny patio table, talking over each other at an exuberant pitch they kept up all night. On my subway commute home, after another day of hiding out in my office and following the breathtaking decline of civilization in articles and essays from the half-dozen websites I visited, I would pray for them to take their never-ending party to one of their friends' places and leave me to spend the night getting high and hanging out on the balcony.

Instead of welcoming, I thought, or at least grudgingly accepting the myriad obligations I have to all the customer service personnel I've spoken to on the phone over the years, the cashiers who ring through my groceries, or the commuters I stand in line with while waiting for the bus, as well as the people I live next door to, or across the street from, or share the alley with, instead of opening myself up to this wealth of humanity and finding within it the very soul of modern life, I thought, I see every interaction with these people as an infringement on my rights. What made me think I could live in a dense neighbourhood in a big city and ignore the people I live next to, without ever having to water their plants, or ask them to take in my mail while I'm away, or help them move a couple bookcases, let alone develop a friendship, or become close, or simply maintain a warm, respectful civility with them? Why did I think I could live like this? Never speaking or even acknowledging people I'd been living amidst for years, like the Shih Tzu Lady, as if I was saying, 'You are nothing to me. I never want to know you. In fact, knowing you is what I'm afraid of.' What were my rights as a long-term tenant of a cheap apartment on a street that was in the middle stages of gentrification, as a citizen in a world-class city that is also an icon of decline and ruin, and in a country that is somehow both very wealthy and extremely poor? I had no idea, but this ignorance was coupled with a palpable and unshakable faith that those rights truly existed, that they were as real as the laws of nature, and that they covered every aspect of the social contract, from fratricide all the way down to listening to an action movie at high volume after 11:00 p.m. on a Tuesday.

Which was why, even though the nonstop party that Judith and Mahdi had been holding didn't qualify as an official crime in the same sense as a murder did, it was still somewhere on the criminal spectrum.

For the twelve years I'd been living in the apartment, I'd never had an issue with noise. But after Mahdi and Judith moved in, I started to notice how every sound they made came into my apartment with almost perfect clarity. Of course I could hear my other neighbours to my right and below me, but for some reason with Judith and Mahdi it was so much worse. At times I had the feeling they were right there in the room with me. The bathroom had a vent, and if I stood at the sink and listened, I could make out the difference in pitch as one of them clipped their fingernails and then moved on to their toenails, or vice versa. There was the dull plastic clink of the toothbrush being placed in the tin cup they kept on the edge of the sink, or the tiny double tap of earrings being set down on the narrow ledge that ran along the bottom of the mirror. I could make out the sound of their thighs lifting from the lacquered surface of a toilet seat. I heard the loud and sometimes volatile video chats that Mahdi carried on with her parents, and the only consolation was that I couldn't understand anything she was saying since she spoke to them in what sounded like Arabic to me. I had to listen to Judith and Mahdi talk for hours in the kitchen, or as they lay in bed together, arguing in low voices about some minor offence or insensitive remark. They started talking to each other the moment they woke up, and they kept it up all day and night. They were apparently incapable of being together without keeping up a steady stream of small talk. At any given moment I might be subjected to a long meandering debate over how they should arrange their houseplants, or a critical evaluation of the career prospects of one of their friends. The small talking was like a compulsion, or an illness, and throughout their nonstop small talking I thought I could sense the yearning on both their parts to keep silent, to refrain from commenting, or to keep their thoughts to themselves.

To be fair to Judith and Mahdi, I thought, when I was in my twenties I had a reputation for talking enthusiastically and at length about the minutiae of my day-to-day life, and for being an oversharer. Revelations I should've never revealed, confessions I should've been ashamed to confess, disclosures even the most indiscreet person would have refrained from disclosing. When I think about all the time I have spent telling my colleagues about my life and listening to them tell me about theirs, I thought, and if I think of all the other offices in our building, not to mention all the other buildings in the downtown core, and if I think about all the cities in the world full of office buildings like the one I work in, I am amazed that the global economy hasn't come to a standstill, since most of the people in power seem to do nothing but small talk about flat-screen TVs and all-inclusive vacations. It doesn't matter where you are or what time of day it is, there is hardly ever a moment of the day when you're not listening to people talking about the intimate details of their lives. Whenever I am at work or out in public, I am always within earshot of at least one person complaining about the way they are treated by their significant other. So, for me at least, there is something almost miraculous about two people who live together and spend every day talking to each other while somehow never running out of things to say, or at least happy to keep saying the same thing that they've already said many times before, with only slight variations. I sat at my kitchen table and listened at the open window, sometimes with genuine admiration, at the resourceful and ingenious way Judith and Mahdi spent hours cycling through a handful of themes in practically the same order every time—things people had done or said that bothered them, things that hadn't happened yet but which they spoke about as if they had, and things that they wanted to do right at that moment, or in the very near future. They improvised on these themes with masterful ease, and if it hadn't been for the fact that the endless conversational jam sessions were shattering my fragile state of mind, I may have even enjoyed listening in on them, and followed along as if they were one of my favourite long-running prestige TV shows.

'You should try talking to them?' my mom suggested one night when I had called my parents in a fury because Judith and Mahdi were partying on their balcony with some friends. 'There's an article online about how if you don't buy now, pretty soon you won't be able to afford it,' my dad said. 'Online?' I said. 'Which article was this?' Mom said. 'You never told me about this article.' 'I didn't know you were interested in real estate,' Dad said. 'Oh, would you listen to your father,' Mom said. 'Doesn't think anybody can be as interested in stuff as much as he is.' I was having a hard time hearing them over the impromptu singalong that had broken out on Judith and

Mahdi's balcony, so I left my spot at the kitchen table where I'd been sitting and held the phone up to the window so my parents could hear. 'That's unbelievable,' Mom said. 'You need to say something to them.' I went to the couch and rolled a joint. 'It really does sound like this might be the last opportunity to get in on the market,' Dad said. 'I'm pretty sure the banks write those articles, Dad,' I said. 'Tim Miller just bought the house down the street from us. You remember Tim Miller?' Mom said. 'Well, he moved into the Hunters' place. You knew that they moved to Florida? Last year, wasn't it?' 'No,' Dad said, 'that was three years ago.' 'Well, whenever it was, another family moved in but they sold it for God knows how much, and now Tim Miller lives there. He moved in with Julie Newton. They got married last summer.' 'I know,' I said, covering the receiver so they wouldn't hear me lighting the joint. 'You two used to date, didn't you?' 'Can you hear that?' I said, holding the phone to the wall that was shaking with the pulse of dance music. 'This is so crazy.' 'Maybe you should speak with the other tenants in the building,' Dad said. 'Was Julie the one who used to be friends with Sarah Fielding?' 'Yes,' I said. 'You dated her too, didn't you?' 'Here it is,' Dad said. 'With an increase in the interest rate projected for next spring at the latest, and the recent surge in foreign speculation, particularly from China—' 'Sarah went to medical school, didn't she?' Mom said '—the window for first-time buyers is closing fast,' Dad said. 'I honestly don't understand when they buy their groceries,' I said. 'Or clean their apartment. Do laundry. That sort of thing. They are literally partying every hour of the day. I can't remember the last time I was able to sit here and read without having dance music blasting through the walls.' 'Well, at least they're not like your previous neighbour,' Dad said. 'Are you kidding me?' I had let the joint go out and was pacing in front of my TV. 'That guy was probably the best neighbour I've ever had.' 'Who's this?' my Mom said. 'You mean Sean McPherson?' 'No, Mom,' I said, 'not my old roommate. My neighbour. The one who killed himself.' 'Good Lord,' she said. 'When did this happen?' 'He told us this already,' Dad said. 'Many times,' I said. 'What?' she said. 'The Middle Eastern man? The barbecue?' 'Mom,' I said, 'who else would I be referring to?' 'You told the Wrights the story just last week. The barbecue? The dead body? The 911 call? You seriously don't remember?' Dad said. 'Jeez,' Mom said, 'I know who you're talking about. Just relax there, mister.' I relit the joint. 'You should see your father right now,' Mom said. 'Look at you.' 'I'm on the government site for tenants' rights,' Dad said. 'I'll send you the link.' 'It's not really like that, Dad,' I said. 'That's more for dealing with landlords.' 'Well, that's who you should be dealing with,' Mom said. 'It's your landlord you should be talking to.' I was lying on the couch, scrolling through my social media feeds. 'What about the police?' Dad said. 'The police are too busy for this sort of thing,' Mom said. 'It's precisely the sort of thing that they are paid to take care of,' he said. 'What do you think? They're busy every night catching murderers? The lion's share of their job involves doing this exact sort of work. Noise complaints, domestic disturbances, and traffic tickets. That's what they do. That's it.' 'You really do have to see him right now,' Mom said. 'When your father gets worked up like this. You have to see it.' 'I can imagine,' I said.

'I have a very clear mental picture of the both of you right now. It's very vivid.' 'I'm fairly certain they're not allowed to exceed a certain decibel level,' Dad said. 'And then there's the hour they're playing it at. At least here I know you're not supposed to play loud music after eleven, I believe.' 'What time is it there, Peter?' Mom said. 'Same as you.' I kept hitting refresh on my feeds. 'We are in the same time zone.' 'No,' she said. 'Isn't it an hour ahead there? Or is it behind? I could've sworn there was at least an hour difference.' 'Mom,' I said. 'What are you saying? You've been calling me here for, like, fifteen years.' 'Well, I can never keep track of where you are. It's always five hours this way, or twelve another. I thought when I called you there it was an hour's difference.' 'Dear,' Dad said, 'we're only a three-hour drive away.' It sounded as though one of them had covered the receiver. 'What does that have to do with it,' Mom hissed. 'She's got a point,' I said. 'Distance doesn't really matter, does it? Like you could live right on the border of a time zone, right? So, you could cross over the border daily, to gain an hour or lose one, depending on how your day is going.' 'Yes,' Dad said. 'I suppose you're right.' 'What was that?' Mom said. 'Oh,' I said, 'you heard that?' I'd returned to the kitchen table and was smoking carefully so they wouldn't hear the little inhaling and exhaling sounds. 'That's them. They're playing a drinking game, I think.' 'A drinking game,' Dad said, sounding very suspicious, as if he'd never heard of drinking games and doubted that they really existed. 'I'm not going to explain this one to you,' I said. 'You'll have to look it up.' 'Look it up,' Mom whispered, but without lowering her voice or moving away from the receiver. 'Just wait,' Dad whispered back, just as clearly.

'There,' Mom said. 'Click on that.' 'I can't see with your hand in the way,' Dad said. 'Guys!' I said. 'I meant for you to look it up later. Not while we're on the phone.' 'Peter,' Mom said. 'Just tell us. Is it like a board game?' 'Oh my god,' I said. 'We can definitely hear that,' Dad said. 'Good lord, Peter. What is that?' 'Dance music,' I said. 'It's like Middle Eastern dance music,' I said. 'Middle Eastern?' Dad said. 'Dance music?' Mom said. 'How could anybody possibly *dance* to that racket?' 'They seem to manage,' I said. 'Wait,' Mom said. 'I thought you just said your neighbour from the Middle East was the one who did himself in?' 'I don't even know where to start,' I said. 'You don't have to be from the Middle East,' Dad said, 'to listen to Middle Eastern music.' 'Oh, listen to your father,' Mom said. 'Don't you talk to me like that.' 'Like what?' Dad said. 'Like what, he says!' 'Well, I'm pretty sure one of them is from the Middle East. Or her parents are,' I said. 'I thought he was a man,' Mom said. 'Who?' I said. 'The one who killed himself.' 'Jesus,' I said. 'Dear,' Dad said, 'he's talking about his current neighbours. Not the one who killed himself.' 'Oh,' Mom said. 'Well. I thought you said he was from the Middle East too.' 'He was,' I said. 'Well, he was Libyan…or Lebanese…I can't remember now.' 'That's Persia, I think,' Dad said. 'They're Persian?' Mom said. 'No,' I said. 'Please listen carefully and I will explain.' I lit another cigarette. 'My old neighbour, the one who killed himself, *he* was from Lebanon. I think. My new neighbours—who are still alive and who you can hear right now playing a drinking game and listening to Middle Eastern dance music—are also from the Middle East, or at least one of them is. The other one is from here, her parents are Latin American, I think.

And, to make things even more confusing for you, they're lesbians.' 'Lebanese?' Mom said. 'You said she was South American.' 'I'm going to hang up now,' I said. 'He said LESBIANS, dear,' Dad said, 'not Lebanese.' 'What are you saying?' Mom said. 'LESBIANS!' my dad and I shouted in unison. 'Don't you shout at me, mister,' she said. 'I can hear just fine. You hold the mouthpiece too far away. You have to speak into the mouthpiece.' I butted out my cigarette, 'I *am* talking into the mouthpiece,' I said. 'Well, you are now,' she said. 'Do their parents know?' Dad wondered, with more than a bit of skepticism. 'I don't know,' I said. 'I would imagine so. What does that have to do with anything?' 'Just that people from conservative cultures aren't as accepting of other lifestyles.' 'It's not really a lifestyle, Dad. You know that right?'

I enjoyed getting offended on behalf of my neighbours. I had told my parents that Judith and Mahdi were lesbians in the hope they would have this very reaction, so I could get a little jolt from feeling superior to my parents' old-fashioned values. They've never been to any of the exotic locales that I've been to on my foreign assignments. They haven't had the experience of sitting down to dinner with a farmer's family in a remote jungle village, or riding through berserk megacity traffic on the back of a scooter, clinging to a guide you've only just met and who hardly speaks your language. Even in their own city, my parents never bothered to go beyond the limits of their own small sphere of experience, so whenever we spoke I fell into the role of explaining how they should think about the world they were living in, talking to them as if they were a couple of idiots, and of course I always felt awful about it after I hung up.

'And I don't know if their cultures are any more backward when it comes to this sort of thing,' I said. 'Oh, I don't know about that,' Mom said. 'Well, I do,' I said, even though I agreed with her. 'I've worked with a lot of people from Middle Eastern and South American countries, and I've travelled there a lot too. I've spent a lot of time in those countries, and I think you'd be very surprised. It's not like what you see on the news.' 'What's going on with that, anyway?' Dad said. 'You must have something coming up soon. This must be the longest you've gone in the last ten years without being sent off to the other side of the world.' 'Like I told you before,' I said, struggling to recall what I had told them about why I'd stopped going on foreign assignments, 'a few senior guys left all at once, so they need me here right now.' I waited for them to say something, but they both kept silent. 'Things have changed a lot in the previous quarter and they want someone who's been around a while and who understands the company culture to focus on rebuilding. So, I think they want to keep me at home and let the newer guys handle the international end of things.' 'Are you okay with that?' Dad said. 'What about your Air Miles?' Mom said. 'What will happen to those?'

They didn't want to hear about my three-hour lunches on a bench at the dog park, I thought, about how I read celebrity interviews and ate noodles from a cardboard box, or how I smoked a bunch of cigarettes while stretched out on the grass, sometimes jolting awake after drifting off for as long as an hour, and they definitely didn't want to know about what I got up to on the days I worked from home, or to listen to me talk about how I basically got paid for showing up, and how everybody who looked and sounded like me (and who didn't drop the ball or shit the bed) was guaranteed to succeed, and how the prize felt more like a bribe, or blackmail, or blood money, and also impossible to refuse, it wasn't even a prize really, because in exchange you had to spend at least eighty hours every week systematically destroying your ability to do any other sort of work than the fundamentally useless kind you were being paid so much money to do. My parents didn't want to hear about these sorts of things, I thought. The only thing they wanted to hear was that I would always have a well-paying job until I retired with an enormous pension. I shared their dread of financial problems (like not being able to buy a nice new car if I felt like I needed one) but I still hung on to some youthful ideals that I believed somehow set me apart. So I was deliberately vague and even a little contradictory when-ever they asked me about work, which must've left them feeling uneasy. 'Maybe we don't understand the corporate culture he comes from,' they probably said to each other. 'Or maybe he's not telling us everything.'

'Besides,' I said to them as I lit another cigarette and opened a can of IPA, 'it's probably time for me to make a move. It's not a good idea to stay at one company for too long. You get rusty. It's important to stay in circulation these days. I'm an anomaly. Most people don't last more than four years, five max.' There was a stunned silence on the other end of the line. 'But, Peter,' Mom said. 'Your pension.' Judith and Mahdi boosted the volume on the dance music so I couldn't hear the sound of my own voice. 'That's it. This is unacceptable,' I said. 'What?' Mom said. 'I said that this is totally unacceptable.' 'You don't need to shout,' Dad said. 'What?' I said, pretending I couldn't hear him. 'Peter,' Mom yelled. 'What about your pension!' My parents must've had some idea of what my life was like, and the sort of person I was beyond our conversations on the phone, but through years of withholding information, distorting what little I did tell them, and painstakingly misrepresenting my day-to-day life, I had effectively destroyed any trust and intimacy with them, and in its place I had created a grotesque familial farce. Instead of real emotions, I could only manage a sort of emotional kitsch. When my mom told me that she loved me, she didn't realize that what she actually loved was a kitsch version of her son, a freakish cartoon with only the most strained relation to who I really was now. Because I lived a completely debased and morally vacuous life, I had to carry on this sham relationship, this kitsch charade, in place of something real. Of course it would've been easy to do away with our kitschy phone conversations, to give up this elaborate farce and just be honest with them, but I worried that they would try to intervene, and intrude on the precious solitude I had been developing ever since I moved into this apartment, and that I would have to give up the host of addictions, vices, and bad habits that felt so necessary in my daily life. I wasn't willing to take the risk, even if it meant that my relationship with my parents would continue to deteriorate until it was no longer possible to talk to them, not even in the form of kitschy parent-son banter.

A couple of weeks later, I came home from a day of onboarding a couple of new hires who were being sent on foreign assignments at the end of the month, assignments that typically would've been mine but for reasons that were never explained to me and I knew better than to ask about, I was no longer considered for. All I wanted to do was sit out on my balcony and read about Serbian jewel thieves and the animation industry in North Korea. When I got home, I listened for Judith and Mahdi, but it sounded like they weren't there, and for the first few hours I let myself hope that it might stay like that all night. The Shih Tzu Lady was fiddling with her flower boxes while her dog looked for a comfortable spot on the lawn to lie down. The dog would settle for a minute or two then get up and plod over to a new patch of grass. A man a few units over was hosing off an enormous canoe. The Pseudo Homeless Guys had a small fire going and were watching videos of downhill ski accidents. Anyone else in my financial situation would have left this neighbourhood years ago, or they would've purchased one of the nicer units on the other side of the street and then immersed themselves in renovations, so I was proud of myself for staying on in this rundown apartment and I felt something like affinity for these alley people.

When I heard the sounds of Judith and Mahdi coming home, I retreated to my couch, which is where I remained for the rest of the night. There must've been at least a hundred people there at the highest pitch of the party. The volume of the music, the way the smoke seemed to seep through the walls, the way the walls shook, the crazed shouts and screams that cut through everything, all of it came over me like a sudden and terrible sickness, and with it humiliation, indignation, jealousy, impotent rage. But for the most part I was in a state of utter disbelief. How could they think they would get away with this? I thought, and I sat there all night in this state of disbelief until things finally quieted down by three or four in the morning and I was able to get to sleep.

Even though I had it easy at the office, spending every day slacking off at work and then getting messed up at home was very demanding, and to keep this up required the discipline and restraint typically attributed to professional athletes and start-up founders, except, instead of world records or innovative breakthroughs, the thing that drove me was an insatiable craving for free time. During the vacancy period, I thought, I experienced one of my best runs of free time since I'd started working for the company. When Judith started coming out every night to bum cigarettes and tell me about her life, I knew that my free time was under threat. Because of her constantly ambushing me with stories about online shopping, fractious family get-togethers, or the office dynamics at the call centre that she was always on the verge of being fired from, or on the cusp of quitting, the quality of the free time I looked forward to every day as I waited out the hours in my office, and that I considered to be one of my natural rights, had been repeatedly and now permanently violated.

When Judith and Mahdi first moved in and the biggest threat to my free time was if I got stuck on my balcony listening to Judith, I still believed that it was a temporary problem, and that she would eventually pick up on my disinterest and impatience, and after a while she'd leave me alone. But after Mahdi completed her dissertation, and they started having people over and partying all the time, it was clear that I was in a free-time crisis. I hoped that if I told them how disruptive these parties were to my *way of life* that they would realize that it wasn't reasonable to be throwing parties in their apartment until 4:00 a.m. every other night. The walls were paper-thin, I would explain, so maybe they could try to be a little more considerate since I could hear them as clearly as if we were in the same room together.

The next morning I rang their buzzer. Mahdi came to the door. I was polite at first. I wasn't suggesting that they shouldn't have parties. One of the reasons I still live in this apartment, I said, is because I couldn't stand living in a place that was quiet all the time. I wanted Mahdi to understand that there was a time in my life when I also liked to go out and party, so my complaint was coming from a place of sympathy and understanding. 'Seriously,' I said, 'it's not a big deal.' I listened as Mahdi apologized for what she said was only supposed to be a small get-together, but some people she hadn't invited had basically forced themselves in, and that's when things got out of control. 'Hey,' I said. 'We've all been there. And I really don't mind. It's actually good that this happened, because I've been meaning to talk to you.' I explained about the paper-thin walls and that I could hear everything going on in their apartment as if we were in the same room. She seemed genuinely surprised, and said that she hadn't known the sound was that bad. I said that was probably because I didn't make that much noise, but she said that she hadn't noticed her other neighbours either. 'And you said you hear everything. You said *paper-thin.*' I insisted that I wasn't complaining, or suggesting that they should live their lives any differently than they were currently living, but I asked if we could work out some sort of system so when things got out of hand I had a way of letting them know. 'Like maybe I could text you,' I said. 'It's not like I'd expect you to stop doing what you were doing, but just be a little more mindful is all.' Mahdi said it was a great idea, and she was also glad we'd had this talk. We exchanged numbers and she texted a smiley face to confirm she'd taken mine down correctly. 'You should've said something earlier,' she said. I told her that I didn't want to be the sort of neighbour who made noise complaints. 'We live in a city, close together, you know what I mean?' I said. 'There's going to be noise. It's part of the deal. I can't stand those people who try to force their routines on everyone around them.' Mahdi nodded along to what I was saying but she also looked offended. 'We're not trying to force anything on you.' 'No, of course,' I said. 'That's not what I'm saying. I wasn't suggesting that you were...I was saying that I didn't want you to think that I was telling you how to live your life. My personal philosophy is *mind your own business.*'

After spending hours the night before fantasizing about all the things I wanted to say, I had lost all my anger now that I was talking to Mahdi. By the time we exchanged numbers and I had reassured her that in the future I wouldn't be shy about letting them know when they were being loud, I found myself apologizing for *making it sound worse than it was.* But there was something hostile about the way I was being so gratuitously polite, and once I was back on the couch I started to worry that by complaining not only about the party the night before, but about the way they lived their lives in general, right down to the way they talked on the phone, I hadn't solved my free-time problem, and had very likely made things worse. Now I couldn't hide behind the pose of the laid-back neighbour, I thought, because I had exposed myself as an uptight neighbour. I had been acting like nothing bothered me, I thought, but now Mahdi and Judith knew that I had been irritated by them since they had moved in.

For weeks after this encounter I tried to act laid-back and pretend that when they had friends over that I was *cool with it*. Mahdi and Judith made a conspicuous effort to keep the noise down at first but eventually it all went back to the way it was. One morning I woke up to the sound of Mahdi talking on the phone to her parents. I have spent a lot of time in Arabic countries, but even though everyone I worked with there was very gracious and generous with their time, and I'm sure they would've been happy to indulge a foreigner's curiosity in their language, aside from a few rhetorical and functional phrases, I never bothered to learn the language. And like I said before, it's not even accurate to say I learned how to speak a few phrases, because that implies I understood what I was saying. Mahdi paced the floor on the other side of the paper-thin wall and spoke without interruption for so long I started to wonder if she was reading aloud from a script. But then she would pause briefly so her parents could interject a question or an exclamation before she resumed in a breathless Arabic monologue while I lay there on the couch and tried to focus on a social media controversy between two famous white women accusing each other of racism. I tried to suppress my mounting irritation over having to listen to a one-sided conversation that I couldn't understand. I wondered if my irritation was a reaction to the sound of the Arabic language. Just like whenever I hear the German language, I immediately see images of Nazis in my mind, whenever I hear someone speaking Arabic, all of the images and videos I have consumed over the years of Arabic-speaking terrorists play in my thoughts like a highlight reel of negative stereotypes. I consider myself to be a thoroughly modern, liberal, open-minded person, and I believe that for the most part I am free of the prejudice and bigotry that is so prevalent in my profession, but I often catch myself indulging in crude and racist thoughts, and sometimes I worry that my progressive political opinions actually conceal my real political character, and that instead of being liberal and open-minded I am reactionary and closed off. I knew that far from being grating or harsh, Arabic is a beautiful and musical language, but I still lay there on my couch, grimacing at the sound of Mahdi's one-sided phone conversation and thinking that it might not have been so disruptive if she'd been speaking Spanish, or Polish, Japanese, or even Russian. Of course, it has nothing to do with the language she is speaking, I thought, it's just that it is 8:00 a.m. and she is arguing with her parents on the other side of a paper-thin wall. 'There is nothing bigoted, or racist, or misogynistic, or homophobic about my irritation over this early-morning phone conversation,' I told myself. So I felt it was okay to send her a text to ask her to speak a little bit quieter.

'Sorry,' I texted, 'I hate to do this...' I sent the message and then immediately followed it up with 'Sorry, but it's just so early.' The next thing I heard was Judith and Mahdi talking quietly, followed by the sounds of them leaving the apartment together. Even though Judith's constant presence on the back balcony had been a huge free-time disruption, and the loud parties they hosted brought on a frenzied and enraged state of mind that I found increasingly unsettling, I truly believed that I had no bad intentions toward them. I knew that the problem I had with them was entirely due to the paper-thin walls that did such a poor job of soundproofing our apartments. I knew that it was unreasonable to expect them to bend their lifestyle to suit mine, and that they had every right to have friends over and host parties and generally carry on in whatever way they liked in their apartment provided they didn't cause harm to the other tenants or damage to the building. Unfortunately, I thought, none of these reasonable and liberal beliefs I held mattered when I was trying to watch the season finale of the McCarthy-era prestige TV series and I couldn't make out the award-winning dialogue because Judith and Mahdi were blaring dance music from the portable speakers they had set up on their balcony.

After that text, a whole week went by where I didn't see them, and I hardly ever heard them. 'You must've pissed off Mahdi,' I thought, 'when you sent her that text.' I hoped it was a sign that things were going to change. During this weeklong reprieve, I spent every night out on my balcony reading long-form journalism and getting drunk and high. But I was in a state of constant low-level anxiety. They could come back at any moment with a few of their friends, I thought, and start partying in their kitchen, or on their balcony. All that week, as soon as I got home from work, I would go around my apartment in a frenzy, starting up an award-winning documentary on the Iraq War only to pause it after a few minutes so I could tend to my social media accounts, which I'd been neglecting for the last couple of weeks because I'd been so distracted. And after a week of going from one form of entertainment to the next, moving from my living room to my kitchen, from my kitchen to my balcony, full of anxiety over when they would come home, I wound up having a minor epiphany.

The reason you can't stand all the noise that Judith and Mahdi make, I thought, is because you spend all your time alone and in complete silence. You never have friends over for dinner, or for coffee, I thought, and there is never anybody sitting next to you on the couch, or lying next to you in bed. You never sit in the kitchen with a friend, I thought, and talk about your day or about an article you read or a TV series you're watching, there is never a jam session, or a dance party, or a card game, and aside from the occasional call to your parents, I thought, you spend all your time in your apartment in a sort of absolute quiet. The only sound you hear in your apartment comes from the TV, which you keep at a reasonable volume. You spend every night alone *in your own head*, I thought, and so you have become exquisitely sensitive to *anything that is not you*.

This was the mindset I was in when, after the weeklong reprieve, Judith and Mahdi gradually resumed partying. It had been a while since Judith had last come out on her balcony to bum cigarettes and tell me about the arguments she had on Facebook. Instead, now when Judith came out on the balcony she would be joined by Mahdi, and they would make a point of sitting at their little table without looking over to where I was sitting at my own little table, and even though I found it impossible to focus on the article I was reading about single-payer health care or the history of the Kalashnikov rifle, I made a point of staying out there until they went back inside. Whenever I ran into them on the street, which was increasingly rare, we smiled coldly at each other and nodded.

I would've welcomed this chill in our relations, and it would have been a relief to openly acknowledge the hostility I'd had for them since the day they moved in, but I felt ashamed for overreacting to Mahdi's phone call with her parents and I felt as if I'd given them something that they could use against me. I vowed to keep an open mind, to be more laid-back and easygoing, to put myself in their shoes, to see things from both sides, and to try not to let the noise get to me. After a few more weeks of sitting in my living room as Judith and Mahdi partied so hard I could hear it through my state-of-the-art noise-cancelling headphones, never once texting them about the noise or commenting on it when I went outside on a rare occasion to smoke a cigarette and they were sitting on their balcony, after weeks of being open-minded, laid-back, and easy-going I told myself that this *had gone on long enough*. It would be completely reasonable to send Mahdi a polite text asking them to turn the music down, I thought, so I paused the season finale and composed a short, friendly message. I hit send. A few moments later everything got a little quieter, and even though within an hour the party had worked itself back to a deafening roar, I spent the rest of the night feeling as though some sort of truce had been established. When I ran into them coming out of their apartment a few days later they didn't say anything. They just nodded and smiled coldly. But over the next few weeks I sent dozens of texts, and I was even hopeful that this low-impact form of communication might lead to a lasting compromise.

'You think it's going to be a late night tonight?' I would text them after they'd been on the balcony for a couple of hours. A little later, I might add, 'You think you're going to be on the balcony much longer?' Sometimes I would put in a scheduling request—'You mind partying inside? Was hoping to sit on the balcony for an hour or so.' I'd send them little tips—'You could at least get some rugs for your floors.' Or pointed inquiries—'You wearing high heels?' But no matter what the text said, the subtext of my message was always the same—'I'm not going away.' I wanted them to know that I was prepared to keep up this text barrage for as long as it took. Judith and Mahdi adopted a strategy of non-engagement and refused to get drawn in by the incessant stream of passive-aggressive texts I sent them. When I sent them a text first thing in the morning to complain about the music they were playing in the bathroom, they would usually turn it down, but they never replied. And when I texted them during their parties they would play along for a bit, but before long they'd get right back to it. Eventually I had to concede that it was no longer working. They stopped responding to my complaints altogether. When I saw them on the street or out on their balcony they didn't even bother with the nodding and the cold smiling anymore. The uneasy truce we'd established by text message had been broken. So we started banging on the walls.

In my opinion, there is no greater sign of disrespect, of contempt even, than banging on the walls of somebody's apartment. If you are having a good time with your friends and family, enjoying a loud and spirited potluck supper, or letting your hair down at an impromptu dance party or singalong, there is nothing more unpleasant, infuriating, and vaguely humiliating than being interrupted by the sound of someone banging on your walls. Even if your neighbour comes to your front door and screams at you to *keep it down* or to *shut the fuck up*, it doesn't have the same demeaning impact. There is something literally dehumanizing about being silenced by wall-banging. So once I started banging on their walls, I was basically telling Judith and Mahdi that I no longer respected them as my neighbours. 'You do not deserve the common consideration and basic respect that serves as the very foundation of civil society,' I was saying. 'From now on,' I said by angrily pounding my fist on the wall, 'I will act as though you don't deserve to be treated with *common human decency.*'

On one of the rare nights when, instead of hosting at their place, Judith and Mahdi had gone out to a friend's apartment or to a club, I spent some time on the balcony reading a long-form article about a debilitating cyber attack on the Ukrainian power grid, and then I rewatched a couple episodes of the McCarthy-era prestige TV show, without having to wear my state-of-the-art noise-cancelling headphones. I heard Judith and Mahdi come up the stairs a little after midnight. They turned on their music and started having loud drunk-sex. It had been weeks since they had responded to one of my texts.

Just a few days earlier I had sent them a string that had devolved into craven pleading, resorting to cute emoticons in a desperate attempt to arouse their sympathy. But they had ignored them completely, and when I had gone out on the balcony the next day, they continued talking to each other as if I weren't there. Since the night Judith had given me the tour, I had often heard them moaning through the thin walls. Why hadn't I heard them before? I thought. Were they playing it up as revenge for all the complaints I had made? Whether it was on account of an increased sensitivity on my part, or because, with time, they had grown less inhibited, and allowed themselves to let loose, I now heard them having sex all of the time. At first I found the sounds of Judith and Mahdi having sex to be a huge turn-on. I would imagine the positions or acts that corresponded to the sounds they were making. I wondered whether they left the lights on, or what tools or aids they might be using to facilitate such powerful and enduring sexual climaxes. I felt like a voyeur, a pervert, a peeping Tom, and these feelings of shame and guilt, as it turned out, were almost as arousing as all the moaning and bed-creaking. But after a while I started to suspect there was something staged about these sex sessions, and that Judith and Mahdi were putting on an exaggerated and clichéd sexual performance in order to get under my skin. These loud sex sessions, I thought, were a way of communicating, and while I was by no means anything like an active participant in their sex life, they must have known, considering all the complaints I had made over the paper-thin walls, that I could hear them. And because I was convinced they knew I could hear them, I thought that they must be trying to provoke me into making a complaint. So even though I'd initially been turned on, it wasn't long before these protracted sessions of moaning and screaming were just as irritating as one of their impromptu karaoke parties. What had once inspired an intense longing and almost unbearable desire, and had fired up my imagination with scenes of baroquely clichéd lovemaking, now brought on the same feelings as when I had to listen to them talk about their favourite reality TV shows. The initial excitement I felt, the arousal of an illicit or forbidden pleasure, was replaced by outrage. They were holding up their healthy sex life for me to see, I thought, and they were rubbing it in my face. Just as they blared their music all night long as a way of rubbing their dynamic social lives in my solitary and socially impoverished face, so they had loud and ecstatic sex as a way of rubbing their robust sex lives in my more-or-less celibate face. 'They're trying to make you feel like shit,' I said to myself as I lay there on the couch listening to Mahdi experience a protracted orgasm.

Once they had finally brought each other to violent, multi-stage climaxes, they finally stopped. As I lay there listening to their weak, post-coital murmuring, I thought about moving, taking out a mortgage on one of those waterfront condos, or buying the top floor of a brownstone in one of the old neighbourhoods. Maybe a change of scenery, a new environment, and an improved atmosphere, living in the midst of people in the same socioeconomic bracket as me, would have a positive effect. Even though things were a little sketchy at work, I thought, I could easily afford to move into a nicer apartment, in a nicer neighbourhood, away from Judith and Mahdi, the

Super and the Grim Reaper, the Shih Tzu lady and the Pseudo Homeless Guys, and if I got laid off then I could sell it if I had to. Maybe it would get me out of the professional and personal rut I'd been in ever since I'd gotten back from my last foreign assignment. It's possible I drifted off to sleep for a second in the flow of these pleasant thoughts, but at some point I became aware that the moaning had started up again, and without thinking of what I was doing I sat up and started banging on the wall.

The moaning stopped. I lay there for a long time listening for them to start up again, or to start talking, but I didn't hear a sound and I fell back to sleep. A few hours later I woke up to the sound of blaring dance music.

We've entered a new phase, I thought.

I banged away on the walls constantly. I pounded on the kitchen wall at dinnertime and I banged on the TV-room wall every morning. There was angry banging, when I would unleash a rapid flurry in a fit of exasperated rage, but there was also calm, almost indifferent banging, where I might smack the wall intermittently throughout the night. Just as with the first text-complaints I sent them, they initially responded to the wall-banging by turning down their music, and lowering their voices, though after a while the music creeped back up to the same gratuitous levels as before. Unlike the text diplomacy, I was no longer trying to maintain some semblance of the laid-back neighbour pose, and I kept up my relentless wall-banging campaign for weeks.

I avoided running into them on the street and never went on the balcony while they were outside. I was smoking more than I'd ever had, even though before Judith and Mahdi had moved in I almost never smoked indoors. The TV room was always hazy with smoke and the arms of my couch had gone pale from the ash. And even though I was effectively in a siege state, I started to feel for the first time since the night I sat on the bed with Judith that I might have a slight advantage. I could tell that the wall-banging was wearing them down. Of course, they had started their own wall-banging campaign. One night—after I'd been banging on their walls fairly steadily for at least a couple hours over what had actually been a fairly low-key party by their standards—one of them started banging back. For some reason I thought it was Judith, though it could just as well have been Mahdi or even one of their friends. I was so shocked and intimidated by this inevitable response that for an hour I just lay there silently on my couch, hardly breathing. I was terrified that they were going to come over and confront me. Here they are, I thought, a young couple just trying to have a good time in their apartment, while their miserable neighbour, who is always at home, is ruining their lives with a relentless wall-banging campaign. The overwhelming shame I felt when they started banging back, the regret for allowing myself to become the sort of person I despise, the uptight neighbour, the fear of having to face them at this very moment of feeling so weak and vulnerable, and as always the memory of fleeing from the sight of my neighbour's corpse, as well as the lies I had told the next day and the problems I'd been having at work ever since, all of this churned through my thoughts as I listened to them banging on the wall. I rolled over on the couch and tried to sleep.

For a few days hardly any noise came from their apartment. I moved through mine as if I was afraid of waking a sleeping child, or an animal, or more like I was afraid of setting off a trap or an alarm. But eventually they started partying again and almost immediately my fear and shame dissolved and I went back to banging on the walls. Now that they had mounted a wall-banging campaign of their own, I was forced to adapt my strategy and change tactics. At the start of my wall-banging campaign I had gone with a saturation method, which meant that I kept up an almost ceaseless barrage of wall-banging. But now I was more sparing, and only banged on the wall when I thought there was no other option. And on their part, it wasn't long before they moved past a largely defensive position and deployed a formidable wall-banging offence. Every time I turned on the TV, even with the sound turned way down, they started banging right away. If I listened to the radio they kept banging until I shut it off. When I took a shower they would pound on the bathroom wall a few times and even shout at me to keep it down.

It was during the wall-banging period that I completely lost control of myself. I had been stuck in a siege mentality for so long. In the way a lonely soldier occupies an outpost, or a bunker or trench, dug in and under constant threat of attack or bombardment, savagely loyal to their little piece of ground, I occupied my apartment with the same sort of damned devotion. The boredom and anxiety that came over me the moment I woke up, or when I lay down on the couch, I thought, were probably similar to the feelings experienced by battle-hardened soldiers as they waited for the next assault on their vulnerable position. Living in my apartment during the wall-banging campaign reminded me of the long-form article I'd read about people who had been kidnapped by Mexican cartels, and while it may seem like an obscene comparison because I was never in any danger of injury, or of losing my life, nevertheless I felt as though this next-door-neighbour dynamic I had with Judith and Mahdi was kind of like being held hostage.

These days it is now more or less generally accepted that you can do an extraordinary amount of damage to another person without ever having to lay a finger on them, so to speak. An insult can be just as violent as a punch in the face, and the wound it causes can last much longer. There isn't much distance between telling someone to go fuck themselves and punching them in the face. When we tell someone that we hate them and wish they were dead, it's obviously not the same thing as pushing them down a flight of stairs, but they are related. And when someone acts in a threatening and violent manner, the consequences, or results, or effects—in the long term—can be the same as if they had followed through on their threat. But while this is now considered to be almost common knowledge, I suspect that most people in their day-to-day lives still act as if speech, while it can certainly be harmful, is not the same thing as violently assaulting another person, even though this argument is itself now considered to be a form of violence and saying it out loud is basically the same as pinning someone to the ground and sticking your knee in their back. The long-standing tradition of keeping these two forms of violence separate, privileging and elevating physical violence while simultaneously devaluing and diminishing the linguistic variety, now seems naive, or confused, or simply ignorant of the whole history of modern civilization, since it is of course impossible to distinguish these forms from each other, or determine where one might end and the other begin. Every text-complaint I sent to Judith and Mahdi, every time I asked them to keep it down, or to move things inside, all of this was wrapped up with a vague but very real threat that if they didn't respond to my texts or turn down the volume after I pounded on the walls, if they kept it up, then one of these days I was going to call the cops. Behind every single interaction I had with them was the threat of making an official noise complaint. Every text I sent, every time I banged on a wall, I was also warning them about the more serious complaint I was on the verge of making, and of course behind my noise-complaint threat was the implicit threat of actual violence. This is what is at the bottom of every customer complaint, I thought, every salary negotiation, marital spat, or market research survey, even brief exchanges with strangers on the bus, and most certainly everything we do online. Most, if not all of our relationships, I thought, are full of implicit threats of actual violence that we have become accustomed to overlooking and excusing.

I finally went to their front door one night when I had been on the phone with my parents, but the noise from Judith and Mahdi's party made it impossible to hear them. I considered going to a movie or taking a long walk to the old part of the city and maybe getting a drink at one of the waterfront restaurants, but I immediately decided against this idea because I knew that when I returned they would still be there partying with their friends. The thought of having to spend one more night on the couch listening to them laugh and scream until three or four in the morning made me so angry that I ran at the wall and started banging, and within seconds they started banging back. At first it was probably Judith, but soon Mahdi joined in, and before long their friends got in on it too. When I was a kid, my dad liked taking us to the ruins of a colonial fort, where he would talk about what he knew, or what he thought he knew, of the history of this ruin. He told me that even when countries were at war with each other, there were still rules that everyone had to follow. It struck me as bizarre that while people were killing one another they would have to maintain a certain decorum, and discipline. I sat there, stunned by their thunderous wall-banging, but then a surge of adrenaline made me feel like throwing something large at the wall, like a chair, or the TV. They finally let up, but then they burst out laughing, and at the sound of their laughter coming through the walls I ran down my stairs and rang their doorbell.

They were calm at first, and listened while I asked them what they expected me to do when they had people over all the time. How was I supposed to live if there was dance music constantly blaring through the walls and smoke pouring into my kitchen window? I knew that they didn't have any respect for anyone else in the building, not to mention any self-respect for that matter, and I no longer expected them to stop partying on my account or for anyone else in our building who was forced to listen to their obnoxious music and inane conversations, but I thought that by now they would've gotten bored with each other and their friends, or exhausted by their relentless drinking. But apparently they were never going to get tired of this, I said, so we were all going to have to suffer through it, but there was no fucking way, I said, that I was going to put up with being deliberately terrorized. I was sure, I said, that I wasn't be the only one in the building who was sick of being terrorized by Judith and Mahdi.

Actually, Mahdi told me, I was the only one who ever complained. I found this hard to believe, I said, and they said, 'Go ahead. Ask around.' I said that it didn't really matter if the other neighbours hadn't complained. I could only imagine why they hadn't. Maybe they were too intimidated, I said, or they were afraid that by complaining they would only make things worse. 'Or maybe,' Judith said, still standing at the top of the stairs, 'maybe the noise doesn't bother them. Maybe it's not such a big deal to them. Maybe they have a higher tolerance, or they're not as sensitive as you are.' I said that you didn't have to be all that sensitive to be bothered by the incessant noise coming from their apartment. 'Maybe they're being considerate,' Mahdi said, 'and they get that if you live in this building there's going to be a certain amount of noise that you just have to put up with.' 'I have been living here for over twelve years,' I said, 'and until you moved in, I never had any problems with my neighbours.' 'But you said you used to travel all the time for your job,' Judith said. 'And since we've moved in,' Mahdi said, 'you've been home every night, or at least that's what it seems like to us.' 'Maybe the last guy who lived here liked to party,' Judith said, 'and you just weren't around enough to notice.' I told them that the guy that lived in their apartment before them definitely did not like to party. 'You told us you never even met him,' Mahdi said. 'So what makes you so sure he wasn't throwing huge parties every night?' 'Exactly,' Judith said. 'After all, he *did* die from a heart attack.'

She had come down the stairs to stand right behind Mahdi. The three of us were not so much talking as shouting over each other. I had been obsessively rehearsing confrontations with Judith and Mahdi for months, sometimes spending hours in front of my computer typing out the things I wanted to say, and the order I wanted to say them in, and then practising how I would say them, as well as imagining how they would respond and what they might have to say against me. Some of these confrontations I envisioned as calm, methodical presentations, sitting at their kitchen table, or having a smoke on the balcony, as if it was all one big misunderstanding that could be easily sorted out with a friendly chat. Other confrontations I imagined as bitter, devastating monologues that I delivered like a TV lawyer while Judith and Mahdi sat silently, ashamed. But I had never considered a scenario like this one at the threshold of their front door. I was like someone starting a fight on the floor of a dance club, or in the stands at a sporting event, someone who has never been in a fight but thinks he is in fighting form, and who has spent so much time watching the clean and tidy choreography of men fighting each other on TV and in movies that he has convinced himself that he's actually a fighting machine, but when he finally throws a punch he is shocked by the chaos that this violent act unleashes, and just like this man, I thought, I was unprepared for how, rather than unfolding in an orderly sequence, the fight with Judith and Mahdi unfolded as a disorderly and confusing confrontation that was over as soon as it began. I couldn't come up with any of the clever remarks I'd spent so much time rehearsing, and instead of a devastating monologue I found myself shouting childish insults and incoherent threats. 'You're the loud ones!' I said, and 'Your music sucks.' 'This is the last straw,' I said, and 'I'm not going to be responsible for what happens next.'

After weeks of plotting things out and planning what I would say, I had thought that when the time came to finally do something about the Judith and Mahdi situation, when I finally confronted them face to face, I would be calm and clear-headed, I would speak with fluency and focus, and act decisively, without any hesitation. But on the threshold of their front door I fell apart completely. 'First you'll say this,' I had said to myself so many times before, 'and then you'll do that.' But when I was finally standing there in front of them, I said something else entirely, something I had never come up with during all the weeks of rehearsal, and instead of doing what I'd always imagined I would do, I ended up doing the one thing I had promised myself I wouldn't do—I lost control. Alone in my apartment, I got to indulge in the most elaborately scripted fantasies of confronting Judith and Mahdi, but the moment I found myself in an actual confrontation with them I forgot all of my lines. I had been completely unprepared for the real thing.

'Are you fucking kidding me?' I said. 'The guy before you was a dream. The ideal neighbour.' 'I would've loved to have met this guy,' Mahdi said. 'He must have been a very tolerant person to be able to stand living next to you.' 'Seriously,' Judith said. 'He must've been in a coma or something.' 'Not a coma,' I said. 'He was dead.' And as I told them my well-rehearsed version of the previous tenant's suicide I watched as the expressions on their faces shifted from horrified and confused to disgusted and outraged, to sad and concerned. Their obvious distress over what I was telling them made me want to embellish the grotesque aspects of the story, and when I reached the moment in my story when I opened the door and looked into my neighbour's bedroom, I lingered over my description of his body on the mattress. The seething yellow film over everything. The swollen, basketball-sized mass, the misshapen form I told them I had thought was merely piles of clothes. 'He just lay there for a month?' Mahdi said. 'That's so fucked up,' Judith said. 'Why did it take so long for someone to find him?' I told her that I didn't know. 'When I got back from my business trip, I noticed the smell as soon as I walked in the door. I complained to the Super right away and that's when we went to check on him. I don't understand why nobody here said anything before me.' 'That poor guy,' Judith said. 'What an awful way to die,' Mahdi said. 'I've heard it's quite peaceful,' I said. I told them that I hadn't planned on telling them this story. 'It's not my place,' I said. 'The Super should've told you.' 'Well, I wish you hadn't told us,' Judith said. 'But we're not moving out,' Mahdi said, 'if that's what you were hoping for.' 'You can live here as long as you like,' I said. 'It's a free country. But if you don't keep things down I'm going to call the cops.' Mahdi didn't even look at me as she shut the door in my face.

'Holy shit,' I said. 'I can't believe she just shut the door in my face.' I looked up at the window, where I could see people dancing. 'Who the fuck do you think you are?' I screamed. The window was partially open even though it was freezing outside and I thought they might be able to hear me over their music, so I screamed again, 'Who do you think you are?' The Grim Reaper was watching from her front door, and the Pseudo Homeless Guys were coming up the street carrying a huge case of beer. I kept on screaming, 'Who do you think you are?' as I walked up the stairs to my apartment, banging on the wall all the way up. A pure, incandescent rage surged through me. I paced between my kitchen and the TV room, screaming, 'Who do you think you are?' and stopping every once in a while to bang on the walls. There was something extremely comforting, reassuring, and somehow even relaxing about giving into my anger. I felt as if I were simply a bystander to what was happening. I could sit back as this fury fed off itself, my rage rising and building with each new angry thought, and even though it got to a point where I was almost out of my mind there was a part of me that got to calmly watch this happen. 'Who do you think you are?' I screamed, banging so hard on the wall that a fine mist of plaster rained down from the ceiling. But they didn't bang back. Maybe if they'd given some sign that I was getting to them then I would have been satisfied. It's possible that if they had, I might have calmed down enough to start thinking clearly, and I may even have realized that it was pointless to keep up this war with Judith and Mahdi, that the only solution was to admit defeat and start looking for a new apartment. But, without any response, my anger continued to feed off itself. 'Who do you think you are?' I screamed. 'You think you can treat people like this? You think you're going to get away with this? There are laws against this. In this country,' I screamed, 'there are laws.'

I sat down on the couch and called 911. The dispatcher explained that they didn't deal with noise complaints, and warned that if I called again I could be fined, then he transferred me to my local police department and I made my complaint to someone who hung up on me without saying goodbye. Why does it seem worse, I thought, when Lord Jim abandons his ship, leaving hundreds of pilgrims to drown, that the boat didn't end up sinking and all the pilgrims survive? It's as if Joseph Conrad was suggesting that if the boat had sunk, and all the pilgrims had died, then Jim's actions would have been justified. But it's precisely because Jim's actions are so beside the point that makes them seem especially cowardly and pathetic. And when Jim overcorrects for his past by sailing to a remote Polynesian island and transforming himself into a grotesque colonial saviour of the native population, he takes things too far, I thought, as I sat on my couch waiting for the cops to show up. Even Marlow, I thought, who sits not just patiently but utterly engrossed by Jim's long digressive confession, gets fed up with the extravagance of Jim's guilt. Marlow points out that it takes a perverse form of pride to make so much out of one's failures and lapses. As bad as Jim's actions were when he jumped ship, the way he made it the focal point of his life was almost worse. Jim, Marlow thought, I thought, made the mistake of thinking that people could be divided into good and bad, and that if somebody was good they were good all the way through, and if they were bad there was nothing they could do about it. And of course Jim assumed he was one of the good ones. So when he jumped overboard and saved himself, he lost the boyish fantasy, the hackneyed moral order, the kitschy vision of manhood, that had served as the moral backdrop for his life.

The buzzer rang next door and I heard someone go down the stairs. Maybe Judith had been expecting some friends from another party, I thought. She would've been stunned at the sight of the cops and maybe she considered saying no when they asked if they could step inside for a moment, but before she could even process what was happening she found herself leading them up the stairway and into her apartment. It would take only a moment for the fact of the cops' presence to make itself felt throughout the apartment, that interminable interval when Mahdi would be standing next to the cops as her friends and acquaintances continued to party, not yet realizing that it was all over. It's like that engineer I read about in a long-form article, who had been working on a bridge, or a skyscraper, and because of some faulty equipment he fell off some scaffolding from an enormous height, but when he hit the ground he got right back up and ran for a few seconds before collapsing. That in-between place, that limbo that sits in every event, where things keep going for a little while longer even though everything has already come to an end. Everything had gone silent next door, as if they all had vanished, or frozen in place. You should be able to hear them, I thought. Even if they are all standing there quietly as the cops search through the apartment, I thought, you still should hear the sound of boots on the imitation-wood-grain linoleum.

You should be able to hear the cops questioning Judith and Mahdi. Maybe, I thought, they're checking on their citizenship status. Just a few days earlier, I had read a long-form article about the increasing role of municipal police departments in the enforcement of immigration law, and the article profiled one woman who had been living in this country for thirty years when she was detained after going to her local police station to register her daughter's bike, and within a couple of weeks she was deported to a place she hadn't seen since she was three years old. Maybe the cops were asking to see everyone's ID and now they were sitting at the kitchen table, reviewing them while Judith and Mahdi and their friends watched in silence. Of course I had no idea what was really going on, and it was just as possible that the cops were speaking with Judith and Mahdi in their stairway, and as thin as the walls were, they could've been talking so quietly that I simply couldn't hear what they were saying, but in my mind I could see the cops in Judith and Mahdi's kitchen, sorting the guests to one side of the room or the other, depending on whether their paperwork was in order. A terrified hush had descended, I thought, once they realized they were being detained. I had only wanted to frighten them, I thought, to show them that I was serious. But my noise complaint may have ended up destroying their lives. Maybe I should go over there and try to intervene, I thought, to explain that I had overreacted. 'They're good neighbours,' I would say. 'They're generally respectful and considerate and while they do have their friends over a lot, they mostly just talk and play music, and these get-togethers only occasionally get out of hand, which wouldn't even be a problem if it weren't for the paper-thin walls.' Is it too late, I thought, to do anything except watch from my window as they are carted off to a detention centre where they will be processed and ultimately deported to their countries of origin? What have you done? I thought. You're supposed to be against noise complaints. You've always seen yourself as a tolerant and open-minded person, but you are actually intolerant and close-minded. I had always thought I was one of the good ones, but now I knew that I wasn't, now that I had called the cops on Judith and Mahdi and their friends, now that they might be facing deportation procedures, which was something I hadn't considered when I made the complaint. In the long-form article about the unprecedented rise of deportations happening all across the country with the help of local law enforcement, all the people that the journalist profiled weren't new arrivals, but had been living here for years, if not their whole life, though I hadn't considered any of this when I made the noise complaint.

It was madness the way I held on to this apartment for so long, I thought. I could afford to hire a rental agent to find a new place. I could throw money at professionals to take care of the few things worth the trouble of moving to my new place.

Illicit drug convictions were enough to get you kicked out of an international exchange program, I thought. Or to have your temporary work visa revoked. Some of their friends might be enrolled in medical or law school, where getting arrested could jeopardize their chances for a career. In many countries, and even in parts of this one, reporting someone to the police was as good as a death sentence. In an award-winning documentary I saw about the Vietnam War, many of the historians and witnesses who were interviewed talked about how it was common for people to call the cops on their neighbours over property disputes or some petty grudge. By the end of the war it was estimated that thousands, maybe tens of thousands, died this way. And I read in a long-form article last year that during the Russian Revolution, people would call the cops on each other and then swoop in and marry the victim's widow or take the position in civil service that their victim had left vacant.

I could hear people talking, but it was coming from the right-side apartment. It sounded like the guys who lived there were taking a rare break from their never-ending video-game marathon. Maybe the cops had already left and I just hadn't heard them walk down the stairs? Maybe the silence I was hearing was the sound of Judith, Mahdi, and all their friends standing completely still and listening to me through the wall. When I looked out the window I saw a cop car parked on the street.

Just go over and set things straight, I thought. Apologize for wasting their time. I saw the cops leave Judith and Mahdi's apartment and they walked up to my front door and pressed my buzzer. I went down to meet them and they asked if I was the one who had made the noise complaint. I denied making the call. But the caller gave this address, they said. I said they must have taken it down wrong, or maybe the caller didn't want to give their real address.

'Are you Peter Simons?'

'No,' I said.

'Are you sure you didn't make a noise complaint? Because the girls next door are pretty sure it was you.'

'I get why they would think that. I'd just been complaining about their music earlier. But it's a big building, and they were being pretty loud. It could've been anybody.'

'Well, if you find out who it was, please tell them that we're very busy and don't appreciate being called out for a petty dispute between neighbours.'

'I'll be sure to pass it along.'

I watched them drive away before closing my door and going back upstairs to lie on the couch. I turned on the TV and chose an episode of the McCarthy-era prestige series. During a scene between Joseph McCarthy and his high school sweetheart, a scene that I had already watched a couple times and that was in every way completely unremarkable, I started to cry. Even after the episode was over and the credits had played through, I stayed there on the couch and stared at the screen with tears streaming down my face.

A few days later I was sitting on my couch—just sitting there without even bothering to watch an episode of prestige TV or check on my social media feeds or smoke a joint—when someone pressed my buzzer. The man at the door explained that he was related to someone who used to live at this address. 'Ahmed Elhassan,' he said. I was confused for a moment. 'I've been living here for over twelve years,' I said. The man also seemed confused. 'I was given this address,' he said. 'My brother used to live in the building, I think. He died a few months ago.' My first thought was that he had come to confront me. That the landlord had told him about my minor role in his brother's suicide and he'd come here to ask me why I had waited so long, and why I had run away and let his brother's body lie there until the Handyman called 911 the next morning. But I convinced myself that I was being paranoid. I expressed my condolences. He thanked me and then asked if I could let him in to his brother's apartment. He must've noticed my confusion at this request because he apologized right away. 'I'm sorry,' he said, 'aren't you the superintendent for the building?' This is ridiculous, I thought. I may spend my days monitoring my social media feeds and obsessively reading long-form articles about the culture wars happening on university campuses or the worldwide decline of commercial fisheries, and I may no longer travel to exotic locales, and I may live in a depraved state since I returned from my last foreign assignment, but I'm still a successful young bachelor, and it should be obvious to this elegantly dressed man standing at my door, I thought, that we belong to the same socioeconomic sphere.

I considered closing the door in his face without even bothering to clear up the confusion, but since I had come to the door wearing my housecoat, and I likely looked a little stunned and dishevelled after spending the night on the couch, it maybe wasn't unreasonable to assume that I might be the superintendent for a building full of cheap, rundown units. I was smiling now and trying, through my confident and relaxed manner, to show him that despite my appearance I was actually an extremely well-paid corporate executive, but he kept staring at me with a slightly irritated look on his face. His clothes were beautifully tailored to fit his large, low-slung frame and I could see they were made from very expensive material. His hair was luxuriously groomed as if he'd come here straight from the salon, where he must've also gotten a shave because his skin was smooth and faintly gleaming. He looks great, I thought, and I felt embarrassed at my appearance in front of someone so beautifully turned out. 'You're not the superintendent?' he said, not looking convinced.

'The Super lives there,' I said, pointing at her door. 'I tried already,' he said. 'There's no answer.' He seemed to hold me responsible. 'I was told by the landlord that someone would be here.' 'She's usually always at home,' I said. 'She's never gone for long. I'm sure she'll be back soon.' He looked as though he still didn't believe that I wasn't the superintendent. 'I'm sorry,' I said. 'I wish I could help. I could give you her number, but she just has a landline. Do you want me to call the landlord?'

'I'm just here to get my brother's things,' he said. 'I'm in a bit of a hurry.' I expressed my condolences again. 'I'm very sorry for your loss,' I said. 'I keep an apartment in the building. I'm away a lot, for work. I use this place for when I have to check back in at the home office.' I mentioned the company I worked for, but he kept looking at me as if I were the superintendent. The whole time I was talking he never reacted or gave any indication that he was listening. This only made me want to keep going, to cover up his silence. I told him that I didn't think that I'd met his brother, but that it was possible I'd seen him around. 'I'm afraid I'm not a very good neighbour,' I said. I told him that his brother's things were probably being kept in the basement storage area but that the landlord and Super were the only ones with keys.

'You've lived here for how long?' he asked. 'Thirteen years,' I said. He went silent and appeared to be working out some math in his head. 'You like it?' 'It's exactly what I need,' I said. 'You never met him, my brother?' I said that I wished I had. 'My brother was not a weak person,' he said. 'He was the strongest person I've ever known. He was always helping people. Always.' He looked up the street again impatiently. 'When we were kids he never had any money. If he got any he would give it away. When we came here it was the same thing. We had nothing. But when we got a little money I was in charge of it because if I wasn't then he'd give it away to someone he met earlier that day. But he wasn't stupid. He was really smart too. Really smart. But coming here was hard. It isn't easy,' he said. 'I can't imagine,' I said. 'We were lucky. I've done well for myself. I'm not bragging. I'm not smart like my brother, but I work hard. I guess I am bragging a bit, but my point is I have a life here we never could've had at home. It's not the same for everyone. It can be hard, and for some, like my brother, it can be unbearable.' 'Yes,' I said, 'it must be incredibly hard.' 'It is,' he said. 'I'm happy here. The people here are good people. But it is impossible to describe what it was like to leave, and then to come here. And for my brother,' he said, 'I think it was just so much worse than it was for me. Some people are able to control their feelings. My brother was not one of those people.'

As I listened to him talk, I felt oddly relieved by everything he was saying about the sad trajectory of his brother's life. It doesn't matter that I took five weeks before complaining about the smell, I thought, or that I ran from the apartment and then waited for the Super to take care of it. I have been moving through each day as if the weight of some terrible crime was crushing me, as if there was blood on my hands, as though I had forsaken my neighbour. But that's ridiculous, I thought. How could I be responsible for someone I knew nothing about, not even his name, and whose only relation to me was that he rented the unit next to mine? It was obscene the way I had been luxuriating in my own bad conscience for months now, as though I was guilty or complicit in some way. But now, I thought, as this man told me about his brother's quasi-professional acting career, it was obvious that I was nothing more than an innocent bystander to a tragic event.

A SUV turned onto the street and pulled over to the curb. The brother rang the Super's doorbell again and then checked his phone. 'I can't wait around,' he said. 'I'll just have them ship his things instead. It's what I should have done in the first place.' 'I'm sorry,' I said, because I felt implicated in how obviously put out he was for having to wait on the Super, and then I expressed my condolences again, this time much more emphatically, but he shrugged them off. 'Thank you. That's very kind. But you don't need to keep saying this. After all,' he said, and I thought I detected a knowing look in his eyes, 'there's nothing even I could have done.' He waved his hands in front of himself dismissively, as if he suddenly found our conversation to be a complete waste of time, and before I could think of something to say, he turned to leave. I asked if he wanted to leave a number where he could be reached, 'In case the Super shows up in the next couple of minutes.' He handed me a textured off-white card that was blank except for the initials V.S.N., and a web address.

All my life, I thought as I went back upstairs and lay down on my couch, I have justified my actions by pointing to similar actions by other people. Something I would never do on my own becomes perfectly acceptable when I see somebody else do it. If I am suffering from shame and guilt over something I have done, I thought, or if I didn't do something but should have, then all that it takes to put everything in perspective and make me feel better is a story about someone else who did something similar or maybe even a little worse. Through a perversely simplistic moral arithmetic, I thought, I can cancel out the most atrocious and destructive actions with the knowledge that the very same actions are being performed by other people. Even if I had done something sooner, I thought, what difference would it have made? Whether the body was found within five days or within five weeks didn't matter. Don't be so hard on yourself, I thought. Anybody else in that situation would've acted the same way. I bet this sort of thing happens all the time.

Photo : Nikki Tummon

MIKE STEEVES was born in New Glasgow, Nova Scotia and lives with his family in Montreal, Quebec. His first novel, *Giving Up*, was published by Book*hug Press in 2015 and was a finalist for the Concordia University First Book Award.

Colophon

Manufactured as the first edition of
Bystander
in the spring of 2022 by Book*hug Press

Edited for the press by Meg Storey
Copy edited by Shannon Whibbs
Proofread by Charlene Chow
Type + design by Ingrid Paulson

Printed in Canada

bookhugpress.ca